Prai

'A clever, compulsive read that asks big questions about the nature/nurture debate'
Good Housekeeping

'A clever spin on the *Sliding Doors* trope. Captivating'
Fabulous

'I fell in love with Fern and think she belongs to the all-time character canon, like Dodie Smith's Cassandra or Jean Rhys's Anna. There's so much truth, vulnerability and joy in Catherine Gray's prose'
Daisy Buchanan, author of *Insatiable* and *Careering*

'Catherine is such an exquisite writer and what a stunning debut this is. A bold concept executed brilliantly'
Poorna Bell, author of *This is Fine*

'Gorgeous. I was drawn in from the very first page. I defy you not to be deeply moved'
Jennie Godfrey, author of *The List of Suspicious Things*

'I was pinned to the sofa all weekend because I couldn't stop reading it. Funny, moving and so bloody cleverly plotted'
Frances Quinn, author of *That Bonesetter Woman*

'One of the best debuts I've read in a long time'
Caroline Corcoran, author of *Through the Wall*

'An ambitious kaleidoscope of a debut novel. Fierce and unflinching about so many important themes'
Kerri Maher, author of *The Paris Bookseller*

'It's refreshing to find such a profound work of fiction. Remarkable'
Joshua Fletcher

'Compulsive, edible, I devoured it'
Holly Whitaker, author of *Quit Like A Woman*

'I really, really loved it. It touched me in so many different ways and made me cry. It was one of those books that I didn't want to finish because I knew I would miss it so desperately'
Nadia Sawalha

'Very hard to put down, and will leave a warm glow for a long while afterwards'
Sophie Walker, author and founder of the Women's Equality Party

'As always, Gray's writing is inspiring, fearless, and viscerally entertaining'
Laura Cathcart Robbins, author of *Stash*

'A dazzling, whip smart story . . . I couldn't put it down'
Laura McKowen, author of *We Are the Luckiest*

'So honest. So inspiring. A true page-turner'
Shahroo Izadi, psychologist and author of *The Kindness Method*

'Transfixed me from the first brilliant sentence and held me in its grip until its poignant, perfect end. I loved this novel more than I've loved any novel in ages'
Joanna Rakoff, author of *My Salinger Year*

'Deeply engaging, fiendishly smart and compulsively readable'
Isabelle Broom

Catherine Gray is a *Sunday Times* bestselling author, who has sold over half a million books in English-speaking territories alone. Her books have been translated into ten languages and received acclaim in the likes of the *New York Times*, BBC Breakfast and Radio 2.

With a background in journalism, Catherine has been a guest columnist at *Grazia*, is a regular guest on the Woman's Hour, and her writing has been published everywhere from the *Guardian* to *Stylist*.

Catherine was born in Northern Ireland, and lived there until she was ten. When not writing, she can be found running to nineties indie, trying to master the art of only eating three biscuits, or oversharing because she can't do small talk.

She lives in a little house by the sea with a high-maintenance dog, a medium-maintenance partner and a low-maintenance toddler. *Versions of a Girl* is her debut novel.

Versions of a Girl

Catherine Gray

MLP

Copyright © 2024 Catherine Gray

The right of Catherine Gray to be identified as the Author of
the Work has been asserted by her in accordance with the
Copyright, Designs and Patents Act 1988.

First published in Great Britain in 2024 by Mountain Leopard Press
An imprint of Headline Publishing Group Limited

This paperback edition published in 2025

1

Apart from any use permitted under UK copyright law, this publication may
only be reproduced, stored, or transmitted, in any form, or by any means,
with prior permission in writing of the publishers or, in the case of
reprographic production, in accordance with the terms of licences
issued by the Copyright Licensing Agency.

All characters in this publication – other than the obvious
historical characters – are fictitious and any resemblance to
real persons, living or dead, is purely coincidental.

Cataloguing in Publication Data is available from the British Library

Paperback ISBN 978 1 8027 9549 3

Designed and set by EM&EN
Printed and bound in Great Britain by Clays Ltd, Elcograf S.p.A.

Headline's policy is to use papers that are natural, renewable and recyclable
products and made from wood grown in well-managed forests and other
controlled sources. The logging and manufacturing processes are expected
to conform to the environmental regulations of the country of origin.

MIX
Paper | Supporting
responsible forestry
FSC® C104740

Headline Publishing Group Limited
An Hachette UK Company
Carmelite House
50 Victoria Embankment
London EC4Y 0DZ

The authorised representative in the EEA is Hachette Ireland,
8 Castlecourt Centre, Dublin 15, D15 XTP3, Ireland (email: info@hbgi.ie)

www.headline.co.uk
www.hachette.co.uk

For Mark,

one of the best humans I ever met

We always may be
what we might have been.

– Adelaide Anne Procter, 'A Legend of Provence'

The Police Station

HOW IT ENDS
March 2014
Ballymena, Northern Ireland

In a way, she's looking forward to prison. Unlimited time to sleep and read, hardly any TV, no mobile phone, wonky Wi-Fi. Haven't all those things been the centrepiece of every holiday she's had lately?

She wonders if she'll get super fit and start bench-pressing the equivalent of small humans. Learn Egyptian for a future trip to the pyramids, maybe. Solve the riddle of the Dorabella Cipher. It's uncertain why she'll become a weightlifting, language-learning cryptologist just by virtue of walking through prison gates, but she doesn't make the rules.

The terrible food she can do – given her idea of cooking for one is stabbing cellophane with a fork. The only worry will be if she has to join a gang for protection. She's never played well with others. It would only work if she were the boss. The head of the cobra, as such.

She knows she's avoiding the gravity of this situation by being blasé. It's her special skill and, depending on who you talk to, also her most irritating trait. Because this isn't *Carry on Convict*; it really is a predicament. She is at an existential fork in the road.

There aren't many times in life you occupy this space, where you sit suspended between two very different possible realities. Where an action – or the lack of it – has the power to provoke a life-changing reaction.

On the church steps before walking down the aisle. Seeing that your partner forgot to sign out of their email account. Finding a bag of money on the street. Pausing in front of a Belgian Malinois at the animal shelter.

Do you move or stay still, click in or keep out, pick it up or leave it, say yes or say no. It seems like such a small choice but the consequences are giant.

Motor idling, she sits in the car park trying to decide. The police station hunkers just thirty feet away. Lowered blinds give it a heavy-lidded look, as if it needs a nap. The road back to Glenfoot is equidistant.

There's a deep temptation to speed out of this car park and keep going. Like Thelma, or Louise . . . whoever it was that Susan Sarandon played in the film. Mind you, that road only leads to Glenfoot Beach, not the Grand Canyon, and Glenfoot Beach is about as deadly as a kids' ball pit. You could drive into the surf at full speed, only for the spearmint waves to push you safely back to shore, so she'd need something more dramatic, much more—

Rap, rap. Sweet Jesus: that made her jump.

A man asking if she's coming or going – his wife is doing laps of the car park in her mud-brown Lada. She makes the universal sign for 'staying' by pointing into her own lap.

She turns the engine off and the silence closes in. The windows mist up and despair takes hold as she thinks of all the sunsets she won't see, the horses she won't stroke, the babies she won't bounce . . .

Oh, do get over yourself. The melodrama of you. This is no Greek tragedy. Merely a Northern Irish mini-drama.

HOW IT ENDS

You'll be out in five years if you can behave yourself and don't become a prison gang boss. Frankly, she's wasted more time in relationships she was too polite to end.

The right thing to do is obvious. She already knows the answer to that. She was responsible for his death.

The real question is: can she physically do it? Actually move her body from the freedom of this car into the confinement of the consequences.

Because right now, the enormity of it has her paralysed.

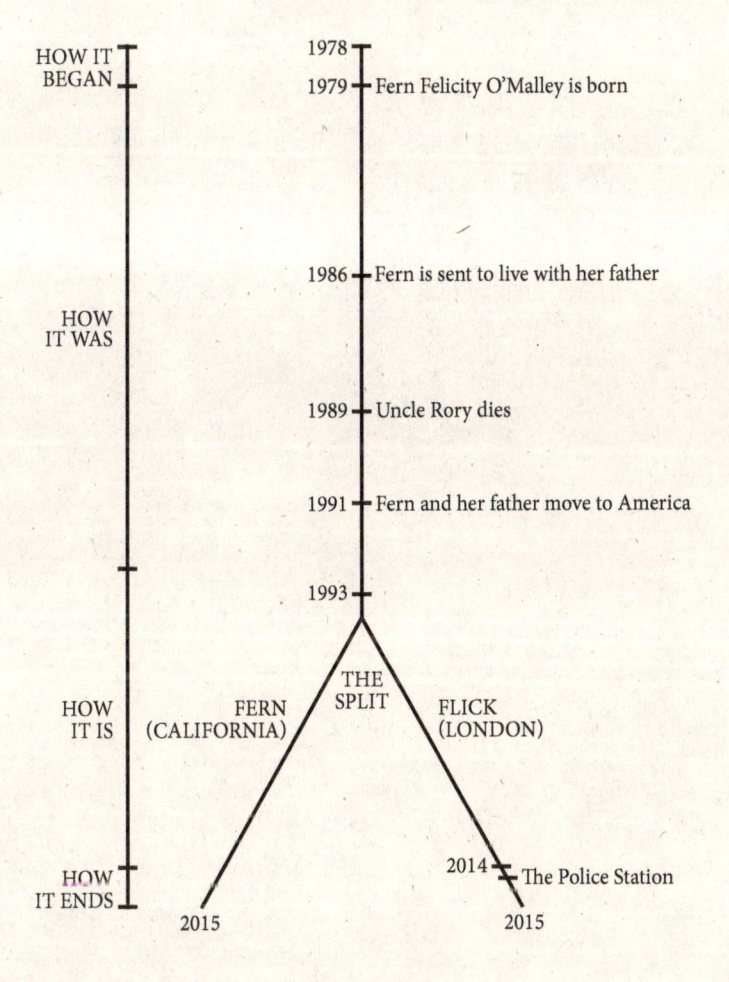

HOW IT BEGAN	1978	
	1979 — Fern Felicity O'Malley is born	
HOW IT WAS	1986 — Fern is sent to live with her father	
	1989 — Uncle Rory dies	
	1991 — Fern and her father move to America	
	1993	
HOW IT IS	THE SPLIT	
	FERN (CALIFORNIA) FLICK (LONDON)	
HOW IT ENDS		2014 — The Police Station
	2015	2015

How It Is

The Campground

HOW IT IS
Twenty-one years earlier – July 1993
Paradise, California

Fern watches them.

'Drew, do you want another sausage?' his apron-wearing mother calls across the campground. Drew runs towards her and wraps his seven-year-old body around her legs. Drew is annoying. But his mum doesn't think so. She laughs, pretends to attack his hair with the BBQ tongs and pops a sausage into his mouth. Then pats him on the backside and says 'shoo'.

Other mothers, like Drew's, love their kids. It's just hers that doesn't. So she's not lovable. That's the only explanation. Where other kids have a soft centre, like the belly of a Care Bear, Fern must have a cave filled with crows.

Drew runs towards the lake and cannonballs into it, shouting, 'Cowabunga!' She bets he will remember this day. If not the whole of it, then at least in part. The day they camped beside Lake Oroville and found a sugar-drunk racoon in their tent surrounded by Reese's Pieces packets; the day his mother loved him and gave him the last sausage.

Sitting on the low-lying limb of a cottonwood tree, Fern picks at the hole in her white plimsoll and feels the needle of potential tears. Focus now. She runs a finger along the inside curve of the shoe's sole, where she wrote F*E*R*N with a marker pen two years ago, when she was twelve.

Mum used to write her initials inside all of her clothes

labels with an orange pen. It was a fuzzy-tipped pen that didn't run. Nowadays, Fern writes her name inside the labels of her clothes, but the pen always runs in the wash, even when she uses permanent marker.

Once, she asked her dad whether he knew about the magic pens, showing him an ink blot on the back of her Fleetwood Mac T-shirt.

'Why are you writing on your clothes, you headcase? Goddamn it, Fern, that T-shirt is a seventies original.'

She'd rather have had a Shakespears Sister shirt, but Da wouldn't hear of it.

'Don't be so uncool, pet.'

Drew's mum is hard to watch. Fern strokes a heart-shaped leaf and slows her breath, trying to stop her heart sprinting as if it's being chased. Look at that tractor instead, *look*, it's so eaten up by plants that it's half farm machine, half forest, like a centaur from the Narnia books she's read. She imagines that it growls to life at night and goes on farming adventures.

She doesn't know why she seems to be the only petty thief in the world who targets campsites. Birds sing while you work, there's always trees where you can hide and the campers leave their cars open, as if the surrounding greenery is a protection spell against crime. Given they're 'getting away from it all', the campers don't notice their credit cards have got away from *them* until they stop for gas on the way home.

It's the perfect place. Da would be proud if he knew. He may have stopped her from ever doing it again – working alone is forbidden – but he'd still pause and throw her a 'You're some kid, Fern Felicity O'Malley'.

It was Da who told her that their way of stealing is called 'petty theft'.

'What does "petty" mean?' she asked.

'In most contexts, it means small-minded,' he said.

She didn't get it. Surely taking what you need and no more is big-minded. 'We're making sure karma doesn't come back to bite us in the bum,' Da added, but she didn't know who Karma was either, or why he liked to bite bums.

If you look at the bigger picture, will these rich folks miss the thirty dollars she needs for food? Nup. They will not. They would drop that on a round of fancy frozen yoghurt served by Daffy Duck at Disney. Will they miss the ten dollars she needs for pharmacy supplies? Nope. They'd throw that at some valet-parking attendant as a tip.

'God forbid they might have to park their own car,' Da says every time they pass a valet stand. She makes an annoyed snort too, even though she doesn't understand why it's a bad thing to have money to pay people to do things for you.

Fern waits. The red minivan's door is wide open. She just needs the people around it to switch their focus. It'll come. A kid choking on a French fry, the need to sing 'Happy Birthday' over a cake, the teens whooping as they find a tyre swing; anything will do. Just fifteen seconds of group distraction and she can sneak into the car, take the wallet she can see sitting there, and be folded back into the forest.

She leans back on the tree's cool trunk. It's relaxing being invisible. Only the sparrows above are aware of her right now. Lately she experiences the world differently. Perhaps it's something to do with having turned fourteen. People keep commenting on the way she looks and, wow, are other people's opinions heavy. She can't walk down a street without feeling them on her.

While she waits, she wonders why the Drews of the world

remember and she doesn't. Her memories before the age of seven are mostly a blank. Kids she meets at the skate park, pool or library, talk in coloured-in detail about their childhoods. Whole hours seem to have remained, like a bluebottle she once saw frozen and perfect in a snowdrift. Sometimes they even have whole *days*. The day they went to the theme park, rode the log flume and had hotdogs; or when they fell off their bike and made a planets project.

Aside from one episode burnt upon her brain (not now, thanks, brain), Fern doesn't have the memories these kids have. She only has flashes, in place of seven years of life lived. As if she were dropped into her skin and yanked back out again a few seconds later.

A seagull swooping on her chips like a jet, stroking a fringed lampshade, a slap right across her face, jumping on a trampoline, coming out of the Irish Sea with blue skin. Feeling lonely under a honeysuckle bush, Da being the tickle monster, fearing she would see a banshee at her window and her whole family would die, sliding the cookie tin off a high shelf, the rush of 'knock door run'. In-out, flash-dark, catch-gone.

And then a tear in her existence, as if a page were ripped from a book. Her mum sending her to live with her dad, when she was seven. She doesn't remember why it happened, or how it happened, or anything at all really.

She's always having to make other people feel better about her being motherless. 'It's OK,' she says, 'really,' and beams at them in her best well-adjusted way. It's like when you tell people your cat just died and they say, 'Oh God, I'm sorry,' and then you have to say, 'Don't worry, it's OK,' even though it's really, really not.

HOW IT IS

Fern hasn't heard from her mother ever since. And while her father has stuck around, these days he's incapable of anything but scratchcards and shots.

Sounds of an argument snap her out of this thought. Drew – the little upstart – has taken another boy's Garbage Pail Kids card without permission and is now waving it above the head of the other kid, who roars with frustration. 'Give me Adam Bomb back, Drew. He's my favourite.'

The adults sigh and gather around the boys. 'Drew,' his mother says, stroking the small of his back. 'What did we talk about this week? Sharing is caring.' Fern shakes her head in disbelief. Drew needs a smack round the legs, not a stroke.

This is her opening, though. She drops down and gets across to the minivan, head low, flattening herself against its red belly, then hopping into the driver's seat. As she pulls herself up, she catches the horn with her elbow. *BEEP*. It's brief, but obvious.

Drew's mother turns, scowls, runs towards the van, quicker than she looks. Fern shuts the driver's door and bounces around the vehicle locking the rest. Spit speckles the window as the mother pounds on it and says, 'Open up this instant, young lady.' Fern is trapped.

The other campers close in on the car. They'll call the cops, for sure. Nobody here appears to be chill about her camping out in their precious minivan. A smug one-armed cheerleader doll grins at her from the floor. The van jiggles from the hammering on the window, making the keys in the ignition jingle.

Keys. Adults now surround the minivan, but the dirt path that heads out of the campsite is clear. And her only exit. Fern

VERSIONS OF A GIRL

turns over the ignition and thinks about how Da does it. As the van wakes, the adults shout.

Da sometimes lets her do the handbrake and gears if they're in an automatic. Handbrake releases first, then D for drive, then foot on the accelerator. The van lurches forward. She hits the brake instead. Whoa.

Then Fern does the only thing that makes sense: drives away. Chased by pretty much the entire campsite, aside from two teenage boys, who are swinging on a tyre swing and cheering her on.

'THIEF!' someone shouts after her. It makes her flinch.

She's an idiot. Tears start to form and spill. They have another car at the campsite, so they'll be after her as soon as they find the keys.

Her only edge is that she's local. Well, ish – she's been in Paradise for a year now. And when kids don't go to school, like she hasn't *at all* in their three years of America, they spend a lot of time in the forest. Often with a big stick and a mashed pack of stolen cigarettes even though they don't like cigarettes.

And so, she knows this national forest's crisscross of dirt tracks like the inside of her own brain. The map of its trails do actually look like a brain. She's stalked every RV park for easy pickpocketings, eaten snacks left behind by holiday-makers at every beauty spot, and used the campsite showers, which are hot and strong, even if you do need to press-press-press the button.

To the west of the campsites there are skinny trees and used needles that she has to dodge, then a path along the highway that leads back to the motel where her and Da live.

HOW IT IS

To the east of here, the forest gets thicker, closer, lovely. Even she still gets lost in it sometimes, so there's a cool circle of a compass in her pocket to help.

Glancing in the rear-view to check they're not on her trail yet, she takes the track on the second right, heading east. Tall pine trees hold her close and sweet air gushes into the van. She realises she's been holding her breath. Exhale, inhale, exhale, you're OK, you're OK.

She swings a left and slows to a crawl, the van bumping along the path as she messes with the fuzz of radio until it becomes a voice. A local radio presenter makes cringey small talk with himself.

What now? Just dump the van and run, of course, but she knows from *Columbo* reruns on TV that this vehicle is loaded with 'physical evidence' from her. Not just fingerprints, but hair, skin, clothes fibres.

To cover her tracks, she'll need to wipe the minivan down and blitz it with bleach. Which would require gloves, probably. Criminals seem to like leather ones. And, of course, she'll need a vacuum cleaner. She enters a daydream where, from now on, she pulls one of those smiley-faced vacuums behind her, like a pet.

Cleaning up the van isn't an option. So, she needs to hide this evidence on wheels. Otherwise she'll end up in a juvenile detention facility for grand theft auto. Given this take was more of a mistake, bland theft auto would be more accurate. She smiles at her own wordplay; she'll tell Buck about that one later.

At a fork in the road she chooses the least travelled path. And then does so again. The minivan bumps on, low-hanging trees stroking and then whacking her roof. Fern can go no further, so she pulls off the road, hiding the van as best she can. Here, the trees are lush and there isn't a primary-coloured flash of litter in sight. People don't come here.

She stops, grabs Drew's mother's purse, plucks a credit card from it, then hops out. Ten seconds later, she dashes back and plucks the keys from the ignition, stashing them in her dungarees. Just in case.

An hour later, she's home. For a moment she stands outside the motel. He hasn't seen her yet and she feels a push of love in her chest. Wally.

He's 'powerless over ice cream' as he puts it, often giving her half-eaten tubs, saying, 'Save me from myself, Fern.' Every day he wears something yellow because it makes him feel happy. One time he made her guess his age and when she said 'eighty!' he went into a big huff and muttered about only being sixty. Whenever guests of The Rest Inn leave things behind in the rooms, he mails them back across country free of charge. He tells several dad jokes involving cheese and the only time he's mean is when he's playing chess. Fern has known him for one year but it feels like ten.

Wally is studying the local newspaper, half-moon spectacles wonky on his nose. He scribbles away in the newspaper's margin, rubbing the back of his bald head and probably thinking up something else kind to do.

She kicks open the door to the motel lobby, *bing bong*. Her arms are full of paper bags, groceries spilling out of them.

'Hunting?' he says.

'Gathering,' Fern replies, putting the bags down.

She chucks a bag of salad leaves in the air while Wally pretends to aim and fire a rifle. Some Twinkies have fallen on the floor and he throws his hands up with delight, picking them like they're woodland mushrooms. She holds a bunch of bananas high as if it's a prize fish on a hook. They belly-laugh at their inside joke.

Fern stops to say hi to the fish. 'Hi, Axl. Hi, Hendrix.' A pair of bored-looking goldfish swim around some neon wavy things and a castle in the shape of a skull. A bug-eyed baby shimmies out of the skull's empty eye socket.

'They made a baby!' she says.

'They did. More to come, I bet. They're probably in there hiding, growing. I was thinking of Dolly as a name for that one there.'

Fern crouches down, tapping the tank to try and attract Dolly. Wally starts to say something – stalls – tries again.

'Um, I mentioned to your dad about this, kiddo, but it didn't seem to land. Somebody's been asking around about you two.'

'What do you mean?'

'Does your dad owe some money maybe? I'm told the guy's Mexican and always wears a Yankees hat. Seems to have been in town for a couple of days now. Nobody's giving him anything, obviously, but just make yourself scarce if you see him, Fern.'

'Don't worry, I can look after myself, Wall.'

Wally frowns. Opens his mouth, then shuts it.

She unlocks room 105, unsettled by what she's just heard. The key is almost just for show. One hard shove and this door would give. Whoever's looking for them wouldn't struggle to get in.

Her dad, Ciaran, is snoring, the air clotted with sleep. His rhythm stalls, catching on a hook, as she flicks on the light.

'Jesus, Mary and—'

'It's not the Holy Trinity, Da, just me.'

'Fern! I, what time is . . . I didn't hear my alarm.'

She opens all the windows.

'Jeez, Da, it smells like booze and bad decisions in here.'

They once played a game where they generated imaginary band names for each other. 'Lanky Angles,' Fern riffed about her dad's skinny dark looks. 'Flint and Snow,' he tossed back at her, given she resembles a black-and-white photo of an olden-days girl come to life. The only colour on her is the zigzag of pink that is her mouth and two halos of hazel, her eyes.

'Why do I sound like a shite folk band while you sound really cool?' Fern said. '"Flint and Snow" is so lame.'

'How did I raise such a smart aleck?' Ciaran replied, ruffling her hair. 'I thought it was a touch poetic, like Dylan Thomas.'

Right now, 'Lanky Angles' pounces on his Marlboros and lights one up, reclining back and crossing his long legs. As Fern goes into the kitchenette, he swigs from a bottle of rum, thinking he's being sneaky. Fern sees him, says nothing, unpacks the food.

'Thanks for shopping, pet. Did you take the money from the jar?'

'Yes, Da,' Fern answers, as she side-eyes the jar on the counter, which has contained thirteen dollars for the past week. She snips the credit card in two and hides the plastic shards under a cupcakes packet in the bin.

Thanks, Sandy; what she now knows Drew's mother is called. Of course she's called Sandy.

She imagines Sandy at home, trying to get through the elevator-style hold muzak to cancel her cards, then being told that only forty dollars have gone, spent in a 7-Eleven on Route 191. Fern hopes it'll be some consolation for her lost minivan. Looking for the van will be like the stolen vehicle version of seeking a needle in a haystack, given Plumas National Forest is roughly ninety bajillion miles wide.

Fern mixes the pancake batter like she's done it a hundred times – because she has – and softens the warm pan with a lick of butter.

They lie back on the couch, bellies full. Ciaran lights up a spliff he's just rolled. Fern opens her neon orange wallet, sliding out the one photo she has of her mother.

'Da, why don't I look much like Mum?'

'Dunno, pet. Why wouldn't you want to look like me?'

He flashes her a grin, a jumble of overlapping teeth he describes as his 'bag o' chips smile'. Fern touches her small neat teeth, her sharp cheekbones, slightly too big nose. The angles and nose are definitely his, to be fair.

Fern wishes she did look more like her mother, Imogen – 'Imo' to her friends. In the photo, she has an elf queen vibe, with her swinging amber hair, cherry-ice skin and blonde-lashed eyes. She looks like she should be sitting on a throne made from shells, overlooking a series of waterfalls.

Come to think of it, Fern does have the same skin tone as her mother, but whereas Mum's skin always looked exactly as it should, Fern's just looks like a blank space in need of a tan.

Ciaran's skin is so brown that people often ask if he's 'half Spanish or something?' To which he replies: 'I'm an Irish Viking.'

'Stop saying you're descended from Vikings – you have no proof of that,' Wally once said. 'Other than your ability to womanise and pillage.'

'Ouch, Wall,' Ciaran replied, laughing and stumbling back as if he'd been wounded. 'So unlike you, buddy.'

'Well, I keep offering to do your family tree and you keep refusing,' Wally said.

'I can't bear to find out that we're the great-great-progeny of peasants,' Ciaran said, winking at Fern, who didn't understand half of what he'd just said, but still grinned as if she did.

Right now, Fern has more questions to ask Da about the past, but the conversation is clearly over. He pours three fingers of ginger wine into a tin coffee cup that says 'Rise and shine' in bubble lettering ('Rise and wine', more like) and heads into the salmon-pink bathroom to creak the shower on. The pipes squeal.

Oh, well. She'll ask him the rest of her questions tonight, after the gig, assuming he doesn't drink too much, stay out too late or bring home company.

OK so. She'll ask him the rest tomorrow.

Perched on a bar stool in Paradise Falls, Fern is waiting for her dad to change into his gig outfit. No, she doesn't know why he can't wear it to the gig either. Instead, he insists on squeezing into the bathroom stall to change.

'I'm not performing as myself, though, am I?' he said. 'I'm performing as Oscar Wolff, so I can't very well just do my set in the civvies I walk in wearing, can I? People want a bit of theatre.'

This is the first time Da has headlined a gig at Paradise Falls, or in other words, the first time he's been allowed onto the stage last. He comes out of the restroom wearing combat boots, tight drainpipe cut-offs, and a scarlet embroidered jacket that says 'mariachi band'. No shirt. An open chest.

He looks ridiculous. He's thirty-three, for godsake, so when will he stop thinking he's still young and start dressing his age? Plaid shirts and dad jeans would be so much less embarrassing.

She wants Buck here to witness this outfit. For the fifth time in the past half-hour, she scans the room. Still no Buck. 'Oscar Wolff' says a hand-painted banner over the stage. They chose red and didn't dry it before hanging it up, so the paint has dripped.

'Do I look OK?' Da asks, his brow furrowed, pulling at his jacket and adjusting the strap on his guitar. Fern's learned that the art of answering questions such as this one is: tell the truth, yet also don't answer directly.

'You look like the lost member of Soundgarden.'

Ciaran smiles, giving a thumbs up.

'Have you seen the sign, though, Da? It looks like a bad horror movie.'

'I know, right. Maybe I'll go on a killing spree after my set. How's my breath?'

He juts forward and breathes all over her. She's not going to sugar-coat this one.

'Like that glass wash,' she says, gesturing to the machine behind the bar, which has just coughed boozy steam all over them.

'Ah, no, really?' Da puffs a breath into his cupped hands. 'Dina's over there – I need to fix that.'

Fishing out a tin of tiny mints, he pours the whole lot in his mouth.

Ciaran climbs onto the 'stage', a cheerful collection of painted upside-down wooden crates.

'Good evening, San Diego!' he calls, to jeers from the crowd. 'Son of a goat, have I forgotten where I am again? These world tours make me head spin. Where are we?' He holds the microphone out to the audience.

'Paradise, California!' they chant.

Among the chant is a shout of 'Go home, IRA scum!' from a muscly guy in a trucker hat. Fern flinches. A hush falls over the crowd. Ciaran laughs.

'Give over,' he says, with a swat of his hand. 'I left my bombs at home, didn't I.'

Da pulls his pockets out, a dollar and a baggy of weed fall on the floor. He places his boot over the weed.

'Why would I bomb you, anyway? You're not English, are you?'

A ripple of dark laughter runs through the crowd.

'Now, enough politics . . . let's have some fun.'

He strums some bright chords and the crowd relaxes; they're in safe hands. Muscly in a trucker hat walks out, kicking a bar stool as he does. Ciaran launches into the opening of 'Hotel California'. 'On a dark desert highway, cool wind in my hair . . .'

Fern admires how Da deals with such insults. They're nearly daily. 'Being Irish in America means being judged with about as much subtlety as a box of Lucky Charms,' he says, and he's right. People either seem to think he's a terrorist, thick or a drunk. Only one of these is true.

Fern, meanwhile, is assumed to be nice, when she isn't particularly nice. They treat her like a wind-up toy that they can place down and nudge into an Irish jig. Waiting for her to entertain them with her Irishness; as if she'll pull a leprechaun from noplace and, *skiddlydee*, *fiddlydoo*, he'll produce a four-leaf clover from his ass.

Da doesn't get tense about it like Fern. If anything, he plays up to it. Catches it, changes it, slings it back as a joke. He's so good with people, unlike her. And so great at singing, unlike her. The crowd love him.

The critics do too. 'Like honey and bourbon served in a bikers' bar,' one music reviewer described his sound. 'As if Icarus fell through the clouds and wound up in Oakland with a battered fender,' said another.

Fern doesn't understand why her dad seems to pursue The Big Time, but then when he's brushing his fingers against it, he'll pull back. He doesn't show for a gig, he doesn't call the guy with the label, they move to another town, and he huddles back into his comfort zone of playing covers themed around California. So original.

Greyhound bus by Greyhound bus, over the past three years they'd moved across the entire midriff of North America, going from East to West. They rode the buses, knees tucked into their chests, socks stuffed into the magazine holders of the seat in front, in desperate search of sleep. Horizontal beds felt heaven-sent. Fern had stopped counting at seventeen towns.

Then they found Paradise. Their off-system existence went unchecked. Nobody seemed very interested in why they were here, everyone was willing to pay Ciaran for odd jobs, cash in hand. The overwhelmed welfare system had bigger fish to fry than a guy with a guitar and his gobby daughter kicking it during the day, rather than working or learning. They asked for nothing from the State, and the State asked nothing of them.

Befriending Wally and knowing he would protect them from controversy – from behind his desk of authority at The Rest Inn – has seen them snuggle down into the soil. Meeting Buck and Dina created a tendril of green, a shoot of a root.

But still, The Big Time remains shimmering in the distance, like Oz, while they circle the Yellow Brick Road.

Da loses his cool for a second as he spots Dina in a white denim playsuit, holding a lighter in the air, her hair crimped. He waves, drops his plectrum, struggles to relocate his rhythm, then finishes his set with Neil Young's 'California Sunset'. The guy next to Fern slings most of his drink down, yells 'Bravo!' at her father and then leaves.

Finally. She thought he might be a good target, moved two stools down to be next to him. He looked together enough to not stay all night, had car keys next to his wallet, didn't look at her for too long, didn't seem likely to talk to her. And as she predicted, he's left a couple of mouthfuls of Jack and Coke.

Fern snatches it and throws it back. There it is. The catch of disgust in her throat, but then – the reward. A warmth spreading through her, as if she's just swallowed a tiny sun.

Looking after herself and Ciaran is hard. She deserves a drink every now and then. Over time the disgust has been overtaken by the hot ball of possibility, which starts in her stomach and licks up into her brain like a fire scaling curtains.

She looks in the mirror of the toilets of Paradise Falls, scanning for a sign of her having swallowed the sun. But she can't see any, other than a light in her eyes and flushes on her cheeks.

Standing in front of the full-length mirror, Fern takes up some space. Now that she's had a drink it's easier not to shrink. She turns side to side, trying to see herself as the world might. Nobody's watching her in here, unlike out there where some of the adults look at her as if she's a snack. She can pass as sixteen, thanks to her height, but her face still looks fourteen.

Almost round eyes, black hair, generous eyebrows, a chapped mouth that's small like a doll's, a right leg that constantly jiggles when she sits, a stomach that shows her ribs no matter how many chips she eats, a blue-tinged mole on her upper lip that people often mistake for ink.

'You've got a little something on your . . .' *No, I don't, world. It's a part of me.*

Fern doesn't want to watch her father get wasted on all the drinks he's going to be bought, so she weaves back through the bar and pushes open a swing door into the kitchen's smell wall of spicy chicken wings. 'Buffalo seasoning and broken dreams', her and Buck had christened the smell.

Where the hell is Buck? Bobbing through the swearing and sweating staff, she pops out the back and drops onto the street. Getting her BMX from behind the bins, Fern wheels it towards the road. Ciaran won't be home for hours and she wants to enjoy her whiskey buzz by riding around the sunset-pink forest trails. If Buck's not here, she'll have to go alone.

'I saw you,' a voice from behind her says. She swings around to see Steve, the second chef. Late teens and pulling on a cigarette, his expression a cocked trigger.

'He looks like a cardboard box on legs,' Buck once said of Steve's squat, cubed and tan physique.

'Saw me what?' Fern says, pulse thumping but face set to unbothered.

He gets up and moves towards her. 'What'll it take for me not to tell?' he says, backing her into a wall.

Clapping twice to turn the motel lamp off, she curls into herself and pulls her sleeping mask on. The eye mask says 'Not now' in diamanté letters.

Dina gave it to her after Fern complained about the curtains at the motel.

'They're meant to keep the sun out, right?' Fern said, pulling the thin fabric out.

'And yet, they almost seem to magnify light,' Dina said, laughing.

Fern lies there for a few minutes, trying to relax, then stops a sob. *Get a grip, idiot.* She feels under her pillow for the hidden plush rabbit she's had for as long as she can remember. She's too old for it now, but too young not to have it.

It's funny. She always thought that out of fight, flight or freeze, which she's read about in the library, she would fight. Everyone knows she's scrappy. Fight – or flight when they're too big – are her happy places. But tonight, she froze. She's never frozen before. Or has she? A memory tugs at her sleeve, then slips away.

Tonight, if Buck hadn't arrived for work and pulled Steve off her . . . nope. Can't complete that thought. She flicks on the TV in her room, her rectangular sleep aid. The opening bars of 'People are Strange' play and the camera swoops down on Santa Monica. *The Lost Boys*: she loves this film. Then the thought rises, bringing with it another sob.

Tonight she was kissed on the thigh, having never been kissed on the mouth.

Fern is woken at 4 a.m. by a muffled crash, a female giggle and a 'Sssh' from her father. She pulls the duvet over her face. The clink of bottles is followed by a smell that creeps under the door and tiptoes into her nose. Weed.

The opening bars of a Rolling Stones track, followed by mutters and mattress creaks that tell Fern she won't have access to the toilet (on the other side of their 'suite') for quite some time.

Da clearly got lucky. She hopes it's Dina. If she gets stuck in here all night, she might have to pee into a cup again. 'I'd rather that than be scarred for life,' she explained to her dad one morning, when he asked why she was pouring a cup of wee into the toilet.

As the parent, he can play music until dawn, getting louder and more obnoxious the drunker he gets, but in the morning she'll have her head bitten off if she so much as stirs a spoon against a cup too hard.

Ciaran reminds her how lucky she is to have the enclosed bedroom, while he sleeps in the lounge on the flip-down bed that can merge with the wall like a chameleon (not that they ever actually flip *up* his bed), but she knows full well that he only gave her the bedroom so he could host late-night gatherings.

Fern hooks a hand behind her head and stares at the ceiling, where she's stuck up seven glow-in-the-dark stars with Blu Tack. They're the only nod to this being 'her' room, as her clothes still spill out of the suitcase, one arm or leg trying to clamber out. There's nowhere to unpack into. The wardrobe is full of Da's stuff.

Staring at the weak glow of the crude plastic stars, she wonders, not for the first time, why her and Da are so skint all the time. It hasn't always been the case. He's always had rips in his jeans and the need for others to buy him drinks, but they used to live in a really nice house, so where's all that money gone? Da even has to do odd jobs for Wally around the motel to pay for their room.

After Mum sent her back to Ireland, she and Da lived in a huge house hugged by ivy, up a l-o-n-g stony drive that crunched. 'You were named after this house,' Da told her, pointing to a stone sign saying 'Ferndale'.

'Your great-granny and grandda built it, many years ago. And it was named after the ferns carpeting those woods there, which breed as fast as the rabbits in them. Your uncle Rory kills the rabbits, says they're vermin, but I think they're cute.'

Ferndale was basically a mansion. It had at least eight bedrooms – maybe more, some doors were locked – and was her home for the next three years. Swinging her leg over fences, water in her wellies, sun pulling the freckles from her face, baby lambs wearing black socks, being folded into a soft body that smelled like bread; Ruth.

Ruth lived in a small house near the front gate, which was kinda similar, but also different, as if a china-boned lady had created a fat-cheeked baby. Fern remembers the stone outsides of both houses – Ferndale's neat jigsaw and the smaller house's higgledy-piggledy ones. 'The Millhouse' said a shy sign on the side of the smaller house.

The Millhouse had a huge wheel, almost as big as the house, that turned in the river alongside it. Fern would lie down under the weeping willow, make daisy chains and watch the water rush. She would ponder whether the house was powering the river, or if the river was powering the house.

Once again, Fern wonders why her memories are mostly a blank before she went to live at Ferndale. The only complete memory she has is from an evening after a wedding, which elbows its way to the front of her mind. She can smell the sharp chlorine of the pool even now.

It's the only fully formed recollection she has of her mother, Imo. But she doesn't quite trust the memory, as it seems too movie-like – vivid and dramatic.

Three motels back, she hunkered down in the dusty stacks of a Salt Lake City library and read about how memories misbehave, in order to try to convince herself that it didn't happen.

All the while knowing that it did.

The Pool

HOW IT WAS
Seven years earlier – June 1986
Surrey, England

She's cold, she's hungry, soon she'll be seven, that cloud looks like a dinosaur. Pushing herself away from the side of the pool, Fern looks at the tiny bumps on her arm.

The rubber ring she's in looks like a pink doughnut with hundreds and thousands on it, she would love a doughnut right now, she wonders if every wedding has a swimming pool for afters.

There were loads of other kids swimming in here too, but they'd been called away by their parents shouting, 'Dinner!' and 'Bedtime!' a long while ago.

Where's Mum? She was here earlier with that guy with the Lego hair, the one who comes round to their flat and eats with his mouth open, sitting at Mum's feet like a dog. His name sounds like 'dog' too. Doug.

Fern stretches her neck up to look at the massive house with black crisscrosses on it, down a hill of stripy grass. 'It looks cheap,' her mum said when they pulled up. But it doesn't look cheap to Fern. Their flat could have fit inside ten times over. She said so to Mum.

All the adults are outside on the patio, far enough away to be the same size as her Sylvanian Families dolls. It's OK, though, she can get out without their help. She flips herself out of the ring and doggy-paddles to the ladder.

HOW IT WAS

Climbing out of the pool, she looks up at the diving boards. One, two, three. The biggest is so high it's scary. Earlier, a boy ran and did a forward roll in the air off the second biggest board. SPLASH, he went. It was amazing and everyone clapped.

Her swimming costume has blue, red, pink, yellow stars. Tugging it down to cover her bum, she climbs the little way up to the baby board, waves down at the house, calls, 'Hey, Mum, look at me,' but nobody looks.

She needs to be higher up for Mum to see. She climbs up really carefully to the second biggest board, where the boy was. Looking down on the water, she shakes from the cold, waves and shouts, 'Muuuum! Look at me!'

The bride looks up. She's really far away and looks so pretty today. Her mouth is an O, she comes towards Fern, she's waving her arms, Fern waves back.

The diving board has water on it. Just before she falls, Fern sees Mum come out of the gardens beside the pool, Doug beside her.

There's a thump after she's in the water. Down down down she goes. Fern feels sleepy; it's quiet at the bottom and the tiles are cold.

Then Mum is there, she's in the pool too, her hair waving in the air like fire, she's angry and has no dress on. Fern's arm hurts as she's pulled up, then Doug lifts her out and onto the side of the pool.

Mum's green dress is folded there with her dangly earrings on top. The earrings look like a peacock's tail. A peacock once hissed at her at the zoo and made his tail really wide.

*

Fern's on the grass, big adult faces above her, she can see up all their noses. Her mum's long red hair falls around, tickling her.

Her head's sore. She puts her hand round and feels a lump on the back of her head. It's so sore it feels like it's moving.

'No, no, she's fine, no need,' Mum is saying, picking her up.

'Are you sure? She might be concussed,' somebody says.

'I saw her fall, I know how bad it was,' Mum says.

'Where were you, Mum?' Fern says.

'Sssh. I was watching you the whole time, silly rabbit,' Mum says. She sounds angry but as if she's trying not to sound angry, like when Da calls the house. 'I told you not to climb up there. Why didn't you listen?'

Mum looks scared. Doug looks confused. Fern is very confused. Mum *didn't* tell her that.

The bride kisses her hand and puts it on Fern's forehead. 'So glad you're OK, sweetie,' she says, pushing a chocolate star from the wedding cake into her hand.

They get into Doug's car, Fern in her clothes now and his big itchy smelly coat, and they drive to the hotel.

'If she was older then maybe,' Doug is saying, voice low. 'But hasn't this just shown what I've been saying? I don't want to raise another man's child, Imo. I've already got a child. I'm sorry.'

'She won't ruin our time together, I promise,' Mum says, placing her hand on his knee.

Then in a louder voice: 'She's a big girl now, aren't you, Fern?'

'Yep, I'm nearly seven,' Fern says, her mouth full of chocolate star.

*

HOW IT WAS

The bright clock beside the bed shows 1:17. All the lights are off, but the bathroom light is on. It's quiet.

Fern gets up, pulls her dotty pyjamas up round her waist, and looks around. Maybe they're behind the door. She looks. No. Maybe behind the shower curtain. Nobody there.

Stretching up, she turns the light on in the bedroom. It's got a little dial so you can turn the light up and down. She plays with it.

Mum and Doug had been here on the bed, drinking some fizzy stuff that made them get louder, watching a boring black-and-white movie. Maybe they're hiding under the bed. She looks. Then pulls the curtains open: nope.

There's a note on the side of the bed in her mum's writing.

Stay here, darling. If you leave this room, you will be in big trouble! XOXO
PS. There are some nuts and fruit if you're hungry.

The peacock feather earrings are placed above the note side by side, like two question marks. Fern strokes them.

Exciting! Fern jumps up and down on the bed. She can watch TV all she likes now. Maybe they're out buying her some toys because of her sore head.

But then she gets scared. What about Baba Yaga, the witch who lives in the woods and eats kids? Are there any woods near here? She pulls the curtain back and looks out the window. There are trees, but they're far away, so that's good.

Some TV will help. She messes with the remote until it turns on. 'Nnnnnngh' the TV goes. There's a girl playing noughts and crosses and sitting next to a weird clown. She waits.

It'll change soon. Any minute now, something good will come.

The Hike

HOW IT IS
July 1993
Plumas National Forest, California

Scout rolls up to Plumas National Forest before it officially opens. A chainmail gate sits padlocked between him and the parking lot, the restrooms, the gateway to all the trails.

Smoke ribbons from a nearby cabin, where cups clank and bacon sizzles, so he's guessing the rangers are having their morning coffee before opening up. Odd, that nature is still closed.

A clutch of just-turned teenagers wearing candy-bright sneakers pass. Given he's over fifty they don't acknowledge his existence. They shove each other, sing a pop song he's never heard, and trip off down a trail that runs alongside the fence. Curious, Scout follows them.

A few minutes later, one by one, the teens slide sideways through a hole in the fence. One kid sees him, elbows another, a third points, there's a murmur.

'Hey, how ya doing?' Scout calls to them, holding his hands up, smiling in his best 'I'm a friendly' way. His East Coast accent, Mexican skin and default mean face tend to unsettle people.

'All good here. I was just looking for the way in. Do you need a hand stamp or something from the rangers? Will I get in trouble if I use this route?'

Most of them shrug and walk on; one thumbs up to him

to indicate it's safe; another smirks, turns and says to the others, 'He's probably used to getting through fences without permission.'

It's loud enough so he can hear, but low enough to be deniable. He prickles, but deep breathes it away. Probably heard similar from his parents. This horse-shit is so often mimicked. Hopefully, once he's an adult he'll arrive at different conclusions; in the meantime Scout has no beef with this kid.

'Be easy,' he says with a wave, pulling his Yankees cap down and heading in what he hopes is the direction of Lake Oroville and Feather Falls. He had high hopes for this generation being the turning point, but so far all signs point to no. Maybe the next?

Being a New York detective may have schooled him in how to handle muggers, Mafia and a maze of rat-coloured subway tunnels, but out here in the woods, Scout can't orienteer his way out of a paper bag.

He feels better already as he makes his way into nowhere and away from somewhere. So this is why people like hiking. The anonymity of the woods reminds him of New York. In Sacramento people look you in the eye, smile, even talk to you.

He loves that in Midtown you can walk down the street bawling your eyes out – not that he ever has – and people will leave you be. The cathedral-tall trees here remind him of the small feeling he gets at home. Except there, it's skyscrapers full of squares of sky.

This job has been rough. Not as rough as being a beat cop in Brooklyn, it's true, but since he retired early from the force and shimmied over into private investigating, his life has been mostly eating pastries in cars. Sitting with a long lens waiting for a cheating spouse, Scout's arteries have hardened and his abs have softened.

Cornering the quarry of Ciaran O'Malley has turned out to be harder than he wagered. A lot harder. When the job request came through from London he bit the hand off the guy. Track down a girl and a thirtysomething drunk who's such a dumb dumb he's using his fake passport name as a stage alias? Yes, please.

The commission was generous and Scout was faxed their leads:

1. The 'wanted for questioning' bulletin from Northern Ireland police, dated September 1990. Detailing that Ciaran O'Malley is wanted for questioning in connection with the unlawful killing of his brother, Rory O'Malley.

   In bulletpoints: no history of violent crime, not believed to be armed, travelling with a minor; his daughter Fern Felicity O'Malley (DOB: 12 June 1979).

2. An update from January 1991 stating that Northern Ireland police now have reason to believe Ciaran O'Malley is travelling under the name Oscar Wolff and his daughter under the name Felicity Felstead. Last known whereabouts: JFK Airport. Underneath is a blurry CCTV grab of Ciaran and his kid in line at Customs.

3. A flyer from a gig in Oakland last year, dated August 1992. The faded font tells of tunes from

Shirley & The Tops plus Oscar Wolff. A picture of Ciaran sits under a promise of pool tables, happy-hour deals and the world's best chicken wings.

Scout flew to the West Coast, hopeful of this being a three-thousand-dollar (plus expenses!) commission that would only take him three tiny days. It'd be a good chance for him to get the lay of the land, anyhow – he's been thinking of moving out West for a while. Once he's solved the case, he'll drive up and down the coast, explore the Big Sur and LA, figure out where he wants to relocate. (If LA, he'll need to work on his soft ass.)

He visited the pool hall where Oscar Wolff played last summer and established that he'd left Oakland almost a whole year ago, that he moonlights as a maintenance man when he needs money, the genius has been using his *real first name* when off-stage, and the chicken wings were not the best in the world.

'Weird thing was,' the bar-keep told Scout, 'he'd just had an A&R man say he wanted to sign him. From Universal Records, I think. Sat right over there, glued to Ciaran the whole while, then gave him his card. But Ciaran did a runner, after having tried so hard to get noticed.' Her multicoloured bangles jangled as she gesticulated 'whatthefuck' in the air.

Scout liked her: she had great energy, wore a Thin Lizzy T-shirt, had a side shave buzz-cut and her laugh sounded like a motorcycle revving. When she turned to answer the phone, he also noted that she had a tight body. But he didn't make a move. He never does. 'You have a great face for radio,' his own mother used to say.

'What do you mean, did a runner?' Scout asked.

'We thought we might have one of those "Oscar Wolff once played here" pictures up one day, so we asked Ciaran for a photo with us after, so's he could sign it,' she said, gesturing to a Polaroid camera behind the bar, a wall of customer photos tacked up. 'But he stared at the A&R man's card like it was a ghost, ran out back and we never saw him again.'

Great. So Ciaran/Oscar may be incapable of thinking up a third alias, but he's clearly capable of making himself scarce.

It took Scout a whole week to find another lead in Oakland. In the end it came from the place where he often found tips: a pissed ex. A note was handed to him by the hotel concierge.

I hear you're looking for Ciaran. I used to date him.
I know that he was planning to try Sacramento.
If you find him, tell him he still owes Kat $100.

This was followed by an entire fortnight schlepping around Sacramento with a photo of Ciaran from five years ago, which Scout already knows doesn't resemble 1993 Ciaran in the slightest.

'Is that Ciaran? Oh, yeah, I guess it is,' foxy bar-keep said back in Oakland, slicing a lime into full-moons, squinting closer at the photo. 'Whoa, California's changed him. He's covered in tatts now, looks about ten years older, skinnier, very tan, much more rock and roll. You know he drinks, right?'

Ciaran is so fiendishly hard to find because he doesn't play by the rules of usual people. He has no family to visit here, no home town to draw him back in, no credit card, and doesn't appear to use any bank. He probably gets paid cash in hand for his maintenance work and takes that cash direct to the bar, burger joint or motel.

What's more, he doesn't have a driving licence for the US, and nobody has reported him having a regular set of wheels. He apparently hotwires, borrows, begs and gets buses. A car is the bell on a cat's collar for a P.I. If you know a make and plate, are in the right state, and have done your bribes right, a car will usually ding-a-ling-ling someplace.

But with this kind of random nomad, the only thing you can rely on is door-to-door questions with photographs. And Scout knows full well from his many years on the force that the observations of passers-by are unreliable as fuck.

The reason police departments worldwide question witnesses on the scene immediately, or a.s.a.p. after, is because the longer ago it happened – even just half an hour – the more the eyewitness accounts of the same event beetle off into different directions.

At his precinct they called it 'contam', short for 'memory contamination'. If you ask three people about a bodega robbery immediately after it happened, chances are they'll all say something in the same neighbourhood. But as the minutes tick by, without even realising it, the eyewitnesses start to change their own memory.

Biases come into play (ageism, racism, sexism, all the 'ism's) meaning that the teenage male who was a bystander, was now the lookout. How they're questioned also has the power to bend reality. 'Was the robber wearing a hat?' seems innocent enough, but it's a contam.

First-hand witness testimony may be king in court – probably the thing most likely to swing a hung jury – but among the cops he has worked with, eyewitness testimony is next door to fiction and a floor above fairy tale.

So, pounding the streets of Sacramento for two weeks asking random people if they've 'seen this man' is Scout's career rock bottom. He needs help.

'What about profiling him?' his buddy Sean suggested, when Scout called begging the favour.

Sean is now a detective inspector someplace in Northern Ireland. He and Scout met in New York when Sean was backpacking around the world, using his Irish accent to pick up as many chicks as possible. They both liked to party hard, which meant they became fast buddies.

Scout knows that if you ask people for too many favours, you get excommunicated, especially now he's not on the force himself. One favour, sure thing, two favours, OK fine, three favours, no response. So he rarely asks, measuring his favour-asking out carefully. This is the first favour he's ever asked of Sean.

'What do you mean?' he asked Sean. 'Profile him how?'

'Just as the psych would on a homicide. Figuring out his character type, motivations, fears, weaknesses, that kinda thing. Why don't you use the files I've sent you to try and get inside his head?'

Right on cue, the fax machine in the guesthouse's office sprang into life. *Chunga chunga chunga* it went, and after the tray had filled up, the pages slid onto the rose-dotted rug. Scout got down on his hands and knees to rescue them.

As he stacked them, on top was a Xerox of a photo: a fine old house. 'FERNDALE' handwritten across it. The next shot: the curve of a staircase from above, the chalk outline of where the body once lay, splintered wood visible along the bottom of the frame. 'SCENE' the same handwriting says; police lingo for 'scene of crime'.

The case notes showed that Ciaran's brother, Rory, took a deathly tumble. Instead of walking down these pictured stairs, or even falling down them, he somehow burst through the wooden banister of an upstairs landing and fell twelve feet onto what looks like a marble floor.

When Lake Oroville appears milky blue behind the trees, it feels like a miracle. Never mind that it's about the same length as Sacramento, he still found it. What a hiking legend.

Scout resists the urge to punch the air and finds the least spiky rock overlooking the water ninety feet below. Sitting down well away from the edge, he pulls out his flask of black coffee and the grilled cheese he got from the deli. Next he draws out the stack of files on Ciaran O'Malley, which ate up all of the guesthouse's paper reserves.

A kid flings himself from a jetty into the lake, shouting what sounds like 'Cowabunga!' This obsession with the 'teenage monster mutant ninjas' or whatever they're called is getting out of control.

The smell of sausages on the grill wafts up the valley, making hunger claw at his stomach. He bites into his lunch and starts to read. Here goes nothin'.

'SUSPICIOUS?' is written on an autopsy diagram, next to an outline of a man. Red slashes show a leg broken in five different places. A thicker red slash sits across the neck. The CoD (Cause of Death) is listed as a 'CF', which Scout knows is pathologist slang for a broken neck. 'FELL BACKWARDS' is jotted next to the CoD.

The death certificate has a nice regal stamp at the top.

VERSIONS OF A GIRL

Date and place of death
27 December 1989
Antrim Area Hospital

Name and surname   **Sex**
Rory O'Malley   Male

Name and surname of informant
Ruth Brady

Cause of death
Cervical fracture

'You Brits and your queen,' Scout teased Sean when he first saw the certificate back at the guesthouse.

'You've lost me,' Sean said.

'The royal crest on the death cert.'

'Don't call an Irish person British, Scout, ever.'

'But you're Northern Irish, isn't that part of—'

'Ever. I'm serious, mate.'

An awkward silence during which Scout felt his second favour from Sean die. Should he apologise? Nah. Too much. Be a man and pretend it never happened instead.

So he cleared his throat and asked: 'If I find Ciaran, do you want me to let you know? You know you could extradite for questioning. It's a serious enough felony.'

Sean paused.

'Rory O'Malley was a reprobate,' he said, voice low. 'Rap sheet as long as my arm of sexual interference with minors, little of which stuck. You know how it goes, Scout: tiny fires everywhere, too many to ignore, but not enough to burn him down.'

HOW IT IS

Sean took a long drag and *yahhhhh* exhaled his cigarette down the phone. Scout could almost taste it.

'On the record, we don't have the resources to investigate a cold case like this overseas. Off the record – and you never heard this from me – if Ciaran O'Malley *did* kill his brother, our unofficial observation is that he did the world a favour. So unless he turns up on our doorstep, we won't be actively looking for this suspect. I say give the fella a medal, a pat on the bum and send him on his way.'

Wow. OK then.

Scout finishes up his grilled cheese, throwing a scrap to a squirrel that's been watching him, rubbing its paws together. Down in the wooded valley a car beeps, then ten seconds later, a bunch of people shout as it accelerates into life. He guesses they're having some sort of drag race.

Oh, maybe not. 'THIEF,' he hears through the cacophony of shouts.

He sees a flash of a red minivan through a gap in the forest canopy. Whoever this perp is, they sure have homely tastes. Scout wonders if they're now on their way to rob a Bed Bath & Beyond. The van takes a corner: they also can't drive.

He goes back to the case notes on Ciaran. The inquest notes are long and dead-ass dull. Scanning them to look for clues, Scout sees a lot of blah di blah from wood experts as to whether Rory's fall could have been accidental. He skims more information about woodworm than anyone would wish to know, getting to the real talk: the upstairs banister was frail, but still needed serious force to break.

A statement from Ciaran's ex-wife, Imogen, in which she really throws him under the bus. Lying, drinking, multiple other women, skipping out on his marriage; a damning character testimony if ever he'd seen one. Scout's ex-wife wouldn't cover him in glory if she was questioned as to his character, but she'd be a hell of a lot kinder than this broad.

He drains the last of his coffee and reads a statement from a Ruth Brady, the housekeeper. Scout finds it nuts that this man grew up in such loaded surrounds – with help, even – and yet turned out so feral. Just goes to show money doesn't mean you're guaranteed to skip the chaos.

The housekeeper says she's known Ciaran her whole life and sketches a different, yet similar picture of the guy described by the ex. The family doctor matches her mixed account. Scout's takeaways are that he's decent, clever, a peacekeeper, but also self-absorbed, a womaniser, a party monster.

Not unlike Scout himself five years back, before he quit drinking.

The pathologist is up next, explaining why the type of cervical fracture meant he didn't fall forwards, yadda yadda, so unless Rory ran backwards into the banister (unlikely) he was probably pushed, either accidentally or with malice.

More testimonies, showing that when Rory died, Ciaran and Fern were the only known residents. Ruth was down the path in a 'gatekeeper's lodge', whatever that is. Scout ascertains it's a house, and that she has an alibi for time of death involving a long-distance call to a cousin in Florida.

The Irish cops know – or at least think they know – the ToD of 11.13 p.m. because Rory's watch smashed when he fell. Ruth says he was meticulous about keeping it correct, while a watchmaker testifies that this type of break could only have been caused by a fall from great height . . . in a few pages of watch chat that Scout can't bring himself to read.

It all adds up to an inquest verdict of: unlawful killing. Which, depending on the circumstances, could be a murder or a manslaughter charge.

The kicker? In the morning, Ruth the housekeeper found Rory at the bottom of the stairs, called it in at 6 a.m., but Ciaran and Fern were already gone.

'They'd always intended to leave early, though,' Ruth told the inquest, an answer highlighted in neon orange by the lead detective. 'They were going off on a road trip – the Wild Atlantic Way. Ciaran told me they didn't need any breakfast, that they'd eat in Ballycastle on their way out, watch the sunrise over Fair Head.'

'REALLY?!' the detective has written on a Post-it beside this. A sentiment with which Scout is inclined to agree.

Minivan Martha

HOW IT IS
A week later
Plumas National Forest, California

'Fern, where is this place? My legs are about to fall off.'

Buck and Fern are bumping along deep in the forest, she on her squat BMX, he on his lean mountain bike. They make an unlikely pair, it's true. She looks like the girl most likely to start a band, while Buck's smile says, 'I have an excellent dental plan,' and his physique says, 'I can throw a ball very far.'

'It looks like a basketball star hanging out with a survivor of the Salem witch trials,' her dad once said, watching them walk into the motel. 'One of the witches they could not burn,' he added, grinning and swiping Fern round the ear.

But Buck's outsides are misleading. There is no dental plan, only a father with anger issues who once threw a spanner at his son. Buck still has the tiny crescent-shaped scar on the back of his head; no hair grows there.

You can see the neglect if you look closely enough – in his moth-eaten clothes, the hammocks under his brown eyes, the dirt under his fingernails and the big-cat-like reflexes. But most people don't look that closely. They don't want to. They want to see a handsome, easy-going boy. And so, they do.

'Any minute now!' Fern reaches the fork and picks the least travelled path. She must tie a ribbon to a tree here; mark it.

HOW IT IS

And there she is. Minivan Martha, as she's now named her. Martha's a solid maternal name, she reasons. She sounds like a mother who would stay. Fern props her BMX against a knuckled tree stump and shows him the key.

'You stole A CAR?' Buck says, scratching his buzz cut and widening his eyes. 'A soccer mom's minivan!'

'Uh-huh,' she grins. 'Last week. I didn't really mean to, I was just trying to get away. I've saved her address and I'm going to pay her back somehow, once I have money. And I will – have money.'

She opens the door. 'After you, dear sir,' she says, bowing low.

The minivan's interior now looks more like a hippy's Airstream than a family vehicle. An ink-blue shawl stitched with fish covers the rear window. Bright pink velvet cushions cover the seatbelt holders. Fern flicks a switch on a battery pack and a string of old fairy lights fizz-fizz-plink on.

There's a pack of tarot cards, a wobbly pile of books propped behind the back seats, a stash of fizzy cola bottles and Mountain Dew, and cassette tapes Fern's ripped by pressing 'record' when a song she likes comes on the radio. She's taken the glow-in-the-dark stars from the motel and has built a constellation here instead.

An oversized white dreamcatcher twirls from the hook businesspeople are meant to hang their shirts on. Adverts for albums have been torn from music magazines and tacked to the back window. The Smiths, Pixies, the Velvet Underground; plus a portrait of Debbie Harry in a pink headscarf and shades.

Fern's written the phrase 'Reality is a hallucination induced by lack of alcohol' around an A4 sheet of paper and has stuck up pictures of Ciaran, Buck, Wally, herself, and the one picture she has of her mum.

'Woah,' says Buck. 'It's like your indie fairy kingdom.'

'It's more of a home than the motel. And best of all, no matter where we go, I can take it with me.'

'But you can't drive.'

'How'd you think I got it here, you ding dong? Our neighbour in Donegal used to let me drive his old tractor around. It's not my first rodeo.'

She slots the key into the ignition and wakes the car in neutral, winking back at Buck. He laughs.

'Seriously, though, Fern, it's stolen. The cops'll be all over your ass like grass.'

She shrugs. 'Not if I leave it here for a few months. D'you think they look for stolen minivans for ever?'

Fern has 'read' Buck's tarot cards and informed him he's destined to be a serial killer who'll be imprisoned after only two kills, and then marry lonely pen pals from Idaho.

'Bloody Useless Buck, they'll call you.'

He's 'read' hers too and saw that she'll be the first Irishwoman in space, but at the last minute they'll replace her with a chimpanzee.

'Safer,' he says. 'Higher IQ.'

She play-slaps his leg and he catches her hand, palm up. He strokes the inside of her wrist in an infinity motion, right where her veins are aquamarine. It's so nice. He searches her face. Fern feels undressed.

She pulls her hand away and grabs a packet of sweets to rip open and offer him.

HOW IT IS

'So when are you going to sort me out a job, now you've graduated from bus boy to trainee chef?'

'You can do better, Fern. Besides, they won't let you start until you're fifteen, like I was. It's cash in hand, but they have *some* standards.'

'*Hate* standards,' she says, flicking through a crossword book, mostly completed. A pamphlet falls out. Buck lifts it.

'Did you do this quiz?' he asks. Fern shrugs.

Buck turns it over and low whistles.

'It says here you could qualify for Mensa. And you want to wash glasses? You're a kook, Fern O'Malley.'

Having spent a half-hour trying to lob cola sweets into each other's mouths and plotting their runaway to Seattle where they will form a band called Tonedeaf Leopard, Buck points out that it's getting dark.

'Jesus wept!' says Fern, when she sees the time blinking on the digital clock.

'I love how religious your expressions are, even though you're definitely headed for hell,' says Buck.

Once, Buck convinced her to come to a Methodist service with him, promising she would have fun; she clapped out of time and burned with embarrassment until he gave her permission to leave.

Fern jiggles on the spot. 'God is about as real as Santa Claus, except God's rubbish at presents. C'mon!'

'OK, philistine, let's bail,' he says, clambering out of the back seat. Then pauses.

'Wait a sec, I've been meaning to ask. Are you OK? Y'know, with what happened with Steve? That was dark.'

VERSIONS OF A GIRL

Fern can't look him in the eye. 'Totally fine. He didn't even get any clothes off.'

'It doesn't matter, that must have scared the shit out of—'

Fern physically places her hand over his mouth. 'I'm a big girl, Buck, and I can look after myself. Thanks for thinking of me. Now drop it, please.'

The Biggest Dog in the World

HOW IT IS
The next day
Sacramento, California

Fern wakes to her dad opening the door, having not knocked. She pulls the duvet up around her chin.

'Privacy!' she says.

'Shopping!' he says.

OK, she's listening. She goes into the 'living room slash kitchen slash dining room' as they like to call it. Dina sits up in bed in a T'Pau T-shirt, yawns, stretches, smiles.

'Dina asked me what I got for your fourteenth,' Ciaran says. 'She near had a conniption when I told her about the penknife. Not good enough, apparently. So shake a leg, pet. We're going out.'

They're in Wally's blue pick-up truck, which Wally only lent to Ciaran after smelling his breath and watching him walk along a line. Ciaran rubs his belly and pats his head while doing so.

'Wiseass,' Wally says, laughing. Then chucks him the keys.

On the cassette player, Pink Floyd ask if there's anybody out there. Wally's bread-shaped car freshener smells like buttered toast.

'Have I ever told you about the summer my friend Thomas and I travelled round Thailand?' Ciaran asks.

Fern shakes her head, chomping on half a cucumber; it was the only thing in the fridge.

'We wanted to try the famous Thai massage, right, but we'd also heard about dodgy places offering happy endings. So we tracked down a massage parlour, walked in, asked what types of massage they offered. The woman at reception, all serious, says, "This is a respectable establishment, please don't worry, sirs." My pal and I looked at each other, turned on our heels and left.'

He laughs at his own joke. She ignores him, staring out of the window at sagging malls, an unkin' Donuts with no D, and supersized empty junctions. Why does he talk to her like she's a drinking buddy? It's gross.

They pull up to a Home Depot where Dusty Springfield sings about spooky little boys. Da tests her on who's singing; gives her a peppermint candy when she gets it right. Ciaran finds an assistant whose name is Betsy, she's happy to serve you today. He explains that it's a surprise for Fern and whispers a couple of sentences in Betsy's ear.

'You two Irish?' Betsy says, as they head towards the stockroom. Nothing like stating the obvious, Betsy.

'Sure are,' Ciaran says, always happy to do this boring chat.

'Me too.' Betsy is happy.

Ciaran does his usual recital of no way, fantastic, small world.

'Well, she sure looks Irish,' Betsy says. 'How old?' as if Fern isn't right there.

'All flint and snow, isn't she, with a touch of rose,' Da says, raising an eyebrow at Fern. 'Fourteen going on twenty-four.'

'That's lovely, flint and snow – are you a poet?'
Betsy goes out back to find the mystery item.
'Bet you Betsy is a plastic paddy,' says Fern.
'I'm going with grandparent.'
'Great-grandparent.'
They slide down the 'Last chance to buy!' aisle, which features items nobody wants to buy. Da holds up a bath mat that turns red when wet; Fern finds a bin cover that makes your trash look like it's wearing jeans. He offers up some coyote urine, but she wins this round with a sexy pirate lady garden ornament.

Betsy's back. They ask about her Irish roots. It's a great-grandparent. Fern's won the bet. Ciaran side-slips a dollar bill into her hand.

Ciaran heaves a great big cardboard box into the pick-up truck's behind.
'Where are we going, Da?'
'To see a man about a dog.'
Fern looks hard at her thumbnail, chewing around it until she loosens a tag of skin, then pulls on it. She sucks on the red bloom.

They're going to see his dealer. To buy weed. Of course. And the stupid thing in that cardboard box is her present. Probably a baking tray so she can make him meatloaf. She shouldn't have got her hopes up.

Da reaches over and swipes her thumb out of her mouth.
'Cut that out.'
'You do it.'
'Do as I say, not as I do.'

She pushes her bleeding thumb into the tiny pocket of her jeans, a pocket inside a pocket.

The Jack Russell puppy is the size of a mouse. His eyes haven't opened yet, outsized paws dangle over the side of her hand, his ears are fuzz-filled triangles. If she closed her hand tight she could crush him.

'I love him,' she says.

'You can have him in a month or so once he's weaned. That box back in the truck is a crate – he'll sleep in there until he learns not to pee all over the bed. Wally will move us to one of the pet-friendly rooms at the motel. They're tired as fuck, but who cares.'

How can a room be tired, she wonders.

'What does weaned mean?'

'See his mouth.' A-shaped and toothless, it's snuffling around her hand. When she offers her pinky finger, the pup sucks it. 'He's looking for a nipple. He'll need his mother for a while yet.'

'But then he won't need her?'

'No, he won't need her.'

Are you sure? she wants to ask, but doesn't want to hear the answer. She runs her finger along his side.

'His little bones.'

'What do they feel like?' Da asks.

'Like . . . the wishbones from a chicken.'

'That we pull like a Christmas cracker to see who wins the luck?'

Fern nods. The puppy's tail flicks to and fro.

'What else?' he prompts.

'He's soft like velvet,' she says.

'That's a cliché. What else?'

She closes her eyes and strokes up and down his puppy tummy. Splodges of brown, black and white, like a finger painting.

'Soft like – moss.'

'Yes! We'll make a poet of you yet. Wishbones in moss. Lovely.'

Since he's small, they call him Digby, like the biggest dog in the world from the film, who ate some magic potion and grew to be the size of a cruise ship.

When they leave the breeders, Fern is so happy that she doesn't notice for a good ten minutes that they're driving in the wrong direction.

'Sacramento: 50 miles' is the sign that slaps her to attention.

'Where are we going? Wally said to come straight home.'

Da has his arm out the window, caressing the oncoming air.

'Wally's too uptight. We're just going to do some busking. Make enough to buy him a pizza for his tea to say thanks. Let's just tell him we got lost, pet.'

'I'm not going to lie for you.'

An hour later, Ciaran strums the opener to 'California Dreamin''. He's close enough to The Grand Hotel to attract their leaving guests, but far enough away from the doorman, who looks exactly like the top-hatted Monopoly man, only much less jolly.

Monopoly Doorman is arguing with a painted lady. Her shopping trolley is piled high with treasure, her dress is dotted with seahorses, her trainers are tie-dye, and she does not like being 'moved along' from his patch of sidewalk.

At the familiar 'California Dreamin'' chords, Fern folds into her own lap and pretends to snore.

'Whatever,' Da mouths at her.

He starts to sing the crowd-pleaser. 'All the leaves are brown, and the sky is grey.'

A couple of shoppers stop, as does a suited high-roller from the hotel, distracted from getting into the back of his car. The chauffeur piles suitcases into the black Bentley while his boss enjoys Ciaran's song. The high-roller chucks a twenty-dollar bill into the guitar case as the song draws to a close, then ducks into the back of the Bentley. It moves into the traffic, graceful like a shark.

Ciaran finishes, the crowd claps, he bows deeply like a Shakespearean actor, then signals to Fern with a jerk of his head. She casts around for what he wants her to nick. On the floor, a room key glints.

'Quick, it's nearly check-out time,' Ciaran says, heading for the back entrance of The Grand.

'What if the staff saw him leave?'

He swings the key in her face, a curly '67' printed in gold leaf on a leather tag. It smells like rich people.

'Doesn't matter, pet,' he says. 'If he didn't give *this* back, then the tab's still running.'

They're at the staff entrance. Someone comes out, already smoking, and they catch the door just before it bangs. The corridor opens on to locker rooms that reek of Lynx body spray, plus a supervisor dozing on a desk.

Above him, there's a pinboard featuring *Sports Illustrated* rip-outs along with rotas. Tits and lists. Lovely.

HOW IT IS

Ding – the staff elevator. An ancient janitor with a mop appears. He barely notices their existence.

Now in the room, they beeline for the rubbish, and Fern makes a pencil rubbing of the notepad. People love to try out pens by writing their name.

'Trent Whitaker, Da.'

Ciaran gives her a thumbs up.

A binned receipt shows Trent's signature too. They're all set.

Ciaran dials 1 for the front desk and puts on a Southern drawl. Fern rolls her eyes while he gives her a 'good a guess as any' look. He tells the front desk that they'll be staying another night, then transfers to room service and orders half of the menu, including a bottle of champagne and six beers.

They put on the cloud-soft robes and lie back on the bedspread. Fern runs her finger along a silky golden seam.

'I feel like a sultan,' Ciaran says. He pours eight-dollar minibar nuts into his mouth and flicks on the telly: Vanilla Ice on MTV.

A pause. Ciaran frowns.

'This guy's a right plonker.'

Fattened by spaghetti bolognese, lobster ('Too much work!' Ciaran said, throwing a claw aside. 'I want a meal, not a project') and a mountain range of different ice creams, their mood has darkened. Night has fallen as Da drinks all of the beers and most of the champagne. It's as if he thinks the answer will lie at the bottom of each bottle, then finds it doesn't, like a cookie without a fortune, so he tries another. And another.

Fern sneaks some champagne while he's out of the room and feels the excited fireflies fizz. He's lost his fireflies and she feels bad for him. He's now decided 'this won't be enough', nodding at the dregs of the bottle and phones room service, too wasted to realise he's lost his southern vowel roll.

Fern raids the bathroom. Anything that's not nailed down is coming with them. She looks at the tray of 'complimentary' bath items.

'Da, why would you want to shower *without* getting your hair wet?' she calls, analysing an item marked 'shower cap'.

'Dunno, pet,' he says, coming into the bathroom, weaving as he goes.

'And what's this for?' she asks, holding up a tiny fluffy stick.

'Cleaning your ears.'

Oh yeah, she has a vague memory of these things. Fern pokes it deep in her ear.

'Not too far. I once punctured an ear drum with one of those fuckers,' Ciaran says.

'Ewwww,' Fern says as she sees the orange and furry result.

She pockets the shampoo, body lotion and dollar-coin-sized soap cake to add to her collection of miniatures.

Da flicks between the TV channels because he can't commit to anything, even a sitcom. The mothers she sees on telly don't exist, Fern knows that. Samantha from *Bewitched* wriggling her nose to magic up a pink room. A perm whisking up Angel Delight. Clair Huxtable going all mama-bear fierce when anyone dares hurt her cub on *The Cosby Show*.

She wonders if the craving she gets after watching the mums on TV is like the craving she gets after popcorn adverts.

HOW IT IS

'Don't be such a puppet, Fern,' Da said, when she whispered to him during *Gremlins 2* that she really, really wanted popcorn from the concession stand, please please please.

'You're playing right into their hands. You don't normally want popcorn.'

'Whose hands?' she asked.

'The movie industrial complex.'

She didn't know who that was, so she left it.

She finds a drunk, high Ciaran crouching by a bathroom ornament, a bottle layered with different coloured sand.

Here we go.

'What are you doing?'

He places the bottle on the counter and squats down to peer at it on a level. Pink, blue, yellow, green . . . it's a flattened rainbow.

'For all we know, these are parallel worlds. Where there are versions of us in this pink layer, living totally different lives,' he taps the bottle. 'While we're down here in this green layer, see?'

Fern sighs. 'Da, are you off your head?'

'Little bit. But seriously. Y'know that nature repeats patterns, right? And matter does the same. There are only so many patterns. Eventually it will repeat. String theory means that like these layers of sand, we *could* exist in a layered universe.'

Even though he's slurring, Fern is a little impressed and Ciaran senses it.

'I was a lecturer in physics,' he says, the line worn smooth. 'At Queen's, which is basically Ireland's version of Stanford.'

VERSIONS OF A GIRL

He wasn't a lecturer. This isn't true. He's forgotten who she is and what conversation they're currently having. While drunk, or hungover, or in the spaces between the two, lies fall from her dad's mouth as easily as 'hello' or 'how are you?'

He uses the lies to get what he wants from people. I was a lecturer at Queen's in Belfast, buy me a drink will you? I am descended from Vikings, sleep with me won't you? I get a big pay cheque next week, be a pal and sub me.

Her father did study physics to Masters level at Queen's University, that's true. He was even junior research *something* there for a while, until he got drunk and 'borrowed' the vice-chancellor's MG from the staff garages, leaving it in the centre of a flowery roundabout after a joyride.

'I drove last night?' Ciaran said, scratching his head when asked about it the next morning. Onlookers later told the local paper that they'd seen him sprinting from the roundabout, wearing no trousers and howling with laughter.

But maybe Da does know what he's talking about. He lies down on the floor and his eyes widen at the light above him.

'Whoa, is that the sun? Inside our bathroom? Groovy.'

Or – maybe he's just high. Fern leaves him to it and goes over to the window to check on Wally's truck. She's not totally sure Da locked it. Pulling the curtain to one side, she sees the truck is safe. Sitting beside it on a low wall, is a thick-armed man in a baseball cap. Something in Fern pings.

He looks as if he's staring directly at her, even though he can't possibly see her from the ground. She lets the curtain fall and hunches down.

Shit.

The Capture

HOW IT IS
A second earlier

He looks up, scanning the hotel. It just so happens that Scout's eyes are on the sixth floor when she draws back the curtain and looks down. *Gotcha*. Passing the blue pick-up truck as he heads towards the hotel, he pats it to say thanks. The truck led him straight to them.

Yesterday, after his very successful first hike ever, Scout stopped at a diner in a town called Paradise for a cobb salad. Paradise is an unfortunate misnomer, turns out, as the place is a bit of a dump.

While he was there, he thought he may as well show Ciaran's picture around. So, as he waited for his salad, he asked a few of the wise guys. Against all odds: bingo. One of them pointed him in the direction of a motel on Route 191: The Rest Inn.

The motel was grimy. A hollow swimming pool had become a sacrificial pit for beer cans and ancient pool floats. A yellow and red sign fizzed over a hotdog vending machine that only the brave or stupid would eat from. But, peering inside the dim office, he could see it was freshly painted, kept tidy, a clean tank of fish, so somebody does care.

Tacked up in the window of the lobby was a sign: 'Back at 9pm. Call the below number if you want a room – ask for Wally.'

He was taught at the academy that it's much easier to lie

on a phone, so, given this is the only freakin' lead he has, Scout made the executive decision not to call, but to come back another time.

~ ~ ~

This morning, Scout pulled back into the dusty lot, in which there were at least two abandoned cars. At the same time, a blue pick-up truck was pulling out.

A flash of recognition – then gone.

Scout wondered if it was really them or a hallucination, the mirage of a waterfall to a dying man in the desert. After all, he's now three weeks into a gig he thought would take three days.

But then he spoke with Wally, the motel manager. Wally started to smile, then visibly freaked when the door bing-bonged and he looked up to find Scout. Then, he was sweating; Scout knew because his shirt darkened around the armpits.

Wally was also gesturing with both hands: doubling the chance he was lying. And when he didn't look away, even once, during their three-minute talk, Scout knew this must be the place.

He left after just a few questions; better to let the guy think he'd done a convincing job. Then had found a payphone and called his buddy high up at the DMV, promising him a steak dinner next time he saw him if he could run an interstate plate search from a name and address.

It just so happened that Wally the motel manager owned a pick-up truck, last known colour blue. And all Scout had to do was find it.

~ ~ ~

HOW IT IS

The girl saw him, so he knows exactly what they'll do. Grifters never come out the front. Scout goes to the back of the hotel, where the staff door spits out and the wrought-iron fire exit stairs zigzag down past all the floors. Squatting behind a cavernous dumpster for cover, he waits.

Sure enough, ten minutes later, there they are. A gutsy choice to come down six floors on the noisy fire escape, but then again scared people never make smart choices. Ciaran's hair is wild and he's wearing a fluffy bathrobe, the overall effect being that of a demented wizard. The girl helps him through the trickier parts of the descent, his pants and boots bundled under her arm.

Scout climbs quietly to meet them on the second-floor landing. Sexy bar-keep was right. Ciaran looks much older than his thirty-three years and as if the wholesome man of the photo had been kidnapped by a tattoo parlour, pinned down and used as a doodle pad. Two full sleeves stretch from his black T-shirt and there's the telltale peeping of a further jungle creeping up from under his collar.

Fern, the girl, also looks older than she is. She already has all the architecture of future beauty, like a line-drawn plan for a building. In a few years' time she'll pop. Fourteen is too young for him – sixteen is also – but eighteen isn't. Scout feels a tug of protectiveness towards her, as he knows not all people share his views.

Hands up to show he's not armed, demeanour humble, he goes in gently.

'Whoa, it's OK, I promise. I'm a private investigator, not a loan shark or hitman.'

He lowers his hand to encourage Fern to drop her father's biker boot, which she's now holding like a weapon. With a surprised look on her face, she lowers it, but protects her dad with her body.

'I'm not after him, Miss O'Malley,' Scout says. 'This is about you. Your mother would very much like to see you.'

The dynamic is an unexpected one. It feels less like a capture, and more like a reunion.

The Diner

HOW IT IS
Twenty minutes later

Fern crams the cheeseburger into her face and sucks the cola up a stripy straw, worried this private investigator dude might change his mind and try to take it back.

They're in a diner for Sacramento tourists, the type where the wait staff wear candy stripes and there's a lot of neon signs telling you to eat fries and be happy.

She doesn't know what 'expenses' are, but she needs to get some when she's an adult, because Scout the investigator said they can order whatever they want 'on expenses', which means it's all free. Waving to a waitress, she orders the most expensive ice cream sundae they have.

'It's on expenses,' she says, making sure the waitress gets that.

Over the road a giant windsock man punches the air above a parking lot with cars for sale. And over by the counter, her dad is doing some similarly big arm movements, explaining something serious to Scout. They both glance back at her. Scout nods and responds, Da says more. Fern wishes she could read lips. Then Da pats Scout on the shoulder, and they come back to the pink shiny booth looking like old buddies with a shared mission.

She likes Scout. He has gnarly scars and looks like he would know what to do in a fight, but his wide grin and open face made her brain relax, even when she told it not to, that it was too soon.

Scout makes some small talk about the burger, diner, service, weather. She wishes he'd just get to the big talk. Fern doesn't understand the rules of, or need for, such pointless chatter. Stop circling the point, world, and just say what you really mean.

'So, you're probably wondering why I'm here,' he says.

Is she expected to answer this? Yes, it seems. She nods.

'I'm here because your mother would like to see you. I'm under instructions to book you onto a flight back to London a.s.a.p. If you're willing to go, of course.'

Fern's breath quickens. She picks at the side of her nails. She doesn't know how to feel about this. It's been seven years, so why now?

'You're coming too, right?' she says to Da.

'Your father can't come,' Scout says.

'Why?'

Scout and Ciaran share a look. Ciaran gives him a nod.

'So you know your uncle died on Boxing Night, four years ago now?'

'I know. And?'

'There was something called an inquest, which ruled it wasn't an accident. And your pa is the chief suspect. He's wanted for questioning. So if he sets foot back in the UK or Ireland, he'll get scooped up by the police.'

Fern is silent for a long time, percolating this new information, staring intently at her fries and clenching and unclenching her fists.

'What about Digby? We get our puppy in a month.'

'You'll be back before he's ready to come to us, pet.'

HOW IT IS

Da reaches over, picks up a fist and uncurls her fingers, placing his hand flat on hers. Scout smiles at her, his eyes kind.

They think she's stressing about seeing Mum again, and she will process that atom bomb of news. But right now, she's thinking about the night Uncle Rory died; a night Da doesn't know she remembers.

The Night Rory Died

HOW IT WAS
Boxing Night 1989
Glenfoot, Northern Ireland

Fern wakes to angry voices. Her dad and his brother. She moans and stretches. The grandfather clock with the swinging circle says it's just after 10 p.m.

They get even more mad. She rolls herself out of the four-poster bed, sneaks outside and looks down into the hall below.

'Send her back! You are not fit to be a father. You're a wreckhead, not a role model for a ten-year-old!' Uncle Rory shouts. 'She's turning out to be as feral as you.'

Her uncle walks round and round, hand running over his thin hair. Fern sometimes wonders if his disappearing hair is what makes him so angry.

'I can't, Rory! She doesn't want her!' says her dad, shaking his fists.

'I refuse to believe it, Ciar!'

'Phone Imo and ask her, right now. SHE SENT HER BACK. Who do you think you are, coming back from Dubai and questioning all of this? It happened three twatting years ago. It's done!'

'Well, if that really is true, then I'll take Fern. You couldn't parent a spider plant. Any court, any judge, any authority will side with me. You're a drunk, Ciaran, and getting worse by the day. I'll petition to be her legal guardian.'

'Over my dead body.'

'Why not?' Uncle Rory says.

'You know why.'

'Nothing's ever been proven.'

'We both know there's not *that* much smoke without fire, Rory.'

'And what will social services think when I tell them what happened last week?'

'Last week?' Fern's dad rubs his hair as if that will make his memory work.

'Fucksake, Ciaran. Your blackouts are getting worse. Last week when your ten-year-old daughter ate marijuana, from a baggy that she found in your belongings. Last week when Ruth had to make her vomit it back up.'

Da now has his head in his hands.

'Send Fern back to her mother. Or I'll take her.'

Silence.

An hour later, her dad hasn't come to bed yet and Fern still lies awake, her heart beating hard.

Da *can so* parent a spider in a plant. OK, yes, he leaves the cooking and washing to Ruth, but he's hardly ever grumpy, they dance about sometimes when he plays guitar, he drives fast over the bridge because she likes it, and they go for long walks in the woods to see the rabbits.

She falls asleep and dreams of Uncle Rory putting her in a potato sack and sneaking off into the woods. She wakes when Da knocks on the door, their secret code knock. Fern unlocks it for him.

'Sorry, sorry, pet.' He tiptoes around like the Pink Panther. 'Go back to sleep. Do you want snug as a bug in a rug?'

She nods. He smooths her hair around her head, tucks the bedspread all around her, makes it as tight as possible, then squeezes her feet, before crawling onto the giant bed beside her and passing out on top of the covers.

Fern's thirsty. Wriggling out of her bug-snug, hoping she can get back into it, she goes into the bathroom and turns on the tap. It tastes like mice and metal. She imagines the mice of Ferndale using the pipes as a waterslide.

Kitchen water tastes nicer. Unlocking the bedroom door, which they always keep locked from the inside, she turns right to pad along the corridor, glass in her right hand.

She's in the West Wing and the kitchen's in the East. Her left hand finds the wallpaper that feels like her dead grandma's fancy writing paper. There's two, three, four gaps for doors before she reaches the 'divider of worlds', as Da calls it.

'In the East Wing is the old servant quarters,' he said. 'In the olden days, ladies got servants to look after their babies, so they would sleep in here – there's the nursery – and the rest of the staff would sleep here as well. Now we only have Ruth, because she's the equivalent of ten men.'

Below the nursery, bedrooms and a bathroom, a staircase goes down to a massive kitchen. Outside the back door there's a vegetable patch, a pig pen, some stables and a chicken coop. The only animals out there now are a few hens who 'think they're no goat's toe,' Ruth said. Fern asked what it meant. 'They've high ideas of themselves, lass,' she explained, her knife thunking through a turnip.

Fern stops at the dividing door, knowing that even though she usually sleeps in the nursery in the East Wing, Da didn't want her over here this Christmas.

'Stay in my room instead, pet,' he said. 'And that means

all night. If anybody but me comes knocking, don't answer. And keep that door locked,' he added, pointing to the gold key that sat in the bedroom door, waiting for its turn.

She's so thirsty. Her thirst opens the door. Up ahead on the landing she sees a person. The clouds are covering the moon so she can't see who. Then the moon shines through and she sees it's Uncle Rory. He's flicking tiny sparks from his cigarette over the landing's banister, onto the kitchen tiles below. Ruth won't like that.

He hasn't noticed her and she doesn't want him to. Half of her wants to run, but half of her wants to warn him about the banister. Da had told her worms are eating the wood, and not to lean on it until they fix it up.

She stands there, not sure what to do. He turns. Sees her.

'I'm just getting a glass of water,' she says.

'Aw, there you are. I was looking for you.' Uncle Rory gestures to the nursery room.

'Where do you sleep these days, little rabbit? C'mere,' he says, crouching down and opening his arms wide, waiting for her to come.

Fern feels a movement behind them. Mice, probably. Ruth tries to block their 'little doorways' as she calls them, with something metal and fluffy, but they keep finding their way back in.

'C'mere,' Uncle Rory repeats, growling, trying to play, but he doesn't know how.

She doesn't want to go to him, but she's been taught that when an adult wants to hug or kiss you, you have to do it. And so she goes.

'You're becoming such a beauty, you know that,' he says, pulling her in for a hug.

She pulls back, hands on her hips. 'I don't want to come and live with you.'

Then closes her eyes up tight against what's coming.

'You'll do as I say and that's the end of it,' he says, incensed. 'Cheeky article. You have your mother's looks, but your father's gall.'

Her uncle lifts her nightgown and reaches round to smack her on the backside, even though she's much too big for that now. One, two, three. She doesn't cry, she won't.

Then he keeps the nightgown lifted, crouches and looks at her pants. Fern's wearing her 'Tuesday' knickers even though it's Sunday. She wonders if she's in trouble for wearing the wrong day.

He reaches out to touch her tummy.

'You're so soft,' he says.

She freezes.

The Heron

HOW IT IS
Two days after Scout finds them – July 1993
Jamaica Bay Wildlife Refuge, New York State

A great blue heron takes flight from the pond at 8.37 a.m., heading in the direction of JFK.

~ ~ ~

A carp jumps out of the water and gets eaten by a great blue heron.

The heron takes flight from the pond at 8.38 a.m., heading in the direction of JFK.

~ ~ ~

8.55 a.m.
Flight 132 from New York to San Francisco takes off without incident.

'Lucky miss,' the pilot says as they climb.

Huh? his co-pilot's face says.

The pilot points out a giant bird approaching just below their flight path, with a wingspan of six feet.

~ ~ ~

8.55 a.m.
Climbing after take-off from JFK, the pilot of Flight 132 hears a thump. Smoke and an odour he'll later describe as like 'three-day-old trash' spread to the cabin of the Boeing 757.

The engine system indicators show damage to the right-hand engine.

Reporting an alert of 3-3 to ground, the pilot circles back and returns to JFK for a one-engine emergency landing.

Remains of a great blue heron are later found in the damaged engine.

Flight status: cancelled. Passengers are placed on a replacement plane to SFO eighty-four minutes later

Runway status: Closed for thirty-eight minutes for cleaning

Cost of damage: $1.3 million on engine removal and replacement

Time Boeing 757 is out of service: three days

Bird ID by Smithsonian, Division of Birds

The Flight

HOW IT IS
Two days after Scout finds them – July 1993
San Francisco Airport

Scout hands Fern her boarding pass. She looks at it with wonder; this is only the fourth flight of her life.

'Why does my name say Felicity Felstead? That's not my name.'

'Your mum will explain,' he says, letting her have her passport at long last. 'It's your middle name and her surname before she married your father. Don't mention to anyone else that this isn't your real name.'

He tells Fern to make sure the attendants show her to the front of the plane, where there'll be 'huge seats that go all the way back' and 'many treats'.

There was a bunch of money left in his expenses stipend, so he'd paid the extra to upgrade her to a first-class ticket, because why the hell not? He wasn't told *not to*. He can just say the only seats left were in first.

Ciaran didn't want to come to the airport, said something about needing to do a job for Wally. But given his red-rimmed eyes, Scout suspected that as soon as they were out of sight, Ciaran was going to go hide in bed, cry and drink.

Over the past couple of days, Scout and Ciaran have become friendly. In Scout's view, drunks and former drunks have everything in common – one is just further down the timeline.

'You're getting her a return ticket, right?' Ciaran asked him.

'Of course.'

'So she's definitely coming back?'

'Yes, buddy, in three weeks.'

Fern is browsing the travel accessories, mesmerised by the tiny padlocks, blow-up pillows, ear plugs, money belts.

'How are you feeling about seeing your mum, kid?' Scout asks, when they sit down to have a soda and wait for the departure gate to open.

The Tannoy crackles like a crisp packet. 'Flight 975 to London Heathrow is now ready for boarding,' an announcer says. She jumps up.

~ ~ ~

'How are you feeling about seeing your mum, kid?' Scout asks, when they sit down to have a soda and wait for the departure gate to open.

The Tannoy crackles like a crisp packet. 'Flight 975 to London Heathrow is delayed by eighty-four minutes,' an announcer says. 'This is due to a technical problem with a previous airplane.'

Scout sighs; leans back. 'Guess we've got ample time to shoot the breeze,' he says. 'So, tell me. What do you remember of your mum?'

Fern eyeballs him, as if sizing him up. She opens her mouth, shuts it again.

He'll probably never see her again, so he hopes she can open up. After all, he's told people in The Rooms his truest, maddest, deepest secrets. Sometimes strangers make for the perfect confidants.

She starts to talk, telling him everything she remembers. Which isn't much; it's mostly just flashes.

Bathtime with candles, a burnt finger, lying in bed hearing Mum and Da yell, a My Little Pony duvet, building sandcastles at Brown's Bay, peanut butter on toast.

Then, in more detail, she tells him about the swimming pool after the wedding, falling from the diving board, the bump on her head, Mum's boyfriend with the Lego hair, the chocolate star for dinner, looking out of the window for Baba Yaga.

Then flash – a slap for being bad – followed by being sent to live with Da when she was seven and not knowing why.

And then, the seven years of no contact since, no birthday cards, no phone calls. Even though she knows Mum visited Da one night at the cottage in Donegal. She woke up the next morning to the smell of her perfume and found strands of her hair in front of the fire. Telling Scout this bit, she struggles, her voice cracking.

He puts his hand over hers, then realises that's probably not OK; removes it.

'It's odd that you don't remember much,' he says.

'I know. It's weird.'

He thinks. 'How does your body feel when you think about seeing your mum?'

She moves her hands over her midriff, as if asking it.

'Worried.'

By the time the gate for Flight 975 opens, eighty-four minutes later than it should have done, Fern tells Scout that she no longer wants to go to London. And so, she doesn't.

The Police Station

HOW IT ENDS
Twenty-one years later – March 2014
Ballymena, Northern Ireland

She uses a hand to clear the fog from the car window, wiping the condensation on her leg. She sees a man being frog-marched into the police station.

Wondering what handcuffs will be like on her wrists, she can already feel the cold metal, but it's a false memory because she's never experienced it. She hears the slide of the cell's bolt, but the only bolt that's ever locked her in has been a pencil-thin one on a bathroom stall.

When she closes her eyes she can still see the outline of his body. Like the outline of the sun on the inside of your eyelids, it lingers. Splayed at odd angles, like a broken wooden toy, his body at the bottom of the stairs.

Once she explains what Rory was like, what he was doing, why he deserved it, surely that'll take the charge down from murder to manslaughter. She knows that circumstances of self-defence reduce a charge and sentence, but what about family-defence? Equally as noble a cause, surely, if not more so.

In *Thelma and Louise*, the detective said he'd get them a reduced sentence because that waste of skin they'd killed had it coming, so maybe she can get the same.

Mind you, she's not sure a Hollywood blockbuster is legal precedent. She imagines her wig-wearing barrister citing it in court: 'in the case of Thelma and Louise versus the American people, m'lord . . .'

But surely there is some sort of vigilante discount, a sentence slasher, when the person killed is a degenerate. If there isn't, there should be.

She tries to open the car door. Tells her hand to do it. Nope, still can't move.

The Split I

Flick and the Townhouse

HOW IT IS
July 1993
Heathrow Airport, London

Imo's leg bounces. Bounce, bounce, bounce go her Mary-Janes.

Heathrow's Arrivals lounge is disgusting. There is – apparently – no VIP lounge. She had to smooth the plastic wrapper from *The Sunday Times Magazine* onto the seat before sitting on it. A kid rubs a biscuit into its own hair while staring at her, then farts and laughs, while his parents smile as if to say, 'Adorable, isn't he?'

'I have a wonderful surprise,' Doug said a couple of weeks back, his caterpillar eyebrows undulating, hands behind his back. Ooh, goody. She grinned and closed her eyes, holding out her hands for whatever it was, hoping for a velvet jewellery case that snapped.

'No, honey, open your eyes,' he said.

She opened them to find – nothing.

'I found Fern.'

She wanted to vomit – then thump him. Before realising that the only acceptable reaction was happiness.

'What, how?' she said, tears starting to fall, but she could style that out, pretend they were joyful.

'Private investigator. It was a long shot, but it worked out. They used Ciaran's trail to find her.'

Her ex-husband can't even make himself scarce in the

whole of America, can he, the dimwit. Ciaran is clever in the academic sense, but otherwise, he's not the brightest crayon in the box.

Imo looks around the seating area, vexed by the proximity of the general public. 'Apparently he's advanced developmentally,' biscuit kid's mum is saying. Biscuit kid has removed his own shoe and is licking it.

Why is Arrivals such a calamity compared to Departures? It's like the grey hangover after a jewel-bright night. There's a tired mini supermarket, a badly stocked bookshop and a high-street café with a pimply adolescent playing a Gameboy. That's it.

Departures is a sexy snake of possibility: alpaca wrist-warmers, staff trying to spray you with perfume, stands with shots of orange liqueur, sunglasses to try on like you're trying on new personas. Can I pull off Lennon-round pink shades? Maybe I move to South America and become a surf babe with ironic eyewear. What about cheetah-print cat eyes – what life might I get if I buy those?

'I've booked for her to come back for three weeks,' Doug said, arms wide and waiting for a hug.

'Three weeks?' Imo said, the tail-flick of her voice a squeak.

Fern's flight has landed, but there's some sort of delay with the luggage. Of course. Never not an inconvenience.

Imo feels wretched with nerves. She could go and get a tub of those bite-size chocolate brownies from the supermarket, chug them down in the toilets, vomit them back up like nothing happened. It's tempting. But she hasn't done that since she was a teenager.

She could leave and pretend Fern never showed and somehow intercept all comms between Doug and this blasted private investigator. That wouldn't be all that hard, given Doug's password for everything is 'Password123'.

She could go to Departures and get a flight to Barcelona, warmed by orange liqueur and wearing the cheetah cat's eyes, then rent a convertible, take a lover, open a candle shop with scents like 'Dying Bonfire' or 'New Tennis Balls', pretend she'd never had a daughter at all.

Instead, she sits, broods, bounces her foot, picks fluff from her black maxi-dress. She can't believe that Doug has placed her back into the role of mother. She was such a disaster at it, on every level. The feeling of being bad at it burns her still.

~ ~ ~

Fern is three months old.

Imo lies alongside Fern on the bed, hair wet from the shower, skin bare, making monstrous faces she would never dare show another human, but her daughter still blinks up as if she's the most magical thing she's ever seen.

She's never felt so loved – so accepted – as she does by this baby. This feels like the love that was promised by rom-coms, but never materialised: unself-conscious and whole. Even Imo's honeymoon periods have felt more fraught, obsessive, jagged.

She and Fern just totally dig each other. Like that trope-y moment in a film, where the two roll over, see each other, and their faces split into grins under a gauzy linen tent.

Regrettably, they're not left to roll around in their love bubble. Nurses keep coming to the house, weighing Fern, asking how much formula she's drinking and when, her legs are cold, do you have any tights, how many times is she urinating, as if that's even possible to count. They're nosy witches and Imo has stopped answering the door.

They're renting a two-up, two-down terrace in Belfast while Ciaran finishes his degree at Queen's University. She expected that they would all live at Ferndale, Ciaran's palatial family home, but oh no. Poor Ciaran doesn't want to do the hour-long drive up and down the coast each morning and evening from Glenfoot to Belfast. It would eat into his drinking time, no doubt.

Imo grew up around money in a three-storey Regency house in London, but Ciaran's heritage is on another level. His house has wings, for crying out loud. She had the private school and ski-ing trips, even a rabbit-fur gilet that had been the envy of her boarding school, but he's from old money.

She expected that, as Ciaran's wife, she would throw lavish parties in the mansion's flamingo-pink dining room, play drunk croquet on the lawn, maybe even host a murder mystery night. She'd seek out the great and beautiful of Antrim and draw them to her – she can't abide boring people – seating ten around the long cherrywood table.

But no, instead they dine on a Formica table with a beer mat underneath a wobbly leg. Ciaran got the table for free from 'a man down the road'. They eat from chipped plates that he foraged at a 'car boot sale', whatever on earth *that* is.

It seems that his dead parents spent all their old sodding money and left him nothing but bricks and woodworm. There's a trust for Ferndale's maintenance, but she can't access it, and besides, it's tiny. Her own parents excommunicated her when she became an unwed teenage mother, even though she's now wed. Nobody comes for dinner and Imo can taste her disappointment in life like the cold tip of a spoon.

Fern's preference for her mother becomes so pronounced that she yells in protest when Ciaran picks her up, so Imo has to do not only nine-to-five, when he's at 'work' (read: studying dusty physics books and doing odd jobs so that they have some money), she also has to do most of the six-to-nine a.m., the five-to-eight p.m., oh, and all through the night too.

'It's not fair,' she says to Ciaran, after a night's sleep smashed into five pieces.

'What, that our little baby loves you best, that we're so lucky we have her, that she's healthy and happy?' he says.

Ugh. She needs a hug – not the bright side.

~ ~ ~

Fern is six months.

Something to do with the introduction of both solid foods and bouncers has resulted in unspeakable nappies. The filth reaches Fern's neck. Ciaran calls them poonamis.

'They don't bother me. I read that being genetically related to someone makes you better able to handle their poo,' he says, while changing his tenth nappy *of all time*.

Imo retches when changing Fern. Some days they get through three outfits. And given dressing a baby is like dressing a cat, that's the opposite of fun.

The highs and lows are intense. When Fern discovers she has a hand for the first time it's beyond enchanting. But if Fern is being whingey that day, Imo will watch her crawl to the edge of the bed and consider not stopping her. In the space between her daughter reaching the edge and Imo pulling her back, there's a tiny thrill. She wonders if it's because she's missing a biological imperative.

Imo confides in Ruth about being a 'tiny bit more irritable' in the past six months. She and Ruth have become close since Nora disappeared.

'I had this after having Nora,' Ruth said. 'It'll go once you get some unbroken sleep.'

Unbroken sleep, you say. When's that likely to happen?

Oh, when she's about a year old. Year and a half, at the latest.

Fabulous.

The truth is, Imo's not a 'tiny bit more irritable'. She's bloody furious. Days frequently come to a close without her having done anything she finds pleasurable. European minibreaks, sunbathing, flirting, driving with all the windows down, fine dining, reading fat novels in bed at midday; all torpedoed. Going to the toilet by herself has become a luxury, and a ten-minute shower is now on a par with a spa treatment.

Imo's expected to be home with Fern all of the time just as she's expected to wear clothes all of the time; what do you want, an award? While Ciaran is lionised for 'babysitting' if he ever takes Fern down to the hardware store for five twattin' minutes in her buggy. His 'babysitting' efforts are rewarded with twinkly smiles, while Imo's parenting only gets heaped with judgement.

Did you have a natural birth? – did you have pain relief? – are you breastfeeding? – she's rooting, though – but how long did you try for? – it takes six weeks to establish a supply – are you swaddling? – how are you swaddling, though? – are you reading to her? – she wants weaning – have you tried baby rice? No answer she gives is the right one unless it exactly matches how *they* did it.

But this is the societal quirk that really boils Imo's blood: 'Who's Fern with?' they ask, forehead creased, if Imo's out for a walk on the beach.

'Her father.'

'Och, he's so good, isn't he? You'll be wanting to hang on to that one.'

~ ~ ~

Fern is one.

The phrase 'petal soft' never made sense to Imo until she felt Fern's skin. A fuzz coverlet over silk. Imo nuzzles it and never wants Fern to grow up.

But Fern herself isn't delicate. 'She's lively, isn't she?' is the euphemism most used for her hurricane of a girl, who tears around yelling full volume, sneaks up on dogs to grab their tails, kicks Imo in the face while being changed, bites her on the shoulder if she wants down. Oh, no. Fern is not delicate.

But Imo is. She's always been in need of soft voices, treatment, fabrics and lighting. Overhead lights offend her so much that she won't even have bulbs in the ceiling lights, lest a visitor should flick it on with a 'It's very dim in here, shall we just . . .' The nerve.

Imo's mother, Penelope, sent the teenage Imo to various therapists to try to figure out why she was such a bad girl. One diagnosed her with ADHD, another with Borderline Personality Disorder. The solution for Penelope wasn't medication or therapy; it was sending Imo to boarding school.

Their family home had a full-time housekeeper, and while she was away at boarding school, her only task was to keep her few personal items tidy. And so nineteen-year-old Imo was spat into full-time housewifery, having never done a load of laundry in her life.

'Do you think you're above a bit of washing-up?' Ciaran sometimes asks, if the dishes mount up. She says no, but means yes, cursing her own mother for never teaching her the art of domestic skills. That Christmas, Fern gets a miniature washing machine and kitchen.

Only, Fern's not very helpful around the house. You can tell which room Fern's been in last because it looks like it's been burgled. Imo trails around after her daughter, going, 'No no no, you bad girl!' as she pulls the entire contents of a cupboard out, upends a file of papers.

Imo finds the disarray maddening. She has to dominate it, she can't survive it. Putting Fern in her high chair, she attacks the housework with all the violence she feels, but has nowhere to put. As she thumps around with the vacuum cleaner, it thrashes around in her wake like a crocodile's tail. She's stunned she hasn't broken it yet.

Sometimes she catches neighbours standing outside her house supposedly having a chat, but clearly eavesdropping on her rage. Sometimes they'll forget to talk and just stand there listening, making gossipy eyes at one another. Imo stands there and stares out of the window at them until they see her.

'Ooh, must dash,' Flowery Apron will say, and, 'Me too,' Violet Perm replies. That's right; off you fuck, ladies. Normally she'd care what other people think, but these streets contain terraced nobodies.

The fury can be useful. It increases her productivity, making her faster, fiercer, stronger, more; like how she's read that adrenaline sometimes means a mother can lift a car off her toddler. But it also begets the risk that she may break the catch on the washing machine door from slamming it too hard, and life without the washing machine is unthinkable.

Ciaran has caught her in her rage whirligig. Once he appeared at the top of the stairs with a badminton racket he'd grabbed from the umbrella stand in the hall.

'I thought we had intruders,' he said, confused.

'This tosser wouldn't clip up,' she said, her face burning, the clothes horse dismembered in her hands.

He laughed and hugged her as she sobbed, suggested a garden burial to make her laugh.

'Are you . . . OK?' Ciaran asked the day after the murdered clothes horse.

His pause before 'OK' said it all. A more honest sentence would have been: 'I know you're not OK, do you want to tell me why?'

'Of course!' she said. 'Just getting used to being a mother, a wife.'

In the privacy of their home, Imo uses swear words Ciaran's never heard. 'And I used to drink down at the docks,' he says, marvelling at her potty mouth. Shitballs, fucksticks, cuntface all dropped in her creamy silver Queen's English.

Outside of their home she floats, smiles and is often told she looks 'peaceful' or 'poised'. When they're out at the pub, Ciaran likes to joke that his wife is 'serene like a cloud until she's saltier than a sailor'.

Imo laughs with her mouth, but tells him to shut up with her eyes.

~ ~ ~

VERSIONS OF A GIRL

Fern is two.

Imo still loves Fern. The first time she toddles over to her and headbutts her with an open mouth, Imo squeals with joy.

'She just ran over and gave me a kiss,' she tells Ciaran, who turns from frying eggs to smile.

And never does she love her more than when Fern needs her. Pain or sadness make Fern pliant and submissive. She'll kiss the tears away, her daughter drops her cheek against her chest, and Imo sings. It's her and Fern against the world. Only she can turn her monsoon girl back into sun.

It's the in-between drudgery that Imo struggles with.

'What did she have for lunch?' Ciaran asks.

'Um, toast. Peanut butter on toast. And juice.'

'And for breakfast?' he wants to know.

'The same.'

'She can't have peanut butter on toast for every meal, Imo.'

'Why not?'

'You're clearly new to this,' the mum at the playground says to her, cocking her head at Imo's book. The woman is braless, ugly and has banana smushed into her top, which is almost certainly a pyjama top.

'You can always tell a newbie by the book in their nappy bag,' the woman continues, even though Imo is giving her a toothless smile that says: Desist, stranger.

Imo opens the book.

'I've got three, how many you got?' the woman says.

'Just the one,' Imo says, not looking up.

'Well, I bet you that you don't even manage to read two pages of that,' she says of Imo's book, punctuating with a sniff.

OK, pleb. Watch me. Imo brings the book to the playground every single day and reads it. She gets to page eighty-four by the end of the week.

Until Fern is delivered back to her howling, with blood and gravel in a hole in her knee, having fallen from the climbing frame. Worst of luck – it's the pleb who delivers her back.

'Can you watch your girl rather than *Anna Karenina*?' she says.

Imo has tried to make friends with other mothers, the ones who look polished and clever, who manage to drag a brush through their kids' hair, but their banter seems to be a language she doesn't speak. Loitering in the church hall, sidling up beside the paddling pool, dawdling at the village fête, she has made many attempts.

'Loving the breastfeeding diet,' one says, bouncing a jolly five-month-old on her hip. 'I weigh less than I have in ten years!'

'When your chips go to someone else's hips,' another mother replies.

Imo smiles wide, on the edge of the group, Fern's hot little hand in hers.

'Oh. I don't know, it looks like your hips have had *some* chips,' she says, in her warmest voice.

An icy stare. Ah c'mon, that was funny, but their gazes slide off her.

'So when are you going to stop feeding?'

'At this rate, I'm not stopping until it's weird.'

'Eight.'

'Ten.'

'High school?'

All the mums laugh, while Imo slinks away, tears pricking her eyes.

In London, that would've got a laugh. An 'ooh, you are wicked' and a wink. But she's not in London, and she's not at ballet school, she's in the provinces of Northern Ireland, where not only does she have the barriers of being upper class, beautiful and a dancer, she also has her Englishness against her.

Friendships with women have always been tricky for Imo. Nora was her only true friend, and Nora betrayed her, trying to steal Ciaran from under her nose. You can't trust women, was Imo's takeaway.

'They're jealous,' Ciaran confirms, grabbing her around the waist, reaching under her paisley mini-dress to squeeze her bum.

'I was only joking,' Imo says. 'Can nobody in this charmless backwater take a joke?'

Ciaran leans back on the kitchen counter, blows his cheeks out.

'Now that sounds borderline anti-Belfast,' he says. 'Also, it's not a backwater – this is a city full of culture. Have you really explored?'

He pauses before adding: 'And even if they are jealous, what you said was mean, honeybunch. You can't just say mean things and then say you're joking, and expect carte blanche in retrospect, y'know?'

~ ~ ~

Fern is three.

Her worship of Imo is still intact. If Ciaran picks her up, the toddler will launch herself headfirst back towards her like a mother-seeking missile. She falls asleep on her chest, while Imo strokes her kitten-soft hair.

Imo has always been beautiful, even as a child, and given her good looks are the number one thing people notice about her, this hyper-focus means she must always look perfect. Otherwise the fairy tale threatens to capsize.

It's essential that she maintains her face. Visible tide marks, stray eyelashes, stowaways in her teeth, and, heaven forbid, acne – all have the power to burst the illusion that she's beautiful. And then what will she be? Nothing.

With motherhood, Imo occupies a new space in the world. She walks with a livid Fern, who planked rather than went nicely into her pushchair, and is now struggling about on Imo's hip, trying to get down.

Attracted by the siren of the cry, the people see her as a bad mother first, a woman second. For those who do get to the woman part, she receives variations of 'If you want another, you know where to find me', as if her womb's an empty public parking space.

Imo smiles but doesn't answer back, for fear of the dark side of their desire: the dethroning. She's experienced it many times, but the most intense was in a queue for a late-night taxi in Camden.

A middle-aged man behind grabbed her hips, pulling her into him. 'Get off me,' she said, forgetting to be gracious and humble and a good girl who can take a compliment. For the remaining twelve minutes of the queue he whispered in her ear that she was ugly, fat, nobody would ever want to marry her, her body hadn't even been worth feeling.

One bedtime, Imo gives Fern the special adult treat of a candlelit bath.

'Don't touch the flames,' she tells her daughter, who nodded her tiny black head in her most sombre way.

Then Ciaran goes apeshit because he gets home and it just so happens that at *that exact time*, the phone went. All Imo did was answer the phone, for Chrissake. She told Ruth she'd have to phone her back.

And she told Fern not to touch the candles; it's not her fault she didn't listen.

~ ~ ~

Czzzzht. A bored voice informs them that Flight 975 from San Francisco has landed.

A few minutes later, she's here. Her daughter. Imo feels a fizz of unexpected love, but then what's this? Fern's wearing a Fleetwood Mac T-shirt that looks like it has fleas, and she's pulling a suitcase that she must've found in a bin. Her hair is an offensive mono-colour, desperate for highlights and a deep condition. If Imo's hairdresser saw it, he'd cry.

She goes to her daughter, feeling the eyes of men on her, always on her, kisses Fern's greasy cheek – dear God this girl needs a wash – and wraps her in a hug that she hopes says: 'I've got you, I'll help you, I'm here now.'

When she and Fern arrive home in the Mercedes, Cordelia is walking past, her arms full of yellow Selfridges bags. She has the skin of an infant, but the soul of a demon.

'Oh, hi,' Cordelia says. 'Who's this you're bringing home?'

Fern climbs out of the back of the car looking like a vagrant. Tremendous.

'This is my daughter, Fern,' Imo says, knowing that Cordelia will interrogate it all out of her anyhow.

'Fern! Such a sweet small-town name.'

Cordelia just said that Fern's name is cloying and provincial.

'Oh, Fern was her father's choice. I didn't want it, felt it was a bit too farmer's daughter.' Imo talks too much when she's nervous. 'I won on the middle name, though. Felicity. So when she's here with us, we use Felicity. Only we shorten it to Flick.'

Cordelia nods. 'Flick, yes, I like it.'

Fern/Flick stands there looking bewildered. Cordelia moves on without further ado, unapologetic as a barracuda.

Imo waits for Flick to express amazement about the house, which rises before her, a pearl-white beauty of a townhouse, twice the size of the one Doug lived in seven years ago. The compliment she's expecting doesn't come.

Their new-ish house isn't unlike the house Imo grew up in, but it's got an extra floor *and* Grecian columns flanking the entrance steps. On a column, '59' is in curly black font the size of her head. That means she's officially made it.

Flick Gets a Mother

HOW IT IS
July 1993
Kensington, London

So she's called Flick now? OK, she'll play along if it keeps Mum happy. She's wanted a mother again for so long, and now here she is, even more fragrant than she'd remembered. For some reason they've stopped at a hotel; she didn't know she was staying at a hotel.

Oh, it's their *house*. Holy cow. She fights to hide her awe. The heavy door groans to let them in. Flick looks down to see a black-and-white floor beneath her battered Vans. A copper umbrella stand is circled by a snake and a vase is stuffed with fluffy raspberry flowers.

Imo busies herself into the house, calling, 'Doug, we're home!' She's loud, but sounds scared. Flick takes off her shoes, lifts her nose to smell the flowers.

She can't smell them. There's water. But no smell. She holds, and then pinches a bud. Fake. The most convincing fake flowers she's ever seen. But why are they in water? Rich people, huh.

Tall and thin, the house unpacks large, reminding Flick of the Flatiron building in New York. Inside an open hall cupboard, she finds shelf upon shelf of other shoes, none of which are as scruffy as her kicks. So she hides hers at the bottom.

Following her mum's voice into the kitchen, she finds her reheating a pie and pouring frozen peas into a pan on the stove. It's not quite like the sitcom mothers she's been craving from the TV, but it's near as dammit.

Doug is lounging on a leather armchair in a conservatory, reading an important-looking book. His square head smiles at her, he gets up to greet her. Lying on a sofa is his seventeen-year-old son, Rupert, who Flick has never met.

Rupert jumps to his feet and shakes her hand. He's so twinkly and tanned, but Doug is uptight and dull. Maybe Rupert's more like his mother, like how her and Da are more alike.

Doug places the invisible cue down on the dinner table. 'It was very good of your mother to come and get you from the airport, wasn't it, Fern, er, I mean, Flick?'

She chews her shepherd's pie and considers it. Um, no, not really. Wasn't that just standard parenting? Even her dad wouldn't expect a trophy for that one.

'Yes, very good,' Flick confirms once her mouth is empty. She's been told to eat more quietly already, which is challenging as she doesn't know how else to eat.

'Thank you, Mum, I'm so grateful,' she says, the pitch of sarcasm designed for Rupert's ears only. He hears it, throws her a half-smile.

'How's school?' asks Doug, folding up his napkin.

She shakes her head. 'Oh, no, I don't do school. I'm an autodidact.'

'A what?' asks Doug.

'Y'know. A self-learner. Da gives me big lists of books I need to read, from Darwin to Dylan Thomas. I get two books a week from the library, read them, make notes and show him. Ask me about anything – we've just done the Tudor dynasty and cloud formation.'

Doug harumphs. Imo places a hand on his to brake him.

'We have *The Wonder Years* on cassette if you'd like to watch it after dinner in the kids' den?' Imo says.

Flick wonders how to put this in a polite London way. There seem to be different rules here.

'Thank you *so* much. But do you have *Columbo*? Or *Cheers*?'

Doug wipes his mouth with a napkin. 'Those are adult shows – you're only thirteen,' he says.

'I'm fourteen, and I don't watch kids' shows,' she replies.

'Don't answer back, young lady,' says Doug.

'But if I didn't answer you, I'd be told off for *not* answering you.'

Rupert sits back and watches the exchange like a ping-pong match, his mouth twitching with amusement.

For the next two weeks, Flick half expects canned laughter to kick in, or for a director to shout, 'Cut!' because this feels too good to be true.

Every morning she wakes up in the same bed, well rested. There are no 2 a.m. shouts of, 'Get 'im! Get 'im, Harry!' from a nightwalker to her pimp; a pimp who is now trying to catch a 'runner'.

The only sounds that she hears at night are clanks from century-old plumbing. There's a floorboard on the way to the bathroom that sounds like Victorian ghosts crying ('It really does,' Rupert says, when she shows him), but other than that, it's so peaceful here.

HOW IT IS

She starts to feel the unwind that comes from a home that isn't a former crime scene. She writes in a journal with a tiny padlock; a gift from her mum. There have been many gifts. Each more thoughtful than the last.

Every morning, Imo greets her with a full-body hug. She cuts an orange into quarters for her, boils an egg, some toast pops up. The 'I love you's, the 'I missed you's make Flick question why her few memories of childhood are so dark and troubled. Maybe they're not real.

When Imo beams her full attention upon Flick, Rupert or Doug, it's like standing in a single ray of sunshine. Only one person gets it at a time, as if it's too special to be shared.

Flick doesn't have to worry about where the next meal is coming from, whether they're about to be evicted from a room, whether they're going to get robbed by a guy with an air gun and an air of desperation. She doesn't have to stress about what the man with the rat's tail wants from her dad. (Money. It's always money.)

Here, money is never mentioned. It's there, there's lots of it and there's no danger of it running out. End of. Flick wraps herself in the cool cotton duvet, stroking the silky trim with her finger.

Then she says something wrong.

Mum is talking about the North American healthcare system, sitting at the marbled kitchen island with a cafetiere of coffee and her friends, Stephanie and Damian.

'People bellyache on about the unfairness of the American healthcare setup, but if you have a job, you have health insurance, so it's only the idle who can't access medical help,' her mum is saying. 'If you ask me, it's genius.'

Last time Flick checked, Mum doesn't have a job, so she'd be OK with no healthcare? Plus, she doesn't know what the hell she's talking about. It's far more complicated than that.

'That's not true,' Flick says. 'Lots of people have jobs but no health insurance. Lots and lots and lots.'

Mum's voice is light, but her face is not. 'Oh, Flick, lovebug, you're *fourteen years old*. You don't know anything. Including how to style your hair, it seems.'

Damian snorts, but Stephanie shakes her head and frowns.

'I'm only kidding,' Imo says, enclosing Stephanie's hand in hers. 'Flick can take a joke, can't you? Off you scoot and I'll show you how to straighten your hair later.'

Hungry, Flick sneaks back into the kitchen an hour later, reaching the pantry unnoticed. Mum and her friends have moved on to wine and they're talking about Da.

'So where is he now? What does he do?' Damian asks.

'He's a session musician living in San Francisco,' Imo says.

Flick bursts out laughing. She tries to cover it up with her hand, coughs to style it out, fails.

'Something funny, dear? Come out and tell us,' Damian calls.

Worried, she comes out holding a jar of pineapple, like it will defend her.

'No, it's just . . . Da's not a whatever-that-is musician. He's a busker and occasional gigger living in a dump called Paradise, which is three hours outside San Francisco.'

Damian throws his head back and roars in amusement.

She's sent to her room. Shortly after, a note is pushed under the door; it smells like daisies.

'I am very angry. Don't talk to me for twenty-four hours. Then apologise.'

The silent treatment, then. Flick hadn't realised they were back at primary school.

That night, the three of them go out for dinner, while she's left at home. Part of her wants to take a spray can of paint, shake it to hear the rebellion rattling around inside waiting to be released and *fsssshttt* – an explosion of colour.

She'd spray 'FUCK THIS, FUCK THIS, FUCK THIS' in neon pink all over this house. That'd blow Imo's hair back.

She wanders the townhouse, fingertips touching things she normally wouldn't dare to. She gets a batshit urge to take a baseball bat to a dresser full of china. She opens the hall cupboard and looks at the shelves of folded scarves, neatly stacked gloves and hats. It turns out that Doug tidies it all up.

'He'll fold you if you sit there for long enough,' Mum said.

She's been left without dinner, so she's now on the prowl in the kitchen, but all she can find are glass jars full of grains, dried fruit and a crate full of veg. Imo has a rule against any 'junk'.

Flick settles for a box of Ritz crackers, the naughtiest thing on offer, and grabs a lump of cheese from the fridge. Flipping the radio on loud, she dances around the kitchen, taking great bites out of the cheese and pouring crackers from the box into her mouth.

Going into the living room, she grabs a soft shawl of Imo's, and twirls with it. On the Art Deco sideboard, there's a photocard from when Imo was at the Royal Ballet School – well over a decade ago – sitting in a gorgeous Japanese dish.

Next to it is a photo of Imo with David Bowie, both popping their hips, clearly taken backstage after a ballet performance. Mum looks deadly and amazing in a goth tutu and sharp crown.

Behind, there are books, many unread. *I Know Why the Caged Bird Sings* is joined by *One Hundred Years of Solitude* and *Wide Sargasso Sea*. There's a massive marshmallow-striped shell that looks like it once belonged to a mermaid, Mexican worry dolls, a Picasso scribble of a bull . . . is that an original?! Sheesh.

It all feels very deliberate, unlike the jumble of other people's houses. This living room is not for living. Even the TV folds away into a cupboard, only coming out at night when Doug is reading upstairs, Flick is meant to be asleep, and Rupert is playing his video games.

Flick once snuck into the hallway to watch as Imo removed the TV remote from a drawer, mixed a cocktail from the drinks cabinet, and threw down one of her little blue pills.

Lit by the blue glow of *The Darling Buds of May*, her mum's face came undone, jaw hanging, skirt riding up to show the lacy tops of stockings, the TV show on so low that Flick's surprised she can hear it.

She looked like the loneliest person in the world.

In the final week of her stay, Flick starts to keep her mouth shut. And she is rewarded for it.

'We're home!' Imo shouts, slamming the door with authority. 'And we've been shopping!'

Rupert ducks into the hallway from the kids' den, curious. Imo's heels click into the kitchen and her face kisses Doug, while Rupert grabs some bags.

'Where are these going?' he asks. Flick points upstairs. 'The spare room.'

Imo overhears. 'You mean *your* room, sweetheart.'

Throwing the bags on the floor in her room, Rupert bounces onto her bed and pats the space beside him.

'You're staying then,' he says.

'Just until next week,' Flick replies. 'My dad won't let her keep me for ever.'

Rupert's voice drops. 'You're underestimating Imo,' he says.

Flick begins to unpack the things she didn't want. A cassette player and classical music, a sugar-spun ballet tutu, tights and a wrap cardigan ('We'll buy you some pointes if you're any good,' Mum said).

There's also a magnifying pocket mirror ('You often have food in your teeth'), plus some tweezers and facial bleach ('You'll either thank me or thump me for these'). Flick pushes these under the bed so Rupert won't see them.

He's too busy looking at the four preppy outfits Flick would never usually wear.

'Wow,' Rupert says, holding up a houndstooth skirt, a navy cardigan with lime-green piping, a grey jumper dress, a black ensemble for a party.

'I know.'

'When's your audition?'

'For what?'

'To be Imo's understudy.'

Fern Goes to the Gig

HOW IT IS
July 1993
Sacramento, California

I'm proud of you, Buck's mouth is saying. And she's trying to take the compliment, really she is, but she just wants to list all the reasons he shouldn't be.

Her dad was impressed too, saying how 'brave' she was, but she doesn't understand. Why is *not* doing something brave? All she did was *not* get on a plane. Surely getting on the plane would have been the braver option.

They round the corner and are swallowed by the dirty bass coming from the Cattle Club. After this warm-up DJ, the Lemonheads are playing. It's a sell-out show that they don't have tickets for, but that doesn't matter, given Buck and Fern know most of the door, bar and catering staff on rotation for local events.

Buck puts his arm around her as they reach the door.

'Well, if it isn't Wednesday Addams and the Fresh Prince,' Steve says, folding his arms across his chest.

She's dressed head to toe in black, a generous amount of kohl ringing her eyes, while Buck's in a white T, stonewash denim and white kicks.

'C'mon, Steve, you know us, you can put us on the guest list,' Buck says.

Fern can't look at Steve. The last time she saw him was behind Paradise Falls. And now she's supposed to just – what – act normal? Even Buck seems to expect it of her.

Dina spots them from the ticket office, their entrance blocked by Steve's Action Man stance.

'Steve, you dipshit!' she calls.

He flinches.

'Let them in or I'll have your guts for garters!'

Fern smiles at her father's potty phrase coming out of Dina's pretty mouth.

Steve thumbs-up to Dina, then hocks and spits on the sidewalk beside Buck, ushering them in.

Buck fist-bumps the bar-keep – another local they vaguely know – and orders two pints of lime and club soda 'and *definitely* no vodka as we're underage'. The bar-keep slips two double shots of vodka into the drinks when his supervisor isn't looking.

'So how long are you and your pops sticking around?' asks Buck, pulling on his straw. 'You said you might move on soon.'

'I don't know,' Fern says. 'Paradise is the longest we've stayed anywhere. I hope we stay.'

'What are you youngsters doing in here?' a busybody with a nose-ring asks.

'We're band kids,' Fern recites. This is always their line, at any gig. Band kids are always allowed. Age restrictions need not apply. The man's eyes light up.

'Evan Dando's?'

'No, the manager's.'

'Can you get me backstage?'
'Can you get us a drink?'

As Evan Dando adjusts his stripy beanie and sings about the cellar door being open, and him unable to stay away, Fern realises that they can't stay, even though she wants to, because America is what's wrong with Da.

In Ireland, her dad had been happier, much happier. He'd overdone it a few times a week, for sure, had got clattered in the pub weekly, yes, but his drinking and drugging had never been this bad.

During the year they'd spent at the cottage in Donegal, there had even been frequent nights of *no drinking*. After asking several local men 'about a dog' only to be bored with details of imminent litters of sheepdogs, Da had given up trying to score weed. There'd been no three-day benders and she hadn't seen any of those empty sachets dusted with white powder.

Aged eight, she'd picked one of those bags up, dipped her finger in and licked it, expecting sherbet. Her mind collapsed and then exploded like a kaleidoscope. When Da saw her with the bag, he shook her hard for the first time ever – and the last time since.

'Never do that! Never ever! These are for adults only!' he said, then made her swill pints and pints of water around her mouth, spitting them out.

Then there was the episode where a ten-year-old Fern had tried to get high by eating marijuana, not realising you either had to bake it into a brownie – or just smoke it. Ruth found her with the bag, questioned her on what she was chewing, and then made her stick her fingers down her throat.

HOW IT IS

Since they've landed on American soil, her dad's behaviour has slowly, surely become worse. She can see this so clearly now, lit in her brain by the flaming torch of the vodka. He can't get better here in hot, deep fried, 24/7 California.

She needs to clear his name with the police and get him back to Ireland, pronto, where he can go back to being the Donegal version of Da.

He doesn't know it yet, but Scout is going to help her. His cell number, scrawled on an airport diner napkin, is in the most important pocket of her orange wallet.

She tosses back the rest of her drink and attempts to escape her own head by moving. She pulls Buck into the mosh pit and joins in, shoving people around. Until she's lifted up and pulled over dozens of hands, who surf her right to the back.

There, she's placed on the floor by a six-foot-five goth, who says, 'Holy crap, you're a *kid* – what are you doing in here?'

Fern shakes herself as she laughs. Buck finds her, his face scribbled with worry.

She grabs him, kisses him full on the lips and pushes back into the pulsing crowd to do it all again. The rush is like a firework. *This.*

Flick Goes to the Ball

HOW IT IS
August 1993
Kensington, London

'I'm Fer . . . Flick,' she says, offering her bony hand. This new nickname is going to take some getting used to. Her hand is enclosed by the giant flipper of the man with the walrus moustache. He looks like a Beatles lyric.

Her mother is shepherding her around the party, a charity ball. Mum's wearing floor-length black velvet and the strands of hair caught on the dress's fishtail look like saffron.

Wally buys saffron at Sacramento market and puts some in his famous chicken tagine. 'Red gold', he calls it, handling it carefully, telling her that per ounce, saffron is more expensive than gold.

Flick pulls at the black skater skirt and itches the collar around the woollen short-sleeved top. 'Why is this so itchy?' she asks. 'Hush. It's cashmere,' Mum replies.

When Mum gave her all the outfits, Flick pulled out a silky label and asked, 'Can we write my name on this?' Imo was confused. 'Like you used to, with the orange pen that doesn't run?'

Mum laughed, found the orange pen and wrote 'FLICK' in lovely writing.

The domed ballroom is gorgeous. It feels like being trapped inside a Fabergé egg. Imo showed them to her at the

HOW IT IS

V&A earlier that week, priceless Easter eggs with trapped worlds inside: three sisters, a golden coach, even a palace.

They're seated at a table with frothy white flowers in the centre.

'Peonies! How glorious,' says Imo, leaning over to smell them. Flick recognises them as the ones her mother has in the hallway.

'You have some pink ones of those at home . . . but these are real,' she says.

Under the table, Imo pinches her thigh.

'Yes, I suppose she is pretty,' Imo is saying, as if she's only just realised herself, to the man next to her.

'Shame she inherited her father's nose, though.' The man honks with laughter.

'Smart little thing,' says Walrus Moustache. 'Fourteen, you say? I wouldn't be surprised if she leapfrogs a school year or two. She gave me an A-level-worthy interpretation of *Moby-Dick*.'

Imo sits back, sits higher. 'Why, thank you, Dean Roberts,' she says.

Flick's overheard enough. She slides back into her spot beside Imo, who hisses, 'Where were you?' and gestures to the food that apparently no one could start until Flick sat down. There's a goblet of green stuff and orange fishes with tails.

'Prawn cocktail,' Mum says.

Flick picks up a prawn and pops it into her mouth whole, crunching through the jacket and tail, then uses her napkin to pull the shards out of her mouth. *Bleurgh*. Prawn cocktail is overrated.

*

'You're quite the dancer!' says Damian.

He's the asshole who laughed at her nose just now. And hair, back in Mum's kitchen.

'It's easy, you just copy what other people do with their feet,' she says, shutting him down.

Flick's had the weirdest doll-sized dinner of her life, which also consisted of gross cold soup ('It's meant to be,' Imo had informed her) and the tiniest chicken she's ever seen ('It's a quail, not a chicken') and a dessert they *set fire to*, which was something to do with Alaska. She's impressed, but still hungry.

The rich people dance to a cover band doing Motown tracks. The band are the only black people in the room. Flick heads to the side of the stage, which is full of discarded wines to sweep. 'Winesweeping' her and Buck call it.

She misses Buck – and Da, and Wally, and Dina, and her future puppy, Digby – but the wine will help with that. She copies the backing dancer's choreography. They notice and beam, giving her harder steps to try.

'She takes after me,' says Imo. 'I was a dancer, before having Flick. I started age five with lessons, then studied at the Royal Ballet School. I played Odile in *Swan Lake* even though I was only a first year. David Bowie saw me dance.'

Everyone looks impressed, apart from Doug, who's clearly heard this story multiple times.

'Well, she's a credit to you,' says Stephanie.

'Remarkable, just like her mother,' says Damian.

Imo's eyes land on Flick; she smiles and then tucks a strand of hair behind her daughter's ear.

They're doing eighty on the motorway in the Mercedes, but it feels like thirty. When Wally's pick-up truck goes above forty, it starts juddering like it's about to explode, wheels rolling down the highway, leaving Wally sitting holding only a steering wheel.

Flick slides down the soft leather of the Mercedes' back seat and realises: she likes expensive things.

'Dean Roberts looked very well,' Imo is saying. Doug agrees. 'Cordelia looked annoyingly well too,' she continues. 'But Stephanie. Heavens. Stephanie looked *dreadful*.'

Flick flinches. Isn't Stephanie meant to be her friend? Doug remains mute.

Flick slouches in the back seat and touches her nose again. She's never loved her nose, but she's never hated it either. The car turns without effort like a river, again and again, moving onto a fairy-tale bridge. Gold and pink, the bridge's turrets have lacy flowers on them, and there are old-fashioned lamp-posts.

'What is *this*?' Flick asks.

'Oh, it's Albert Bridge,' Imo says, bored.

'Who made it?' Flick imagines Mariah Carey summoning it out of the Thames with a wand.

'Some queen or other,' says Imo. 'Victoria? I think it was a wedding gift . . . Did I ever tell you about the time a member of the royal family hit on me?'

She swivels to face Flick, who shows no interest. 'Well, that's a story for another time. It's a corker, isn't it, Doug?'

Doug mm-hmms.

Flick watches the speckled moon moving with them over the bridge's spires, as if it's following them. She wonders what Mariah would stash in those tower rooms. Litters of kittens, probably.

'I'll tell you something, Flick,' Imo says.

She waits on the something, while Imo reaches her velvet-gloved hand into the back seat and gropes around. Flick stares at it, puzzled, then realises and holds it.

'I've loved having you here, darling,' she says. 'We both have.'

Doug turns and smiles, his profile a confirmation.

'So . . .' Imo pauses for dramatic effect, like a presenter giving an award, '. . . stay for the rest of the summer, won't you? We'll go to see concerts beside the lake at Kenwood House, see dinosaur skeletons at the Natural History Museum, go on the riverboat to Greenwich.'

Mum twists in the front seat, eyes dancing. 'Say yes, say yes, say yes!'

Flick is stunned. 'OK . . . yes,' she says.

The car swings onto their street, the townhouses crowded into a tight crescent like clenched teeth.

Sleepless the next night, Flick goes to the bathroom for a glass of water. Downstairs is out of bounds to her after 9 p.m., while Rupert has no curfew. By now, she knows better than to break the rules.

She's two storeys up from the ground-floor hall, but the stairwell behaves like a sound periscope, magnifying what's said on the hallway phone.

'No, Ciaran,' she hears her mother say.

Padding down the thick-pile stairs, Flick crouches on the landing above, looking through the banisters. Imo is sitting on a stair, trying to be quiet, but is clearly drunk. Flick wonders why people keep phones in the hallway, where there is the least chance of privacy.

'No, Ciaran!' Imo says again, her voice rising. She drops back down in volume.

'If you come and get her, I will tell the police everything. They'll find out *exactly* how Rory died.'

A long pause.

'She's staying here. That's the end of it.'

Imo places the phone down and throws her head back to swallow a pill. Flick darts back into the shadows of the stairwell above.

Her mum leaves the tin on the stair and goes into the living room. Flick can hear the opening of the globe drinks cabinet, the tinkle of ice, the pour of a drink.

She creeps downstairs and looks for a redial button on the phone. She's desperate to talk to Da, to tell him she's sorry, she just needs a mother too, that's all. She'll come home at the end of the summer, promise, she misses everyone so much, she can't wait to get Digby home.

But the phone is an antique, gold-leaf ornament. There is no redial.

Instead, she picks up the tin, removes a pill from it. Maybe this'll help.

Not long after, she feels the warm hand of the drug smooth back her hair, stroke her forehead and sssh her. *Everything will be OK*. Flick leans her head against the staircase and watches Imo watching TV.

She doesn't know what this drug is called, but it feels exactly like what she wants from her mother.

Flick Stays in London

HOW IT IS
A few seconds earlier

'If you come and get her, I will tell the police everything. They'll find out *exactly* how Rory died,' she says.

'You'd really do that?' Ciaran is asking her. 'To your own daughter?'

'She's staying here. That's the end of it.'

The antique phone dings with protest as Imo slams it down. God, she misses him. God, she hates him. She throws back a diazepam to avoid feeling her feelings.

~ ~ ~

Fern is four.

Imo and Ciaran are a disaster. They fight and shag, fight and shag, sleep eat repeat. Fundamentally unsuited for healthy co-existence, they're like two magnets that are either way too tight or repelling each other with all their might.

Ciaran tried to make light of their skirmishes in the first couple of years.

'All new parents argue,' he said. 'Your amygdala gets larger when you have a baby, so our brains are more primal, that's all. Maybe we should get some of those Sumo suits and run at each other in the garden, screaming.'

Imo didn't laugh.

Ciaran says he loves her but she knows he doesn't. She

saw the deep love he had for Nora. This is its lustier but shallower cousin; a hot tub to an Olympic-sized pool.

Imo stalks him when they argue, not able to stand the distance, while he flees and asks to be left alone. She chases, he runs. She stands over him disallowing sleep until they reach harmony, but they can never reach harmony without him getting some sleep. He asks for space, she comes in closer.

When Ciaran moonlights as a handyman for cash in hand, he gets sexual favours as tips. She only wears Opium by Yves Saint Laurent, displaying the bottle on her dressing table like art, but he comes back smelling like Charlie Blue and then – cheaper still – White Musk. He starts carrying condoms even though he and Imo don't use them, preferring the rhythm method.

The savagery reaches new levels. He says she's damaged and desperate in a pretty package. She says his dead mother would be ashamed of him.

They've said all the words there are, so he punches a wall next to her face and she throws a mug of scalding coffee at his torso. He dodges it, which makes her roar with frustration. Untouchable, this guy.

From there, they both know there is no place to go. And so, one night Ciaran packs a bag while Imo sleeps, her hair swooshed around her face like Botticelli's Venus.

He sneaks into Fern's room where she is a burrito in a My Little Pony duvet, leaving her a paper aeroplane with 'I love you, pet' written in his curly looping script.

His note to Imo is sealed and up high on the kitchen shelf so Fern won't read it when she wakes at 6 a.m. and tiptoes into the kitchen, humming.

Dear Imo,

She can't grow up in this hostile climate. She deserves better. We deserve better.

You were right, I've been sleeping around. I'm sorry I called you a psycho for being on to me. You weren't a psycho, you were right.

You're Fern's mother so you get to keep her, but I'll always want her if you ever don't. I know you struggle with her sometimes.

I'll be in touch in a couple of weeks to make arrangements. I've gone to Ted's until I find my feet.

Thank you for giving us our daughter. She's everything I never knew I wanted.

Ciaran

Months of trying to change his mind follow. She phones Ted's and threatens to hurt herself if he doesn't come home. They start letting it ring out. She turns up at his university wearing nothing but stockings under a trench coat. She sends him a first edition of Graham Greene's *Rumour at Nightfall*, with a sweet note inside saying she misses him, a pressed flower as a bookmark.

Nothing works. He remains unreachable. Not that she has *ever* managed to reach him, even when he was snoring right beside her.

~ ~ ~

Fern is five.

They move back to England and Imo seeks work as a private ballet tutor. With that income plus a laughable amount of child maintenance from Ciaran and the government, she manages to rent a two-bed apartment off the Kings Road. It's grim, but it's the right postcode.

~ ~ ~

Fern is six.

She completely changes towards her mother. They'd never experienced the terrible twos, apart from a couple of incidents where Fern refused to leave the supermarket without a strawberry pinwheel.

Enter the Satanic Sixes, as Imo has nicknamed them. Always in public, Fern shouts, hits, even twists away from her mother and into traffic. Throws a milkshake over her and calls her a cow.

Imo's ballet students worship her. 'You look like a princess,' one says. Others want to touch her skin. They bring her flowers on her birthday.

Whereas Fern offers nothing but scorn for the way her mother looks, walks, talks, drives, cooks, provides. It's all: your teeth have yellow edges on them. I hate you. Why do you have hairs up your nose? Your toes turn out like a pigeon. I want a Benetton jumper. This dinner is disgusting. You drive too slow, hurry up. Your breath smells like an ashtray. Why is our flat such a dump?

Imo gives Fern the picture from her and Ciaran's wedding day, thinking she might want it for her bedside.

'I can see it's you, but you look so different now,' Fern says. 'Like you're a hundred years old.'

Imo is twenty-six.

Fern looks eerily like Ciaran, and this too seems to have become an unrequited love. First the father rejected her and now his daughter is too. Despite Imo giving them *everything* she is, they both find her substandard.

Then Imo meets Doug. Finally, after three years of scrabbling around for scraps, going on awkward dates in high-street pasta restaurants with men who order the second cheapest bottle on the menu, she's found an eligible bachelor with a diversified portfolio.

The first time he comes round for dinner he sits on her battered second-hand Laura Ashley sofa looking incongruous in his tailored suit. With his city-broker hair, he looks like he should be sitting on a neat Chesterfield instead, swirling a brandy glass and eating something dotted with caviar.

His chosen seat is as ironic as a detective sitting on top of a buried body. Underneath that very cushion, she's started hiding the 'final reminder' bills, in the hope that some sort of vortex under there might make them disappear. So far, no luck.

~ ~ ~

Fern is seven.

Three months into their courtship, Imo is invited to meet Doug's parents. This is the moment they tip over into serious. Like her mother taught her, a man chases a woman until she catches him.

It's been a tough summer for them. Doug is divorced too and already has a ten-year-old son, so he's nervous about taking on someone else's little girl. Fern is asked to stay in her room whenever Doug comes round. Imo buys her a little TV and gives her microwave dinners on a tray.

His family estate is in Yorkshire; a sandstone manor with a family crest above the door, but once she steps inside, Imo sees that his parents have kept everything they ever owned.

Some rooms look like they've just moved in, corners piled high with boxes. With a couple more decades of hoarding, they may need to burrow their way out. No wonder Doug is so neat, aligning his pens like stationery soldiers.

Imo picks her way through the grungy house. They've mopped the pathways through the boxes, wiped the table they take afternoon tea on, bleached the toilet bowl, but the rest of the house is lined with dust and cobwebs. Given she's wearing a two-piece from Karen Millen that she'll definitely need to return, she's as careful as if she were wearing a suit made of live kittens.

'No tea for me, just water, thank you.'

It's a success. She charms his genial mother (lipstick on her teeth the entire time) and his mostly mute father (who stares at her legs as if they're a TV).

They get engaged, and Imo and Fern move into Doug's Kensington townhouse. The week of the move, an eviction notice is sellotaped to the door of her rented flat. She takes great pleasure in burning the notice to ash with a match. Then she stands on her balcony overlooking Chelsea and lights up a lavender-and-gold Sobranie, because she can afford to smoke these now, *bitches*.

~ ~ ~

Fern is seven-and-a-half.

Imo and Doug are at a thirtieth in a five-star hotel, Fern stashed upstairs in a two-bedroom suite with a baby grand piano. She's been given peanut M&Ms, the code to order films and has been told not to leave the room under any circumstances.

'Who has their thirtieth at Claridge's?' Imo says to Doug, who – she notes in a sidebar – is looking his full forty-five years right now. 'A wedding, yes, a sixtieth, yes, but a thirtieth? That's just obscene. What's wrong with Annabel's? I'll have my thirtieth *there*.'

At his suggestion that maybe they can just enjoy it, rather than stab their friend in the back all night long, she click-clacks off to the powder room.

She knits her brow to see that the bathrooms are exquisite too. The door is curved mahogany, the lights are soft and shaped like roses and a golden bird perches above a vaulted Art Deco mirror. The loo even feels slightly heated, for Godsake. A painted cherub offers her a paper towel and she wants to punch him in the face.

She's heading back to the function room – and to Doug – when she sees him. Ciaran, sitting on a red leather stool in the bar looking madly handsome and talking to a rumpled academic. She feels a jump of *gimme*.

Imo finds a mirror in the foyer, fluffs out her navy tulle gown, reapplies her raspberry lipstick and smooths her hair. She then makes her way to Ciaran across a high-shine floor as treacherous as a frozen lake.

She'd thought Fern was asleep, she was sure she'd been asleep. She wasn't asleep.

Imo had checked just before coming upstairs that Doug was safely stashed away with his cronies in the champagne bar, braying about ways they could all continue to get richer. She'd then peeped in on Fern, who was still and silent.

But then Fern was up and standing by the door of the suite's living room, holding a plush rabbit, a smug look on her face, having just walked in on her mum and dad, both topless and rolling around on the sofa.

Ciaran's really helpful reaction is: 'Holy fucking shit, pet, oh my God, Mum and I are just, errr . . . OK I'm off I'll see you soon OK loveyoubye.' He then leaves.

Fern looks at Imo, defiant.

'I'm going to tell Doug,' she says.

'Don't you dare. It wasn't what it looked like.'

'I'm going to tell him. I want you and Da back together anyway.'

Fern turns to go back to bed.

'Come here,' Imo says, her voice low.

Fern comes over, body softening, expecting a hug.

Imo slaps her round the face, hard.

The next day, Imo catches a last-minute flight to Ireland and drops Fern at Ferndale. It's only meant to be for the remainder of the Christmas holidays.

'I can't cope with her right now, Ruth. I need a break. I phoned Ciaran to let him know, so he'll be here tomorrow. I can feel myself becoming like *her*.'

'Like your mother?' Ruth says, arranging macaroons on a floral plate. They've had many late-night chats about Imo's mother over gin.

'It's like trying to resist gravity.'

'In my experience age only compounds it.'

'Did you ever lose it with Nora?'

'Yes, the night she left.'

'What happened?'

Ruth breaks eye contact, turns back to stir the tea. *Too close.* Her walls may be down, with Imo at least, but there's an ornamental border that you don't want to step on.

As she drives away from Ferndale, Imo whoops, rolls the windows down, feels the bite of the winter air, turns Mozart up. A whole ten days of freedom, of not being told she's failing at everything, of not having drinks poured over her in public. Why are fathers allowed to bugger off for weeks at a time, but mothers aren't? It's hypocrisy.

A week later, she writes to Ciaran and tells him he can keep Fern. She wasn't meant for this task. Somebody else will have to do it, just as they should have done all along.

~ ~ ~

Imo lies on the sofa watching *Dallas*. That second diazepam almost unhinged her jaw, like a snake about to eat a meal, but she'd needed it after that phone call with Ciaran.

The last three-and-a-half weeks with Flick have been more pleasing than she ever could have expected. She's enjoyed buffing the girl to a shine, dressing her, hugging her, exposing her to culture, teaching her how to be more considerate.

Mothering a seven-year-old was an entirely different experience, one that Imo felt she was hopeless at. But this kind of mothering? This she can do. Flick is fourteen, fiercely independent, spends a lot of time in her room, and can legally be left alone for long stretches.

This has been more like a makeover meets a mentorship, and Imo feels a push of joy in her chest when she does it; a feeling that she only gets when she's good at something. She can remake this wildling in her image, maybe even coach her to fulfil her own unrealised ambitions.

What's more, receiving all of that praise last night on Flick's behalf had been intoxicating. Pretty, capable of skipping a school year, a great dancer. What had Stephanie said again? 'A credit to you.' Yes, she could well be, with some work.

Maybe Flick could stay even longer, beyond the end of the summer.

Fern's Body

HOW IT IS
Seven years later – February 2001
Los Angeles, California

Fern scrubs her face clean and pulls the cartoonish fake eyelashes off in unison. The rule for any stripper is to take a usual face of make-up and triple it. Subtle doesn't get tips.

Outside of work, she wears sod-all make-up and pulls her unbrushed hair into a tight bun or tucks it under a cap. This means she never gets recognised and she wants to keep it that way. Her regulars are not the types she wants to shoot the breeze with in Target.

'It's not what you think,' Misty, the club manager, told her on their first walk through the club, when Fern paused at the sight of a dancer using heavy-duty stage make-up on her inner thighs. 'The bruises are from the pole. It's a lot tougher than it looks.'

When she interviewed a month back, Fern wondered if Misty was the manager's real name. Now, a month in, she knows that nobody uses their real names here in Stripperland, unless they're a total doughnut.

'You'll want to get yourself some pleasers,' Misty said, gesturing to a row of ankle-breaker heels.

'Pleasers?' Fern asked.

Misty didn't bother to reply.

Fern had been planning to show up in her Doc Marten's rather than six-inch stilettos, but clearly that wouldn't fly.

Feminism doesn't live here. She wonders if the clients like this stuff because they've been conditioned to, or because they actually do.

'If you're good, you'll make around three hundred dollars in a four-hour shift. That's four private dances plus stage tips,' Misty added. 'You'll need to pay us a hundred stage rental upfront per shift, no matter what you take home. You can do drop-in shifts occasionally, but we prefer you stick to the schedule so we don't have too many girls fighting over the same guys.'

Fern didn't really process that last bit. She was too busy calculating this: two tiny little shifts a week would be more than enough, leaving plenty of time to study, hang out with her Jack Russell, Digby, and drive back to Paradise every few weekends to check on Da. The remainder would cover her food, car, rent and the slice of her UCLA tuition not covered by her scholarship. She wanted to do cartwheels, but kept her face casual.

'You can drink on shift given you're twenty-one, and if you get them to buy champagne, you'll get a third of our profit,' said Misty. 'Don't do drugs here unless they offer them. And I advise you to never work in exchange for drugs, unless you want to wind up in the red light real fast.'

'Is it cash in hand, off the books?'

Misty nodded. 'As far as we're concerned, the money that changes hands here – other than your stage rental – is a private transaction between you and the client.'

They were walking past a row of booths, not much bigger than confession stalls, with heavy velvet curtains hooked up to one side, but ready to come down and hide what's inside.

'What happens in there is up to you,' Misty said, pointing into the private booths. 'You're a sole contractor, after all, and we don't have to know. However, prostitution is illegal in this state and I'll have you sign a contract confirming you understand that.

'If anyone gets too handsy without prior agreement, there's a panic alarm.' Misty reached into the booth and lifts a flap of fabric to show the red button. 'If you push that, Tony will come running.'

She pointed to a man with no neck, who flashed a smile at Fern, showing two gold front teeth. Tony, who was perched on a stool far too small for his thighs and reading Ernest Hemingway.

In her last gig as a waitress on roller skates in a sports bar, Fern had worn not much more, earned a sixth of the money and had still got her butt slapped, tits ogled, foul things written on receipts, waited for in the parking lot and her crotch grabbed in the kitchen by the manager.

At least here, a woman was running the show, she'd be protected by Tony – she smiled at him – and the transaction of titillation for money is out in the open, rather than blurred by pretence. At the sports bar, she'd had to pretend to care whether her customer enjoyed his burger, rather than just caring about the imminent tip; while he'd pretended to care about the fries rather than her thighs.

She may be little more than a bag o' flesh to these dudes, but at least she's a profitable one.

Her co-worker Stella ('Star' to her clients), bursts into the changing room to start her shift, giving Fern a biff round the ear.

'What's up, valedictorian,' she says. 'Damn, girl, what happened to your thigh?'

A scar grows across Fern's thigh, vivid and raised, like a scarlet mushroom.

'Fell while drunk dancing,' she shrugs. 'It's keloid, apparently. Means it looks worse than it is.'

'It looks rank.'

'I don't care. I can use cover-up.'

Her friend shudders. 'Anyway, I brought you a joke.'

Stella often does this, like a cat offering up a punctured mouse. She's a stand-up comic, doing open mics before her late shifts on the pole.

She stands, using her electric bikini line razor as a substitute microphone.

'Hey, do you guys know of any cures for sex addiction?'

Stella twirls and delivers the punchline over her shoulder.

'Because I've tried fucking everything.'

Fern's back pockets are stuffed with twenties – even a couple of fifties – as she leaves the Landing Strip via the staff exit. It leads to a separate fenced-off parking lot so that the clients don't try to follow the girls home.

She high-fives Tony, on his way back in from a smoke.

'You look so different,' he says, framing her face with his hands.

'I'm only a part-time hot person, Tony. Full time would be exhausting.'

Leaning against a wall, she smooths out the crinkled bills and rolls them up, securing them with a hairband. Later, she'll put her velvet footstool onto the bed and wobble around until she pops open the ceiling panel above her bed.

Inside a giant Mason jar up there, she already has five hundred dollars stowed away. 'FUTURE HOUSE' is scrawled across the glass.

The back door opens up into the big night sky, the roar of Highway 101 and the dusty Santa Monica mountains beyond. There are mountain lions round here, so she always comes out quiet, half because she wants to see one, and half because she doesn't.

It would likely weigh more than her; she's read they weigh up to 150 lbs. She'd have zero chance if a mountain lion decides to take her down, and something about that excites her. *I surrender, you win.*

Her car's in the shop and so Buck's there, just as he said he would be, leaning against the hood and smoking into the stars above. They used to joke about how the teenagers on *Dawson's Creek* always knew the names of constellations, pointing out the Big Dipper and the Great Bear, while actual teenagers don't have a freakin' clue.

They would mimic Dawson and Joey, Fern talking out of the corner of her mouth, half-smiling like Joey.

'Look, Dawson, it's the Big Ripper,' she'd say, pointing up at the sky.

'No, no, Joey,' he'd correct her. 'It's the *Cake* Bear.'

An electric thunderstorm hovers on the horizon hundreds of miles away, a promise of chaos. Buck's silhouette makes her feel safe, but as always, there's a catch of recoil.

Fern prefers people who are unsure about her. Now *they* are good judges of character. She enjoys the challenge of trying to win them over, like they're a computer game. Whereas she completed Buck when she was fourteen.

And she pretty much knows he moved to LA to be near her, despite all of his noise about the LA chef scene 'being more upwardly mobile than San Fran's'. Uh-huh, OK, sure. Everyone knows San Fran is the hip, artsy food critic you want to impress, next to the sun's-out, guns-out, 'can I have the dressing on the side' nonsense of LA. In LA people barely *eat*.

'Why don't you ever come in, if you're early. Misty knows not to charge you,' Fern says, kissing him on the cheek.

'I don't want to see you like that . . .' Buck says. 'Y'know, unless you ever want me to,' he rushes to add.

Fern fights to disguise her cringe.

'Besides, strip bars just really aren't my bag. I find getting a hard-on in a roomful of other guys somewhat socially awkward.'

'Prude,' she says, swatting him. 'It's just my skin suit, it's not my soul.'

Buck seems to turn this idea over in his mind. Unlike Fern, who has no filter and finds words falling out of her mouth before she's thought them through, Buck deliberates over every word.

'But you only get one body. So doesn't it deserve my – and your – respect?'

Fern shrugs and lights a joint.

The next morning, Buck comes with her to collect her car from the shop.

'They'll charge you less if I front the operation,' he says.

It's infuriating, but he's right. This way, she also has more chance of getting the real story as to what was wrong and what they fixed, rather than the 'little lady' broad-sweeps version.

'I need to go get Scout and drive down to Paradise today,' she reminds Buck. 'Sure you don't wanna come?'

'Nah,' he says. 'It'll be good for you to get some time with your three dads.'

'Like *Three Men and a Little Lady*?' people say, when she tells them about her fatherly trio of Ciaran, Scout and Wally. 'Who's Tom Selleck?' they then ask. It has to be Ciaran at full throttle – he even has the power to grow the legendary moustache.

Feeling her hangover start to rise – Fern always drinks when she works, it makes her feel sexy – she drops Buck off at his condo and loads up on miniatures of vodka and bourbon at the 7-Eleven. Vodka for during the day when she doesn't want to smell; bourbon for the evening when she wants to feel swell.

She tucks two into the driver-side pockets, one into the centre of her bra under her vest, and then downs the remaining vodka while driving one-handed, followed by a gulp of cold coffee and a Juicy Fruit gum. For an ex-drunk, Scout's easy to fool.

Digby cocks his head and whimpers from the passenger seat, his brown eyes plaintive. Lately, he watches her all the dang time.

'What, buddy?'

He looks at the empty bottle on her lap.

'Oh, shush.'

As if her dog is judging her for day drinking.

She wants to tell Buck about this comic moment, that Digby is a fun sponge . . . but if she did, Buck might start judging her too.

HOW IT IS

He's one of those rare people who has one or two drinks and then stops. Fern wants to shake him and say, 'What are you doing? That's not how you drink! That's merely an entrée, *chéri*. You have forgotten to drink the rest of your drinks.'

Some twonk behind her leans on his horn because she has dropped beneath the speed limit. *It's a limit, not a target, dude.* She bets he's the kind of blowhard who audibly sighs in queues; this queue is interfering with his mastery of the universe.

When she exits the highway he sends out a long honk and a few melodic short ones. She laughs.

Fern and Scout's Mission

HOW IT IS
Half an hour later

Hearing a honk of the horn, Scout pinches open his blinds to confirm that, yes, Fern is here. She opens her book on cognitive psychology and stretches her legs out across the passenger seat of the brown Dodge convertible he refurbed and gave her for her twenty-first.

Two teenagers pass, dribbling a basketball between them . . . then stop to double back for a look at her legs in denim cut-offs and cowgirl boots. Fern is oblivious. Scout unpinches the blinds and hurries to grab his bag and get down there. She needs to be more aware, silly girl.

The teens scatter like mice when he bursts out of his complex. On the one hand he hates how people assume he might be Cartel, but on the other, he sometimes uses this assumption as a crowbar.

'Fern!' he says, pushing her legs off the seat.

'Oh, hey!' she says, beaming, then sees his expression.

'What's wrong? Who peed in your cereal?'

'Those guys were cruising on you and you didn't even notice,' Scout says, gesturing at their departing backs.

'How is that my responsibility?' Fern says.

Scout clenches his fists and looks skyward.

'It just *is*, Fern. It's up to you to stay safe.'

Fern frowns and turns the key to wake up the Dodge. *What the fuck*, her face says.

HOW IT IS

As they drive, Scout wonders where he can get Fern a mini-taser. Surely one of his contacts will do him a solid. Pepper spray just isn't going to cut it. Fern is a toddler with a weapon, when it comes to her sexuality. She doesn't realise just how much this plaything could hurt her.

He wonders if the vodka on her breath is from last night or this morning. Probably last night. But then the apple doesn't fall far from the tree when it comes to addictive tendencies.

Thirteen years ago, Scout fell onto the train tracks of the subway and only just managed to haul himself out of the path of the train in time. He will never forget the headlights bearing down on him, the screech and spark of the driver applying the emergency brakes, the disbelief of those who had witnessed it. They were more appalled at his beer-soaked stupidity than relieved he was OK.

He hasn't touched a drop since. It scared him sober. An oncoming train'll do that.

He side-eyes her. She looks great, aside from a nasty new scar on her thigh. Not tired or shaky looking. But then, Scout's also learned that a person can do a fine impersonation of having their shit together, while also having a secret breakdown.

He wonders what will scare her sober.

Being a father figure to Fern has changed Scout, especially since she's moved to LA. Many of his friends on the force had told him that being a father to a girl is a nightmare.

'You know those locker room conversations you had as a teen?' one asked him.

'Uh-huh,' said a wary Scout.

'Well, now they're about your daughter. You've been punk'd, my friend.'

Everyone assumed Scout would have kids, even though he'd never expressed any interest in doing so.

'Too freakin' late, you'll develop the utmost respect for teenage girls,' his colleague added. 'All the while knowing that the rest of the world sees your cute teen the same way you used to look at pieces of ass.'

They were right. For a start, Scout has started to bristle at phrases such as 'piece of ass'. Ciaran, on the other hand, seems to be missing whatever paternal chip activates protectiveness, encouraging Fern to profiteer on her Winona Ryder-esque looks. 'You look like the cat's pyjamas, dear,' Ciaran will say, when Fern dresses up for anything, which always involves far too little clothing, turning her into a grenade.

Wally is the type that has always respected girls and women, no matter what they're wearing or how sexy they are, so he's no use at all. Fern's only hope of getting through this loaded-weapon predicament intact is – Scout. He knows about these creepers because he *was* one. Still is, sometimes, when his higher self recedes and has an afternoon nap.

Scout forces himself to think about other things. Like where they are on their joint mission to solve the mystery of who really killed Fern's uncle, Rory.

In the seven-ish years since he and Fern met, they've formed an alliance not only based on Ciaran's slapdash parenting versus Scout's constancy, but also on their shared belief that someone other than Ciaran killed Rory. And their shared obsession with finding out who and why, in order to clear Ciaran's name.

For Fern, this fixation is born of a belief that Ireland can fix her father's addiction. For Scout, who's more clued-up on how a physical move doesn't necessarily lead to a mental one, he's more interested in righting a judicial wrong.

He doesn't pierce Fern's hope that Ireland might be her father's El Dorado. She's too young to understand that there's no such thing as a 'geographical fix'. He tried it himself when he was still drinking, yet every time he moved, there he was.

Scout and Fern have spent many satisfying afternoons at her apartment, eating Pop Tarts and drinking creamy coffee until their eyeballs twitch, working on this problem. Fern has a giant corkboard on one wall; a mass of index cards, marker-penned arrows, the names of all of those involved, and even a map with drawing pins in it.

'Very original,' Scout said, when he first saw the board.

'Why, thank you,' she replied.

On the wall, 'Ruth' is underlined three times and surrounded by stars; the sixty-something housekeeper of Ferndale.

Given the fact that Ruth was present in the grounds the night Rory died, and she believed Ciaran was innocent, both of them think she holds the key to unlocking the truth.

'Oh, you'll be pleased, kiddo,' says Scout, having to shout to be heard in the vintage convertible. 'I heard back from Ruth!'

Scout called around every post office in County Antrim, Northern Ireland, until he found a postmaster who recognised the house name 'Ferndale' and could tell him the town. He then wrote a letter to Ruth asking if she could help them shed more light on the murder.

Fern beeps her horn with joy, causing a visor-wearing lady with a walker to shake a fist in their direction.

'JACKPOT.'

Flick's Body

HOW IT IS
February 2001
London, England

Flick watches her from the crack in the door. Sita ejects the cassette tape – most likely symphonies – and slides in a bright red alternative. Flick recognises the opening bars of Jay-Z's 'Hard Knock Life'. As the bass line starts to bounce, Sita bounces too, with zero elegance but maximum swagger, like a boxer warming up for a fight.

When the kids from *Annie* start singing, Sita busts out spinning fouetté after fouetté. Flick counts twelve. A coup for any ballet dancer, even a working professional, and yet Sita's pixie face is casual. Jay-Z starts to rap. In tandem, Sita drops into a breakdancing shoulder spin, springs up from the floor, then runs and arcs into a masterful split leap; a *grand jeté*.

Sita's fusion of street dance and ballet isn't the only thing Flick finds interesting. She watches Sita's hips, the swing of her plait, the sweat on her navel, the darkening cleft of her soft grey sports bra. The shorts show burnished upper thigh as she twirls, a peep of black knickers when she kicks. Flick feels a stir in her lower midriff.

At twenty-one, many things turn Flick on, but Sita the most.

As soon as class was over today, Sita pulled the leotard and tights from her body saying, 'This pastel bullshit is burning me – why do they have to be skintight?' Sita keeps her pointes on when she practises after hours, but everything else she wears is anathema to ballet conventions.

Muscle-vests bearing 'I'm hot, so what', harem pants with psychedelic prints, a Rage Against the Machine T-shirt knotted at the front, her brother's old trackies, which have to be fastened to the highest setting, yet still hang low in the middle of Sita's ski-slope hips.

Is it wrong to watch her like this? Flick knows Sita would let her watch regardless. They are best friends. Flick *has* watched this exact routine in a permitted way before. The only difference is, right now Flick doesn't have to work to hide the thoughts she's having.

When Sita finishes, Flick hurries back to the changing rooms, where she's supposedly been this entire time, and scooches her feet up beneath her, reopening her copy of *The Unbearable Lightness of Being*. Sita strips and hits the showers. Flick doesn't watch this part – too far.

Sita calls out over the water, 'Just gimme ten, kitten, then we'll roll.'

Sita sighs as her ancient black-and-white Beetle splutters – dies – splutters – dies. 'We'll get there in the end, you old codger,' she says, patting the vehicle's dash with sympathy. This key turn, the vehicle bursts into life. 'Booyah!' says Sita.

'So, you gonna audition for that production of *Swan Lake*?' she asks Flick, as they exit the Royal Ballet School's car park. 'You know you'll get in. Your form lately is dope.'

Flick cracks a window and noses for the airstream like a dog. The car smells like fast food and worn trainers.

'Yeah, I am. But Mum wants me to audition for Odette *and* Odile.'

Sita low-whistles. 'Black and white swan are a double this time, yeah? That's a giant undertaking.'

Flick uh-huhs. 'I just want a smaller role. I'm not ready for centre stage.'

Sita tears the top off a Pepperami packet with her teeth and rips a chunk off.

'I thought Sikhs weren't allowed pork?' Flick asks.

'I thought Irish Catholics weren't allowed sex before marriage, but you're a massive slut?'

They share an amused look and high-five.

'I'm not, though. Irish, that is,' Flick says, grinning.

'You are, though. Why deny your half-Irishness?'

'You haven't met my Da.'

'Stop calling him Da – you're not in a Werther's Original advert.'

Flick laughs. Sita exits a roundabout without indicating, earning a bip of a horn.

'Besides, you're the most Irish-looking person I've ever seen, so your dad's genes clearly mobbed your mum's.'

Flick stares at the treetops of Hyde Park zip-zip-zipping past. Swans glide around on the Serpentine, gorgeous and menacing with their foamy busts and masquerade masks.

'Did you tell your mum you feel the role's too big? The double?'

Flick nods. 'She's now calling me Swan Flake.'

Sita laughs. 'She's such a bitch. I love it.'

Flick looks mournful. She takes out a magnifying pocket mirror that she got for Christmas, then squints at the blue-tinged mole on her top lip for the fifth time today. She really needs this gone. Mum said she'd pay for her to have it removed.

Straightening her face and clearing her throat, Sita adds: 'I'm sorry, kitten. At least you'll be outta her gravitational force soon – once you save enough dough.'

A car cuts in front, causing Sita to hit the brakes. She winds the window down.

'Oi! Watch where you're going, ya big poppadom!' she shouts, middle finger aloft.

The finger stays outside for a solid three seconds, just to make sure the other driver sees it.

Doug is padding along the hallway on his way out, reading a folded-up newspaper with one hand and unhooking his car keys with the other, when Flick gets back to the townhouse.

'Hello, dear,' he mumbles, not looking up. They pay very little attention to one another, unless Imo insists Doug applies some discipline, which he does with a world-weary lack of gusto.

'You're grounded,' he'll say, looking like he's about to fall asleep. Imo prods him, as if turning a dormant toy back on. 'For a month.' She kicks him with her foot. 'You cannot disrespect your mother that way, OK?'

For the most part, though, things at 59 Kensington Row are tranquil. Rupert moved out a few years back when he got into Oxford. Around the same time, Doug gifted the university a new library wing, which was nice of him.

Imo has embraced the wonders of modern technology, setting up an email address, Imogenanddoug@hotmail.com, with which to regale the Cordelias, Stephanies and Damians of her acquaintance with Flick's status as a rising ballet star.

Mum sits in the study patiently, while the chunky PC bleepy auto-dials the mysterious number that accesses the world wide web – then *beeeepshhhhhhbeebongeebong* for a good minute – before allowing her into her inbox so she can feast on the 'marvellous!' and 'splendid's that her friends (and frenemies) ping back in response.

Flick never sees the emails, but she's berated if she fails to tell her mother of every small win. It's sweet, Mum being so proud. She never thought she'd see the day.

Tonight, her mother isn't in any of her usual places. Flick bounds upstairs, excited by the idea of a free house, and swings her bedroom door open.

Imo is sitting on her bed. The room's dark aside from the reading lamp on the bedside table, which is pointed at the book in Imo's lap, currently covered up by her ring-crowded hands.

'Gosh, a touch dramatic, don't you think, Mum?' Flick says, turning on the overhead light.

She's used to Imo being in her room. Most recently, Flick found her mother poking through her bin, reading a screwed-up note on a scrap of paper.

'I'm emptying it!' Imo had said, offering the proof of an empty plastic bag.

Tonight, Imo lifts the glittery journal up, wordlessly, so that Flick can see. The journal was padlocked – now it's not. *Fuckinhell.*

How could this have happened? Flick had stashed it so carefully, on top of her wardrobe in the dip, someplace nobody would ever look. You'd have to get on top of a stool and grope around in the dust bunnies even if you knew where it was.

The key's hidden elsewhere, so the lock would need to be picked, or smashed.

HOW IT IS

'How did you find it?' she asks Imo. The catch on the diary is broken, bent out of shape.

Her mother sighs, as if this question is irrelevant.

'I was cleaning. It was open when I found it. Careless as usual, Flick.'

Bullshit. Sita will call it out too, when she tells her. 'No wonder she's been gifting you a journal a year,' she'll say later that evening. 'It's the perfect thought-stealing honeytrap.'

Imo pats the bed beside her. 'You're not in trouble. We just need to talk about some of the contents.' Flick sits close enough to satisfy her mother, but far enough away that she's safe.

'So. You need to tell me. I need to know. Are you a lesbian? Just give it to me straight.'

An unfortunate choice of words. Then it lands.

That means . . .

Flick's shame stirs. The diary itself is pretty tame. On some level she always knew this day would come, so she's been redacting her writings of negative chatter about Mum. During the times when she *has* had a rant, she's then scribbled the forbidden words out so hard that the pen tears the page.

But at the back? There's a stash of loose papers folded and tucked into the cover, which Flick usually hides elsewhere. Featuring sexual fantasies. Starring Sita, who remains nameless, and John, their fit ballet school classmate who sometimes joins them, and also stays nameless in the story.

They're merely 'he' and 'she' in the narrative. But as the memory of what she has written, what they *do*, sparks in her brain, Flick burns down into her own lap.

Flick has written her own porn. Because, aside from the house's taboo copy of Nancy Friday's *My Secret Garden* (which weirds her out) and some ancient copies of *Penthouse* that Rupert dumped beside the wheelie bins pre-university, Flick has found no sexual outlet that fits her desires, no safe space to express herself, no language that describes what she likes.

So she's been making up stories that aren't a freaky tale about a dog or a first cousin, nor are they pictures of a skint teen reclining on a hay bale, claiming her name is Sugar and that she loves riding.

'Well, are you? A lesbian?' Imo demands.

'Yes. No. I don't know. Do I need to know?'

Imo starts to cry.

Flick Sees Her Father

HOW IT IS
A month later
London, England

'FLICKKK!' Imo summons her twenty-one-year-old daughter as soon as she hears the front door click. Flick goes to her. Before she pushes the study door open, she draws a pocket mirror out of her bag, checks her teeth for food, her hair for messiness.

Sky the colour of sand fills the six-foot sash windows of the study; the sand whipped up by a distant hurricane. To Flick, who is a catastrophist at the best of times, this is a reminder that the world could end at any time. She best start stocking a bunker.

'How'd it go?' Mum asks, wired with suspense. 'I've been dying to know; did you not see me ringing and ringing you after?'

Flick had turned her Nokia off after it had buzzed in her bag for the ninth time. 'Phone's dead,' she says, shrugging.

'What's the point in you having that thing if I can't reach you?'

Imo's gifts tend to come with fine print, and the fine print of Flick having a mobile phone is that she ought to be reachable.

'I bet you were marvellous, weren't you? Did you get John to record it, like I asked you to?'

Flick nods and hands her mum the camcorder from her bag. 'He had to do it from backstage; he didn't think they'd like it if they knew.'

Imo ignores this and flips open the display to replay the contents. She squeals when she sees the profile of Flick on stage, a curtain obscuring the faces of the audition panel.

'You look gorgeous in that new tutu I got you.' Flick squirms under the compliment.

Silence as Imo listens to the chatting preamble.

'Why do you keep saying uh-huh, uh-huh, uh-huh? You sound like the village idiot.'

Imo watches the audition dance – the Black Swan solo. She gasps when Flick pulls something off; furrows when Flick falters.

Then she pauses the replay, lips thin.

'You land like a bag of bricks after that *assemblé*, dear . . . you know better, so do better.'

But the final sequence of *fouetté* turns pleases Imo. 'Lovely, just lovely,' she says. Flick glows.

Imo clasps both of her daughter's hands and pulls them into her lap.

'My talented protégée. You'll get it. If you don't, I'll march into that school myself and give them what for. You could be the prima ballerina of your own company soon, if you really apply yourself.'

Imo stops, arrested by a thought.

'Oh, I bet you'll be the youngest prima ballerina Britain has ever seen!'

'But, Mum, I don't . . . I won't . . . I don't think that's what I want. The stage fright.'

'But you're good enough.'

'Even if I am . . . I want to be happy, not a stress ball in the spotlight.'

'Success is stress, Flick.'

'Why can't I just be . . . not the main part?'

A sharp intake of breath.

'Because you owe it to me. I could've been a prima if I hadn't had you. I was expected to have kids. What I wanted was irrelevant.'

Imo lights a pink and gold cigarette.

'You get your talent from me, so use it,' she says, exhaling. 'If you owe Doug and me anything for taking you in, it's to shine your light, rather than hide it away and be a layabout.'

Flick's mouth gapes and then snaps shut. *Taking her in?* She's her daughter, not a street urchin she'd offered shelter to.

And *if I hadn't had you?* Imo chose to have her, she wasn't forced. Why did she have her at all, if she didn't soddin' well want her?

She doesn't dare say any of it. Her anger always remains inside, burning her and no one else. Flick knows that her mother's love is writ upon her submission. If she rebels, disagrees, contradicts, even in a small way, the threat of excommunication hovers in the air, much like the Saharan sand. And if she were to be fully exiled, Flick couldn't be sure of survival.

She can't shake the feeling that if she were nicer, skinnier, less clumsy, prettier, kinder, shinier . . . just better all round, then she would gain a more secure place in this house, where Doug and Rupert never risk taking her side. This isn't her home, as such, it's just a house where she's been permitted to live for the time being.

Which is why she can't tell her mum – God, no – that

she's planning on seeing her father. And soon. Sita's family are going on holiday to America, Flick is going with them, and her and Sita have it all planned.

A fortnight later
San Francisco, California

The wind quickens, the sky shifts and the top of the Golden Gate Bridge skewers a fat rain cloud. Flick half expects the steel to pop it, like a water balloon. The sunrise-tinted underbellies of seagulls swoop above, taunting the gridlocked cars. Surfers paddle in Fort Point like glossy black seals.

'Stop being such a bitch, Mum,' Sita calls from the back of the rented minivan, over the pretty, dark heads of her smaller siblings.

'Let us go to Yosemite, for God's sake. We're twenty-one, not ten! We don't need you to babysit us. And you don't even have to ask Flick's mum, so stop gibbering about overseas phone calls being so pricey. She's an adult.'

'Bitch, bitch, bitch!' the sweet siblings start to chant.

Sita's mum rolls her eyes, knowing better than to react. Then turns in her passenger seat to say, 'But there are bears there, Sita.'

'And how often do you hear of British tourists being eaten by bears in Yosemite National Park?' Sita slings back. 'We're not dumb. We'll camp in a permitted area and use those bear boxes and we'll make sure we don't carry minty gum, or use apple shampoo, or wave honey-covered sausages in the air going "c'mere, bear, here, bearrrr, coochiecoochie, bear". All the precautions, I swear.'

Sita's dad says something they can't hear.

'OK, OK, Sita,' her mum calls back. 'If you're going to be such an obstreperous nitwit, we're glad to be rid of you. Flick, that doesn't include you. We love you.'

'We'll drop you at the coach station on the way back. You've got three days to yourselves and that's it. We have tickets for a show on Friday.'

Sita and Flick clasp hands in a silent rejoice. Their cool hands become clammy.

Flick wonders if Sita really wants to touch her. She drops the hand-hold first, just in case. Sita looks at Flick, puzzled, then blows a bubble with her Hubba Bubba, bursting pink across her nose. Peeling it off, she points out the window.

'Look,' she says. 'It's Alcatraz.'

To Flick, the neat island looks more like a battleship than an ex-prison – its peppercorn windows like cabins, its lighthouse a funnel. She doesn't have the confidence to say this aloud, as with most thoughts she has.

'Did you know it wasn't just three people who escaped from that prison, it was five?' Sita says. 'I mean, the prison authorities said they all drowned, but bodies were never found. Imagine making your getaway by paddling on a raft from *there* to *there*.'

Sita points from the island to the shore. 'And then pulling yourself ashore, having made a papier-mâché model of your body to fool the guards. Such a groovy story.'

Flick smiles. She often wonders why Sita bothers hanging out with her. She has so much to say, while Flick has so little.

'Maybe that's how we'll get you away from your mum, one day,' Sita adds in a hushed tone. 'We'll make a robot

Flick that says, "Yes Mum, no Mum, three bags full Mum", on repeat and then we'll paddle off down the Thames.'

Sita picks Flick's hand back up and holds it all the way to Alcatraz, staring out of the window humming 'Baby One More Time'.

By ten o'clock that night, Flick and Sita have hopped from bus to bus to reach Sacramento, then rented a car in Chico. Now, they're rolling towards Paradise with a family-sized bucket of fried chicken.

On a deserted highway running through Butte Creek Canyon ('So. Many. Jokes!' Sita says, hitting the dash three times), Flick is quiet, then sees something that makes her head whip round.

'Sita, can you turn? I know not really, but since there are no other cars.'

Sita indicates left immediately.

'Fuck the law, I laugh in the face of the law,' she says, swinging the car round – but only after checking her mirrors.

Flick directs her down a side road into the forest. Deep they go, until they turn on to a dirt track into the blackness, their headlights the only reprieve.

'Um, OK, have you lost your marbles? What are we looking for down here? Do you think your dad is a forest nymph or something?' Sita asks. 'He isn't down here, Flick.'

'Hush,' Flick replies. 'Here, here!'

They jostle to a stop and Flick – *slam!* – darts out of the car, bouncing off down a path using the torch from the glove box, looking for the knot in the tree where her and Buck used to hide the minivan's keys.

Sita hangs back, unsure, until she hears a yelp of triumph and can't help but follow.

'I knew he'd leave it here,' Flick says, holding a key.

Next thing, she's opening a vehicle's door – a burgundy minivan that looks like it crawled out here to die a decade ago.

'I can't believe she still runs. Buck must've looked after her,' Flick says, the car clearing its throat, the radio a fuzz from a defunct signal that perished long ago.

'It even smells nice. Has it seriously been here for seven years?' Sita asks, opening and sniffing a packet of cookies that went off in 1997. *Crunch*, she bites into one. Spits it back into her hand.

'Almost eight. He's been here,' Flick smiles, holding up a neon tartan blanket.

'We could stay here tonight even, save some dollars?' Sita says, testing the back seats to see that, yes, they do go all the way back. 'We can find your dad in the morning, yeah?' she yawns, and does a small fried-chicken burp.

'Best watch out for those bears, though,' Flick says, venturing a rare tease, 'given you still smell like chicken.'

Sita mimes a bear with claws out, roaring and pouncing on Flick, rolling her over onto her back. They pause, eyes locked.

Then Sita kisses her.

Flick lies awake, listening to the twit-twoos, rustles and shrieks of the forest (foxes, not wolves, she tells herself) while Sita snuffles beside her.

They're naked under the tartan. Flick's shoulder and ankle are brushed by Sita's breast and toe. She's never been more aware – or had as much sensation – in either part of her body. Daring to move them might break the spell, so she lies still, despite pins and needles stabbing her feet.

She plays it back in her head. The long, astonishing kiss. The second, deeper kiss with the flit of tongue-tips. The moving of Sita's hand up her ribcage to brush Flick's nipple through her cotton bra. Flick's hand moving under Sita's grungy floral dress to grab her bum cheek. Moving her face down past the V-shapes of Sita's hips to discover she tastes like the sea. The bliss of feeling Sita's hand pull her knickers to one side.

Flick's slept with one man . . . well, one boy, really. A maternally endorsed boyfriend who was a friend-of-a-friend's son. At a wedding reception in the country club, Imo had watched the romance blossom on the dance floor. When the boy asked Flick if she wanted to go for a walk, Mum had given her a little push.

On the golf course that night, the boy and Flick had stubbly, consensual, underwhelming sex. He'd put too many fingers inside her afterwards, until she pulled his hand away and said, 'It's OK, don't worry about me.'

So Flick's not a virgin, but she has never experienced anything quite like this. This delicious afterglow, where an orgasm isn't a solo event but a mutual miracle.

Taking a deep inhale of the blanket and getting the faintest suggestion of Buck, Flick wonders if he's been with someone under this tartan too. She turns and props her head on her hand to watch the curve of Sita's sleeping cheek. The anti-ageing effect of sleep makes her look innocent, different from her awake self.

For the first time in the three years they've known each other, it occurs to Flick that maybe she'll hurt Sita, rather than the other way round.

But no. That seems unlikely. Flick always loves them more. A chill in Sita's voice, a text without a kiss, an unreturned phone call is enough to send her spiralling off into a story where she's been abandoned.

At least once a day, she wonders why Sita likes her, when she'll realise she's wrong to, and when she'll stop. The only thing that pulls a pastel comforter over that near-constant fear is one of her mother's pills.

A cloud draws back from the moon like a curtain, the new light showing a wolf padding through a clearing up ahead. Flick smiles. For the first time in a long time, she feels safe.

The next day

Flick sees the dome of Wally's bald head first, craning over the chess board, about to move a wooden pawn into a power play.

He and his opponent sit in the porch outside reception. Wally is as still as a mountain, a metronome ticking beside him, wearing something yellow as usual.

He hasn't seen her come round the corner from the car park. She could still run back to Sita in the hire car. She always wonders if people she hasn't seen for years will be disappointed at how she's turned out.

Mum tells her exactly what the people say about her. 'They said you were wearing too much make-up' or, 'They said you're the most beautiful creature'. The pressure to impress pushes on her chest, leaving her breathless.

Wally's chin rests on the hammock of his interlaced hands. A minute, two, three go by. Then Wally's rival splutters, 'Hellfire, Wall!' and topples his own king as a sign of resignation.

Wally stands up and shakes hands over the chequered board. Flick hovers, unsure, her hand twitching for the mirror in her pocket to check . . . but then he sees her.

'Good morning, Miss. How may I help . . .? Well, I'll be . . . Mother of pearl, is that you, Fern?'

'It's me, Wall. But it's Flick now.'

Wally's forehead puzzles, but he says nothing. He reads her body language and doesn't hug her, instead hustling her inside before starting to make hot chocolate.

She sits underneath a selection of clip-framed movie posters: *Goodfellas*, *Pulp Fiction*, *E.T.*, *King Kong*. It smells like flowers from an aerosol can. This place may be a dump, seen by the overseas owner as little more than a decrepit cash machine, but Wally always keeps it as smart as he can.

The goldfish that previously circled the tank, hopefully forgetting they'd just done the very same thing, have now been replaced with exotic fish that flit rather than lap. Neon discs with fins and eyes, they mimic the blues and yellows of the jar of boiled sweets on the counter.

Chattering away with excitement – 'when did you arrive, how long are you staying, so good to see you'– Wally pours a double shot of hot, thin liquid from an 'instant to-go!' drinks machine into fat ceramic mugs, bypassing the paper cups in the plastic chute.

HOW IT IS

Flick's mug says, 'Some people just need a high five' and then in tiny text on the back, 'in the face'. Wally adds whipped cream from a can and miniature marshmallows.

'Hey presto,' he says, handing one to Flick, grinning. 'Your favourite.'

Flick peers into the mug's contents as if it were an abomination. Froyo and fried chicken yesterday, now this sugar syrup for breakfast? Imo would throw a fit if she could see what Flick's been putting into her ballet-hardened body.

Wally catches her expression. 'Oh man, I'm a jackass. You're not a kid any more. Do you want coffee?'

She shakes her head and curls both hands around the cup. 'This is perfect, Wall, ignore my jet-lagged face.'

'I have a surprise,' he says.

Then Wally opens a back door in the office and a ball of energy flies out, throwing itself into her lap and licking her chin.

'Remember Digby?'

'I can't believe you didn't see online or that your mother didn't tell you,' Wally says, rubbing his shiny head. 'She must know, surely – his last single was number one here for *weeks* last year. Or, I guess, maybe she didn't know? He has got a beard the size of a racoon now. And he uses his stage name the whole time – Oscar Wolff. Doesn't want anybody to know he was ever called Ciaran.'

Flick shrugs as if to say 'no biggie', slurps her hot sugar water, scratches Digby's chin and marvels that Ciaran has managed to keep his 'wanted' status across the Atlantic a secret from Wally. She would've thought it'd have come out when her dad was wasted.

155

'Dina's with him,' Wally adds, misinterpreting Flick's quiet for concern. 'But I think she's hanging on by the tip of a fingernail. You know what he's like. He's been attempting to alienate her for, what, seven years now?'

Wally's writing down the name and number of an agent in LA on a flower-shaped paper coaster. On the back he writes down his own email address, his landline number, his fax number even.

'So's we don't lose touch again,' he says, folding a stiff Flick into a full-body hug.

She lifts Digby and gives him a squeeze, lets him lick her nose.

Wally considers his next sentence. 'When you didn't come home that summer, Ciaran and I were both devastated. Him more so, of course,' he says. 'I know it wasn't your call, so I'm not trying to send you on a guilt trip, but since I never got a chance back then to say it, know this . . . If you ever find yourself lost and in need of a home, all this can be your kingdom too.'

He sweeps his hand at the motel; the crouching clapboard rooms, the decades-dry pool full of dead insects. Flick laughs, pockets the details and gives him a shy peck on the cheek.

As she's walking across the parking lot towards Sita, clouds of sand dust at her heels, urging Digby to stop following, Wally calls after her.

'Your dad's different now, kid.'

She turns.

'There's a poem by Charles Bukowski called "Bluebird". When your mum kept you, his bluebird shrank. Got quieter. He almost lost it altogether. Read the poem before you see him. It'll explain why he is the way he is.'

Flick nods. Wally calls Digby to heel, blows her a kiss. She pretends to catch it.

They're in LA by nightfall, thanks to some speeding by Sita and whacking the domestic quick-hop flight on one of Flick's three credit cards.

'How can you afford this?' Sita asks.

'I can't,' Flick replies. 'But when I reach bottom, there's always more money.'

LA is immediately discernible as faster, hotter, merciless, predatory; the vampire of Californian cities. 'Celebrity Bar' a gigantic red arrow promises, a six-lane boulevard of cars charge forward like horses, and low-lying smog makes the bottoms of the skyscrapers vanish.

The mustard cab drops them at the Chateau Marmont.

'Bit of a cliché for outta control rock stars,' Sita says. 'But, bloody hell, your dad must be doing well.'

They peer up at the whimsical structure, rising from palm trees.

'It looks like a Lego castle my little sis once built,' Sita says. 'Did you know the drummer of Led Zep once rode his motorbike through the lobby? And Jim Morrison said he used up eight of his nine lives here. Once he fell off the roof.'

A sizzling cigarette butt lands beside them, chucked from a balcony above.

'Well, there you have it,' says Flick, gesturing to the butt. 'The spirit of Jim has spoken.'

Sita laughs, grabs her around the waist and kisses her. Flick backs away and looks around to see who saw. Sita's mouth sets into a straight line.

The receptionist eyes them warily until she confirms via a clipboard that yes, Oscar Wolff's party are expecting them.

'You're a little early, though, so please enjoy a drink at the lobby bar while you wait. Courtesy of Mr Wolff's tab.'

'Good job these are free – they're fifteen dollars to buy,' Sita says, consulting the drinks menu.

'He doesn't think much of us,' Flick says of the scowling barman with a quiff.

'Who gives a damn? Not everyone has to like you.'

Sita leans back to look at the domed scarlet ceiling and the Japanese art.

'I feel like I'm inside a geisha's uterus.'

Flick downs her drink and rises to her fate.

'Good luck, kitten,' Sita says, squeezing her hand.

The soft boom of her heart in her ears, Flick pushes the elevator button. As the numbers ascend she feels the inevitability of what's about to happen rise.

Ciaran opens the door with an, 'Och, pet! C'min, c'min!' He's smaller than she remembers. Although that's to be expected, given she's bigger.

She's script-written and directed this reunion in her head many times over. But no. Their sentences overlay, stumble and trip each other up, and they headbutt when they hug.

'Your nose looks different,' Ciaran says.

'Mum paid for me to have it done for my eighteenth,' Flick says, turning to show it off in profile. She wonders if he'll notice she's had the upper lip mole removed too, the one everyone always thought was ink.

He says nothing. Nods and gestures to a sofa.

HOW IT IS

They sit either side of an enormous glass coffee table. Other people move in the honeycomb walls of the cavernous suite; more church than hotel room, with its arched windows, gothic candelabras and wooden-beamed ceiling.

'How's your ma, how's Dina, how's life, how's work?' Their small talk skates the rink of the table, pretty and polite, while the unsaid moves beneath the surface.

Ciaran offers her a drink, from a bar crowded with crystal decanters, the colours ranging from geyser clear to amber deep. She accepts. Flick's already a diazepam down, but she needs all the help she can get.

As they get stuck into the strong drinks, they both unclench and move to a balcony. It overlooks terracotta rooftops, the starburst tops of palm trees and a fat sapphire of a pool.

Flick looks directly at him for the first time. His usually tan skin is wan, his eyes haunted, his hair slick with grease. Money may have bought him health insurance but it hasn't bought him health. He's now so covered in tattoos, from primitive stick figures to elaborate botanicals, that he's more ink than flesh.

'What do those say?' Flick asks, gesturing to the letters inked on his knuckles.

Ciaran holds them up so that they form two words. 'LONE WOLF,' he says, winking.

He starts to do a small 'awoooo' howl, but Flick laughs.

'But, Da . . , the start of the N slides off the side of your knuckle. It looks more like a V. As if you've named yourself the "LOVE WOLF".'

She remembers herself and shrinks, waiting for the blowback. Oof. She knows better. Why did she say that?

Ciaran's face splits into a wonky-toothed grin. 'There she is,' he says, throwing his arm around Flick's oyster silk dress and giving her a whoomph-there-it-is of body odour.

'Who?' Flick asks, sinking into his hug.

'My piss-takin', smart-arsed little delinquent Fern. I knew you were still there underneath uptight Ms Flick.'

Ciaran pretends to flick long hair from his shoulder. Flick pulls out of the hug. Why do people think she's stuck up, when she's actually shit-scared? If there's a secret to being shy without being misconstrued as in love with herself, Flick would like to know what it is.

'It's Flick now,' she says, a chill in her voice.

He squares her shoulders and looks at her. 'Fern, you're not your mother, so stop aping her.'

She smooths her hair. 'Like I said, it's Flick now.'

Ciaran reclines back on a striped chaise longue, stroking his beard, raising his wizardly eyebrows and taking a long pull on his bourbon.

Da gets Sita and Flick a room in the Chateau, only it's five floors down.

'This is nothing like Da's penthouse,' Flick says, throwing her bag on the bed. The bed smells like unwashed hair, the colour scheme is cappuccino, the ashtray even has ash speckles from the last guest.

'It's free and it's not a car,' Sita says, blipping the TV on. 'Did you find that poem Wally was going on about?'

Flick's been down in the business centre, using a PC to look up 'Bluebird' by Charles Bukowski.

'Yeah, it's kinda beautiful. All about a secret bluebird inside this bloke that he won't let out. He pours whiskey on it during the day so that nobody knows it's in there, but then sometimes talks to the bird late at night.'

'Maybe it's a metaphor for his soul?' Sita says, painting her toenails deep pink.

'So is Wally saying me leaving killed Da's soul?'

'Or maybe the bluebird's his vulnerability. Hidden by bravado.'

Flick shrugs. They order one burger and fries to share on room service, having learned that American portions are double the size of English ones. 'And a bottle of Sauvignon Blanc, please,' Flick adds, while Sita shakes her head to say no thanks.

Sliding Doors is on the movie channel, nearly finished. They curl up to watch the end.

'Ugh,' says Sita as the credits roll. 'I hate that they're making out that a romantic relationship can save you. Why can't she just go blonde and set up a PR agency without meeting whatshisface?'

'But it can save you,' Flick says, sitting up, pulling her feet in beneath her. 'The right relationship can change everything.'

'No it can't,' Sita says. 'A relationship doesn't have the power to propel your life in a totally different direction. Unless you're talking about your first relationship . . . then, maybe.'

'Like a first love?'

'No, like your main parent.'

Sita turns off the TV and looks directly at her.

Flick makes a face and walks into the bathroom to start her three-step process of cleansing. Sita's toiletries are on the left-hand side of the sink and total four items. On the right-hand side, Flick's are a cityscape.

'I hate that you're a pop psychologist now,' she calls, as she foams apricot cleanser into her cheeks.

'I'm not a pop psychologist. I'm training to be a psychotherapist,' Sita replies.

Flick goes back into the room, picks up the wine bottle and a glass.

'I still don't get why you're doing that evening class.'

'Because by the time you're good enough to be a pro dancer and young enough to still do it, you're only looking at about ten years.'

Starting to run a bath, Flick kicks the door shut.

'I'm Ciar— Oscar's daughter, Flick,' she says to the ticket desk. Their manner switches from cool to toasty as they hand her two lanyards with 'Savage Tour 2001' on them, plus a picture of her father wearing a leather waistcoat and a veneer-perfected smile.

They're ushered backstage into a room with fifteen other people, buckets of iced beer and packets of pretzels. The other people in the room turn, eyes hungry, upon the newcomers. When they see that they're nobodies, they turn back to their conversations and wait for the somebodies.

'Ugh. Let's find your dad,' Sita says, but not before grabbing two beers and using the side of the table to flick them topless. They enter a long corridor where A4 sheets of paper with the band members' names are taped to doors. OSCAR WOLFF.

Flick knocks. No answer. Sita pushes the door open.

'Oh shiiit, sorry!' she says, as the crack in the door reveals a twenty-something brunette in black stockings and not much else sitting astride Ciaran.

They wait a couple of seconds. No sign of the door re-opening.

'Fern, FERN!' a voice calls from behind. 'Well, smack my ass and call me Susan, is that Fern O'Malley? Your dad said you were in town.'

Flick turns to see Dina. Her familiar pretty, round face is the same, but wearing a lot more make-up, her already blonde hair is now platinum, and there are two new additions to her chest that were definitely bought on a credit card.

'Dina! It's Flick these days. Da's . . . busy . . . let's go get a drink.' They shepherd Dina away.

'Dina's getting wil' old, honeybunch,' Da says post-gig in his dressing room, wiping eyeliner-smeared sweat off his face, as an explanation for what they saw.

'She's nearly forty!' he adds, shrugging.

Sita crosses her arms, smiles sweetly. 'I might be missing something, but aren't you older than that?'

Ciaran laughs, points at her. 'She's a pistol. I like her,' he says to Flick, turning to do a line of cocaine off the dressing table. He lobs his grenade casually, like a tennis ball.

'So how long have you two been together?'

Sita smiles, Flick shrinks.

'Bet your ma loves that,' he says, chuffing with laughter.

'This isn't about us, Da,' Flick says. 'You're going to bugger things up with Dina once and for all, if you carry on.'

From a drinks sidecar, Flick pours herself a double, triple – make it a quadruple – vodka, and throws in some rocks, a tremor in her hand as she uses the ice tongs. Sita shakes her head when Flick angles the glass towards her in enquiry.

'Dina knows right enough,' he says. A pause. 'Make your oul' da one of those drinks too, wouldja?'

The next day, Flick cowers as a *toot-de-doo!* announces somebody has won the jackpot, followed by an onslaught of quarters. A hen party whoop down the boardwalk, wearing cut-out masks of what she can only assume is the groom's face.

'This is like Guantanamo Bay for the hungover,' Flick says to Sita. 'Can't we get out of here? Please?' She squints at her face in a pocket mirror. 'I look like a zombie today.'

'I've wanted to come to Santa Monica Pier my whole life, and you need to feel the consequences of your actions,' she says, punching Flick in the arm and confiscating the mirror. 'If I could've dragged your dad down here too and made him ride the rollercoaster until he detoxed all over himself, I would've.'

Sita stuffs a cloud of cotton candy into Flick's mouth and pulls her onwards, asking: 'Is this the pier they used in *The Lost Boys?*'

Flick shrugs and starts to hum 'People Are Strange', despite her kicked-dog mood.

'Why are you so anti-fun, Sita? You *seem* fun, but then you go all party pooper when things get extra fun.'

'*This* is extra fun, Flick. Last night was dark. When you say "extra fun", are you talking about the part of last night where I dragged you out of that camper van? The camper van driven by two men you had only just met an hour previously, who you wanted to go with, to play pool in a "dive bar"? Or should I say, *die* bar?'

'They were fit!'

Sita is stern. 'Sure. Those *fit* rednecks who probably would have killed, stuffed and mounted you for their log cabin wall?'

'You're just jeal—' Flick starts to say.

'Nope.' Sita places her in front of a pinball machine in the arcade. She charges it with quarters and pulls back the ball-launcher.

'See this ball, Flick? You're this ball.'

Ker-ching goes the ball.

'And you're shooting yourself into the night like this, to randomly ping around in whatever madly unsafe manner. You total knob.'

The ball ricochets down tunnels, is super-launched by electrified buttons and judders through zigzags until it finally slows and clatters down towards the levers. Sita attempts to save it and fails.

Flick catches the ball in her hand.

'I hear you,' she says. 'I promise I do.' Flick shows Sita the ball in her cradled palm. 'But see this hand – know what this is? This is me settling the fuck down whenever I get married and have kids. That's what'll calm me down.'

Sita nods and walks away.

Fern Sees the Photos

HOW IT IS
February 2001
Los Angeles, California

Using the master key Wally just furnished her with, Fern braces herself before opening the door. She and Scout have been knocking for a good twenty minutes. It's 7 p.m. and coyotes howl in the distance.

Da is most definitely in. With the lights blazing and the TV blaring, they can even see his silhouette through the papery curtains. But he's not moving.

She centimetres the door open and at the squeak of the hinges, a naked girl who Fern recognises from Walmart – not much older than herself – darts into the bathroom and locks the door.

Ciaran is spreadeagled on the bed, unconscious, mercifully wearing Y-fronts, and surrounded by the debris of a bender . . . but his chest is rising and falling. Thank fuck.

A lime-green bong, empty bottles with ash on the rim, the vestiges of a drug binge on the bedside dresser. They've been at it for days by the looks of it.

Now dressed in a black playsuit, flecks of eyeliner crawling down her face like ants, the girl bolts through the room for the door. They let her go without comment.

'Christ,' says Scout. 'Him and Dina musta split again.'

Fern isn't listening. She's cross-legged on the floor beside Ciaran's bed, fanning out dozens of photos.

HOW IT IS

'Sssh,' says. 'Don't wake him. Check this out.'

'I bet this split is the full stop, rather than the comma,' Scout adds, raising his eyebrows as he uses a coat hanger to lift a pink thong from the bed into the wastepaper bin.

For the past eight years, Ciaran has jerked Dina around, ricocheting from guitar serenades underneath her window, to a few months of normality together, to him feeling 'suffocated' whenever they create anything approximating intimacy. They're caught in a sickening dance where the moment she comes closer, he runs away, but when she tries to move on, he pursues her.

Scout crouches beside the photos.

'This is Ferndale,' she whispers, waving a faded photo of a grey manor house that looks stern but fair.

'Oh, wow. This is Da when he was young. And look at all of these pictures of him and my mum! I've only ever seen photos of her on her own.'

There's an exquisite redhead with a heart-shaped face, her hair a mixture of plaits and wild fuzz, lying in the lap of a spectacle-wearing and heavy-eyebrowed Ciaran, who looks up at the camera. She looks only at him.

In another faded shot, there the couple are again, but this time with another man; he has similar bone structure and features to Ciaran, but arranged in the wrong way.

'Ohhh. Could this be Rory? Boy,' Scout says. 'This is the first time I've seen him.'

He flips the photo over; written in slightly smudged fountain pen is 'Imo, Rory and I'. He shows Fern, who averts her eyes from her dead uncle – he gives her the creeps – but flips it over to read the caption. She recognises her father's hand, but whereas then it was flowy with generous loops, now it's spidery with scratchy triangles.

'His writing looks different now,' she says, keeping her voice low. 'Can your mental health change your penmanship?'

Scout shrugs. 'Who's this, I wonder?' he says, pointing out a slight figure in many of the pictures. Embracing Imo, standing stiffly next to Ciaran, she has a pointy face and cobalt hair. 'Maybe a sister? Has your dad ever mentioned one?'

Fern shakes her head. They flip photo after photo, looking for a caption. On the back of a shot of the girl sitting on the edge of a well, squinting into the camera like she fears it, they find 'Nora'. Her dad's handwriting, with a tiny ink heart drawn next to it.

'He's mentioned a Nora,' Fern says, her voice rising. 'Definitely. A few times. She was Mum's best friend. I think she might have split my parents up. He said something about being in love with her.'

They look at the picture. She's peculiar looking – not a patch on Imo – but hypnotic somehow.

'She looks familiar,' Scout says, bringing the photo closer.

Ciaran starts to stir. Every time either Scout or Fern have asked him about Rory's death, or Ferndale, or anything related, he shuts them down. Fern's even tried asking him when he's buzzed, in the hope the rum will loosen his tongue, but the shutdown then was even more gruff.

She hurries to stuff the photos into her fringed suede satchel before he sees them and remembers getting them out last night.

'We need to take these to Ireland and ask Ruth about them,' she says to Scout, whispering. 'Maybe she'll know who Nora is and how she connects to this whole jigsaw.'

Ciaran wakes, looks at them with astonishment, rolls over and vomits into a wastepaper basket that contains torn Rizla packets, a burger wrapper and a cerise thong.

Fern Goes to Ireland

HOW IT IS
Six weeks later
Glenfoot, Northern Ireland

As Fern takes the gilt-edged floral teacup, it trembles against the saucer. Scout looks up, his expression sharpened. *He knows.*

Last night on the red-eye from LAX to Belfast, while Scout's mouth hung open like a cave, the rhythm of his snores tidal, Fern had hit it hard. I'm nervous, she told herself, but she wasn't.

That little service button – with what looks like a French maid on it, even though it summons a man – had proved too tempting. Press: wine. Press: beer. Press: vodka.

For some reason, having a different beverage each time made her feel like she was drinking less. What could be more civilised than having a flight of drinks while literally flying? She could see the air steward start to tire of her thirst, start to consider cutting her off, so she bought a bottle of premium vodka from duty free, as well as some perfume to throw him off the scent. Then she just decanted her own drinks.

So today her head feels like a grey dishrag, wrung out but still dirty. Her hands vibrate, jonesing for more of the dog that bit her.

Fern puts the juddering cup and saucer back on the coffee table. Stupid cup and saucer. Who has a hand steady enough for *that*? She'll drink her tea later when nobody's paying attention to her. Nibbling a sugar-sparkled 'Nice' biscuit, she looks at the curio display that is Ruth's home.

Around a faux gas fire, in which fake logs sit fooling no one, is a collection of at least ten ceramic figurines, most female. One cradles a lamb, another twirls in an evening gown, one embraces a groom – him in black, her in white.

They stare out at her, with black, unblinking dots of eyes. I am nurturing, says the lamb holder. I am beautiful, says the twirler. I am loved, says the bride. We are women, they say. What are you?

Fern mouths 'fuck you' at them.

'I'm delighted to see you, of course,' Ruth is saying, looking far from delighted. 'But I expected you to write rather than show up.' She smiles to sweeten it.

Scout has removed his Yankees hat in deference, and now twizzles it awkwardly, eyes downcast like a boy. Fern rarely sees him unsure like this.

She must be, what, sixty-something? But she's a badass, in a grand dame kinda way. Her blue eyes twinkle out of her face, as if they're backlit. She reminds Fern of the old lady at the start of *Titanic* who later drops the diamond necklace into the sea. Minx.

A wooden mantelpiece clock ticks, its numbers roman numerals. A Madonna is caged in a frame, rosary beads draped around it, and almost everything is beige. It all feels staged.

Scout explains that, as a retired detective, he has had access to the case files of Rory's unlawful death, quickly skimming over the how and the why.

'As you know, ma'am,' he says, stroking the rim of his hat like it's a comforter, 'Ciaran O'Malley has been wanted for questioning about the unlawful killing of his brother, Rory, for what, over ten years now? This is what's kept him and Fern from returning to Ireland. And from living where they should be living. Right here.'

Ruth shifts in her seat, brings a teacup to her lips and peers over it like an alligator. Wow, strong start, Pops, Fern thinks, mentally saluting him. Maybe it's an interrogation tactic when you meet an alpha: to disarm them by making yourself as big as possible.

Scout clears his throat, goes back in. 'I can see from the interviews you gave the Northern Irish Police that you *don't* think Ciaran did it. But that begs the question: who did? The forensics show it wasn't an accidental fall. It required the force of a push to break through that wooden banister. But then, you know all that.'

Ruth nods, lips pursed, hands clasped. Fern can't see a speck of dust in the entire place. This woman must clean every damn day.

'Ciaran won't come back here to clear his own name,' Scout says. 'He's incapable, totally lost, his drinking is chronic now. He doesn't have the grit to face the inquisition he would get back here. So, it's up to us, and we're hoping you'll help, so that Ciaran and Fern can come home, here to Ferndale, where they belong.'

Fern feels like clapping. What a speech.

'I would love to have Ciaran and Fern back at Ferndale,' Ruth begins, wording everything with precision. 'But I don't know how I can help. I told the police everything I know.

'The only people in the house were Rory, Ciaran and Fern,' she continues. 'Obviously Fern wouldn't have been capable, aged just, what, ten?' Ruth looks to Fern for confirmation. Fern nods.

'I'm guessing you don't remember seeing anything amiss that night?' Ruth asks Fern.

Scout interjects for her. 'Fern doesn't remember anything about that night at all.'

Ruth leans forward a little, having exposed Scout's weak spot.

'Well, I know Ciaran doesn't have the character for such malicious intent, you're right about that,' she says. 'So I can only surmise that Rory ran at the banister in order to smash himself through it.'

'*Backwards?*' asks Scout, in disbelief. Ruth bristles.

Fern takes a biscuit, feeling like she's watching an episode of *Poirot*.

'He could have flipped or twisted in the air,' she says.

'We both know that the inquest ruled out the possibility of that,' Scout says, shutting her down.

'I only know that the house was locked and those three were the only people in residence. And given Ciaran wouldn't have done it, and nor would Fern, Rory must have done it to himself.'

Scout nods, adjusting his body language so that he has both palms up in supplication. Fern wonders how much of this is psychological training from his detective days.

'OK, I hear you,' he says. 'But let's play devil's advocate and assume there was someone else in the house. Who could have gained access? Could you make a list of any other employees, past or present, who could have pocketed a key? Or known the brothers well enough to be let in? Any lovers, friends, frequent visitors to the house?'

He removes the wallet of photos from his jacket pocket and slips out the topmost photograph. The magnetic, straight-faced girl by the well.

'For starters,' Scout says, 'you could tell us who this is?'

Ruth slides the photo across the table and picks it up, her hold tender.

'Well, that's an easy one. This is my daughter, Nora. She disappeared in 1978. Over a decade before Rory died.'

Fern feels the tragedy of this, but can't make her face look sufficiently sad. A year or so ago, she'd done an online test to find out if she's a sociopath, given she doesn't understand why her face won't do what people expect it to. This is sad – look sad, please, Fern – she can't look sad.

'Here, follow me,' Ruth says, standing up and smoothing her tweed skirt, after what feels like for ever, but is probably only three seconds. 'I'll show you.'

Scout and Fern follow, cowed, as Ruth leads them to the mausoleum of her missing daughter's room, unchanged since 1978.

Ten minutes on, they're led to the front door. Oh. It's possible they've overstayed their welcome.

'I'll make up a couple of rooms in the house for you both,' she says to Scout. 'There's a lovely walk through the woods over there, if you want to do that in the meantime? Stay as long as you like, obviously. I'll get you that list in the morning.'

Her formality is impenetrable; she practically curtsys.

Scout and Fern set off down a path into a scene from a Constable painting – a blaze of bluebells in a woodland glade

– immediately regretting their box-fresh white trainers. Furry tails twitch and upturn as rabbits run to hide.

'Well, she's a treat,' Fern says. 'Did you get the vibe she's a kung fu master impersonating an old woman? I'm gonna nickname her Mr Miyagi.'

Scout is silent. Fern play pushes him.

'What's up?'

'When we were going up the stairs to see her daughter's bedroom, did you see all those photos of Nora?'

'Um, kinda, but it doesn't matter, does it? She was gone by the time Rory was killed.'

Scout draws a tissue from his pocket and opens it to show a tiny bird's nest of hair. 'I swiped this from Nora's hairbrush when Ruth wasn't looking,' he says.

'Why would you do that?' Fern asks.

A blackbird lands on the path in front, its wingspan clearing a clean circle in the leaves like a helicopter. It regards them with a curious orange-rimmed eye.

'Because, *mija*,' Scout says, 'I'll be really surprised if Nora *isn't* your mother. She looks just like you.'

How It Was

The Cottage

HOW IT WAS
27 December 1989
Glenfoot, Northern Ireland

Ruth gets smaller and smaller in the back window of the car. Uncle Rory was nowhere to be seen this morning. Ruth said he fell down the stairs and was hurt, and not to go in the East Wing.

Da's acting weird. This morning, he packed up all their stuff and said, 'We are going on a trip.' Then he gave his amazing red car to a friend in Derry. Now, he's buying a rubbish car that's all scratched, from a man as fat as a hippo.

They go to Dunnes store to buy clothes. Fern wishes they could go to Tammy Girl.

'Work away. Just make sure it's warm,' Da says, gesturing to the girls' clothing.

'What, I get to choose?' she asks.

'You bet your ass you do. I don't give a flying shite!' he says. Da swears too much. She's going to get a swear jar so that she can make money out of it.

'But maybe give that section a hard swerve,' he adds, pointing at the party section. Noooo. That means she can't have the glittery llama jumper. Da walks off towards the men's section, his legs like the BFG's.

She wanders about, half happy and half scared. She chooses a T-shirt with Penelope Pitstops all over it, plus a long green and purple striped scarf that reminds her of *The Worst Witch*.

Da chucks in thick black tights from a display beside the till – in sizes XS and XL. 'For you and for me. We'll wear those under our jeans. It's a farmer's secret for staying warm,' he says.

Fern laughs, imagining a big serious farmer hunting deer while wearing Dunnes tights. She thinks of her suitcase in the car, the one Mum packed when she left London: frilly dresses, cardigans and even a tutu, all of which don't fit. She doesn't know why she brought them.

'Where are we going?' Fern asks.

'To where no one knows our names,' he replies.

The sky goes purple – like a Parma Violet dropped into water – and tiny robot heads pop out of the road, like they've been buried in there.

'They're called cat's eyes; so you don't lose the road in the night,' her dad explains when she asks about them.

She prefers the idea of road robots, so she falls asleep dreaming that she's rescuing them.

The next morning, she wakes up in the highest bunk bed she's ever seen, taller even than dad. The wind wolf-whistles. She wishes she could wolf-whistle.

'Frickin' Icelandic wind,' her father says, as he blows on his fingers. He's making porridge over a fire.

'How did I get up here? Did you carry me?'

He nods. 'Welcome to our Donegal getaway.'

Fern climbs down the ladder. The porridge isn't so bad. Da puts cinnamon and honey on it. The cottage looks like it's

HOW IT WAS

growing straw hair from its roof and only has two windows, one of which a donkey is headbutting.

'It thinks its reflection is another donkey,' Ciaran says, drinking his coffee.

The other window is filled with what Da calls 'the road to the sky'. It comes up from the beach and is very twisty. Da shows where they are on a map hung up on the wall. The map looks about a thousand years old. They're way, way, way at the top of Ireland, but Da says they're 'not in Northern Ireland any more'.

Of course they are. Adults are such weirdos.

It rains a lot here, even more than it did back in Ferndale. At night Da reads her stories about hobbits; little people with hairy feet who are looking for a ring. Or scared of a ring – she's not sure, but she likes the dragons.

Then they get a dog, Fetch. She's brilliant. She jumps over walls and does paw and roll over but never gets the ball. Next door there's a farmer who owns the headbutting donkey.

'He's the most obedient donkey you'll ever meet,' the farmer says. 'Loki's his name. Feel free to ride him about, wee 'un. He's getting very rotund.'

Without Ruth around, Fern's hair becomes so tatted that it's like a doormat. Da has to cut off the tangly ends. She gets into the tin bath beside the fire – the water's too hot – then he shampoos her hair with a soap that smells like fruit. He brushes it when it's wet and plaits it.

Da makes horrible stew with carrots in it, Fern misses Ruth's food. Sometimes he brings home snowball cakes from the bakery. They stuff them into their mouths whole; she loves the coconut outside and raspberry inside.

Using a wall, she swings onto Loki's back and holds on to his hair as he sways up and down the beach. Crabs sidewalk back into their hole houses. Fetch jumps up and down in the hills of sand. Fern's plait blows into her face and gets full of salt.

She slides off Loki, buries her face in his hot neck and gives him a mint. He crunches it and bats his long eyelashes.

~ ~ ~

Fern turns eleven in June. She hasn't been to school in six months. She asks Da if the police are going to come and arrest them.

'Nobody gives a rat's ass here. People leave you be,' he says.

They spend a lot of time in the caravan park's rec room, where Ciaran likes to play pool and talk to the barmaid, trying to get her to go out with him. 'She wears no knickers! She's a prick-tease!' Fern hears Da say to his mate at the bar. She doesn't know what a prick-tease is, but it sounds bad.

The games room becomes Fern's library. People come on holiday and leave books behind. She reads Jackie Collins, which feels exciting and grown-up. Da finds her reading a page about 'the girl with the golden snatch'. He laughs and replaces it with another book, the best she's ever read: *Rebecca*.

There's been no birthday card from Mum – that's the fourth year in a row – so Fern opens the suitcase full of London clothes and picks out the pink tutu. She takes the tutu out to the bog and pokes it with a stick until it's swallowed by brown bubbles.

~ ~ ~

HOW IT WAS

Every week, Ciaran and Fern go to Annie Kelly's pub so he can use the phone and get drunk in a place that's not the cottage.

First time they went, Da pointed at the ceiling, full of water jugs, scary saws and china cups and said: 'It looks like they covered a jumble sale in glue and threw it at the ceiling.'

Annie's nice. She lets Fern sit behind the bar on a tall chair and eat Scampi Fries. Sometimes she gives her a ginger ale, which makes her nose fizz. Fern draws on a Yellow Pages; cats, moons and witches on broomsticks.

She can't hear exactly what Da's saying on the phone at Annie Kelly's, but he sounds serious and always comes off the phone looking sad.

Until one day he's pink and happy. 'C'mon,' he says, pulling Fern off the stool and into a twirl. 'We're going to celebrate!' They order the pie of the night, he gets to drink loads of whiskey, she gets to drink three Cokes, and they stay at Annie Kelly's all night long.

Fern wakes up in the middle of the night; she's by the fire and curled up under a blanket with Fetch, who's snoring and dreaming about running. She strokes Fetch's belly to tell her she's sleeping, not running.

Da's not there, but it's OK. The fire stops dancing and becomes still. She smiles and pulls the blanket up under her chin.

The Getaway

HOW IT WAS
27 December 1989
Glenfoot, Northern Ireland

Fucccck. Fuck fuck fuckety fuck.

How does he do this? He's never done this before. Are you just supposed to know how to make a run for it; what to take, what to leave, how to not leave a trail, how to tie things up and square things off and not fucking get fucking caught?

Ciaran searches his brain for every TV show and novel he's ever encountered about a fugitive making a getaway.

Fugitive has	Ciaran has
A nondescript getaway car	A tomato-red Triumph Spitfire with a personalised number plate
A safe deposit box. Contents: a stack of cash, a smorgasbord of IDs, some loose diamonds in a drawstring velvet bag	About £840 to his name. A trust for house maintenance that he can't access without the signature of Ruth and his (now dead) brother; a Masters degree in physics; a toolbox to do odd jobs with
A computer hacker guy, a gun guy, a gadget guy	A guy called Ken who shifts dodgy motors. No other guys

HOW IT WAS

Fugitive has	Ciaran has
Access to a cabin in the middle of nowhere	This one he can do; his father left him the keys to a Donegal cottage
A sexy sidekick who he picks up along the way. Usually an assassin who can't bear to kill the hero because she wants to ride him instead.	A ten-year-old daughter who pretty much torpedoes all shagging opportunities that come his way

It's now 4 a.m. Having smoked an entire pack of Marlboro Reds and paced a floorboard shiny, Ciaran still doesn't know what to do about his dead brother.

Four hours ago, after his daughter woke him up and he soothed her back to sleep, he headed for the kitchen to find the wine and padded down the stairs to find his brother's breathless body, legs at freaky angles, face mid-yell.

What's even more confusing is how he feels about it. Beyond the gut-punch of finding Rory, the horror that one moment someone can be alive and the next they're dead, followed by the ejecting of his stomach contents on the kitchen floor . . . after all that, the only adjective Ciaran can find to describe his reaction is: relief.

Rory was always a dodgy bollix. Understatement of the century, that. Silken and impressive, but capable of reprehensible things. Ciaran had made sure that Rory was never alone with Fern, but the older she grew, the more dangerous his presence became.

It was fine when Rory was overseas, which he has been for the past few years, trading something or other in Dubai.

VERSIONS OF A GIRL

But ever since he's been back, Ciaran has felt like history is repeating itself. His brother showed an unnatural interest in Nora from when she was thirteen, and now he was starting to look at ten-year-old Fern in the same way.

He would have told Rory to sling his hook years ago if he could have, but they co-owned the estate. If only Ciaran could buy Rory out, own Ferndale outright, then Rory wouldn't be able to come near Fern at all, but the idea is so outlandish that it verges on absurd.

Ciaran could no more find that kind of money than he could trap a herd of unicorns and open a unicorn petting zoo.

When he found Rory's body, Ciaran went for help, of course, but then the reality landed. He, Fern and Rory were the only people in that locked house. No signs of forced entry. Ruth has a key, of course, but that's it.

So if Rory's fall was foul play, suspicion will land squarely at his feet, particularly as it now means he owns Ferndale outright. And if he goes away to jail, Fern gets sent back to her mother.

Unless he tells them the truth. But he can't.

It physically hurts to give his mate the Spitfire.

'If you scratch her, you're a dead man,' he says, a growl in his throat as he tosses the keys.

He and Fern then walk deep into the Derry council estate, finding the door knocker shaped like a lion's head, the portal to the site of many iniquitous nights. Once, when he was on acid, Ciaran had a chat with this lion.

'What about ye?' says Ken, friendly as he is round, wearing a tank top that shows rather too much side nipple. He leads them to a Fiesta striped with rust, flakes of grey peeling off to reveal gold, like the car version of a coined scratchcard. They take it for a spin along the banks of the Foyle.

'See that wee girl running in the purple top?' Ken says, pointing at a middle-aged woman.

Ciaran confirms that he can see the wee girl.

'Her ma went out for a swim in Portstewart Bay, training for one of those triathlon things she was.' Ken uses air quotes for triathlon, as if it's debatable whether they're real. 'Got caught by an undercurrent out yonder and never came back.'

They pass a graveyard. Ken adjusts his gut and says, 'There's a wee boy laying in there who was hit in the head with a hurling ball. Only twenty-three he was. They started wearing helmets after that.'

'Sounds like fitness is quare deadly round these parts,' Ciaran says, throwing Fern a wink via the rear-view mirror.

'Where are we going?' Fern asks.

Neat bungalows with Romanesque bird baths have dwindled as they drive. Now there are no houses, only inky streams slicing through rusted gorse. A munching ram stares at them, unblinking, horns curling round its head.

He's only ever been to the cottage with women. Nora first, then some women he cheated on Imo with. He suspects his father kept it on the downlow for the same purpose, given he was a womaniser too.

When Ciaran first came to the cottage, aged seventeen, a year after his parents' accident, the only supplies in residence were red wine, matches, turf, Black Magic chocolates, baby oil and an unnecessary amount of sheepskin throws. Takes one to know one.

Maybe that's why Ciaran's father was so furtive about

leaving it to him. The estate was divided clean between him and Rory, but after they signed the final documents, the solicitor asked Ciaran to hang back for a private word. He handed him a padded brown envelope.

'Your father requested you have this from his personal effects, but was adamant that I couldn't open it.'

In the privacy of his bedroom, Ciaran snicked the envelope open with a key, already crying, expecting a letter from his late father, probably telling him to remove his head from his arse and become a lawyer or a doctor.

Instead, a large key wrapped in bubble wrap dropped out. The only message was on a yellow Post-it (thanks for the sense of ceremony, Dad): an address in Donegal, plus 'In case you need some space from Rory.'

Oh, the irony. Maybe their father should have gifted the Donegal panic room to Rory instead.

Warming his hands on bitter coffee, Ciaran stares out of the window. They're just a few miles from the northernmost tip of Ireland. The British checkpoint soldiers waved them straight through when they'd crossed the border into the Republic. Mid jokey banter, the soldiers only glanced at them once; a rust-bucket car with Southern plates, a worried Irishman (they all look worried), some Dunnes bags and a ten-year-old girl. On you go, lad.

The muscular Atlantic is just eighty feet away. It'll devour this cottage within the next couple of lifetimes. Blond sand and heather bow low to the uninterrupted winds from Iceland. Beyond the beach, a lonely road hairpins up Knockalla Mountain and melts into mist: 'the road to the sky'.

Days are spent roaming. They tramp along beside waterfalls, take the Fiesta inland and up high to go dig turf, they head to the amusements at Letterkenny. At night they eat watery, stringy stew, studded with potatoes and juicy carrots, while the rain roars at the trembling windows and the turf burns to keep them warm. He reads J. R. R. Tolkien to Fern by candlelight.

When she's asleep, he allows his fear out, pouring beer onto it, telling himself the booze is a balm. His need to go out and find cheerful oblivion – chase the wee hours, locate women to shag – is less pressing here. Because there's nowhere to go. And all the women – aside from the sexy barmaid at the caravan park – seem to be teenagers or married. Neither of which is his style.

One morning, a Border Collie puppy shows up in the outdoor loo, curled around the toilet bowl as if it were its mother. They call her Fetch because, while she's eminently trainable, she refuses to actually fetch. Her caramel eyes watch the stick fly through the air, she sniffs and licks a paw as if to say: 'If you want it so badly, you go.'

He lets his daughter do what she wants, eat what she wants, say what she wants, think what she wants and look how she wants. His only parenting acts are the morning porridge and the evening meal, plus shampooing her hair every few days with Pears soap, inhaling the sweet metallic smell while Fern complains that both her swimsuit and the tin tub are too small.

The mutton stew is batch cooked once a week, and they rotate it with ham, eggs and waffles, or soup from a can with wheaten bread. They stuff fat cakes from the bakery into their mouths whole and grin at each other, coconut-dusted animals.

After a month or so, he asks Fern if she knows what happened to Uncle Rory.

'Do you remember the night your uncle fell through the banister, down into the hallway?'

Fern shakes her head, her most serious face on.

'You know he's gone, though, right?'

She hadn't known that, no. But she doesn't seem upset.

'I didn't like him,' she says.

Ciaran pulls her into a hug, ruffles her hair.

~ ~ ~

Six months into his exile, Ciaran starts to relax. He even starts to have the odd night off the booze. Granted, the entire night he's not drinking, he thinks, look at me not drinking tonight, on repeat × 1000. But it's a start.

People come to Donegal to escape, to merge into the landscape, to flee small-town talk. Here, people know that you keep to your side of the street, and that's that. But it turns out that if you become a part of that landscape, the people will lie down in the road to help you.

Ciaran decides it's time to place his trust in a chosen few; he needs lookouts. While Fern browses whoopee cushions and erasers that are shaped like ice creams, pretending not to listen to his conversation, he speaks with Mrs Lavery in the post office. According to Fern, Mrs Lavery smells like sweetcorn (aye, well, she does a bit).

'Will you send word if anyone comes knocking, asking about me and her, Deirdre?'

HOW IT WAS

Mrs Lavery nods, snuffing out a flicker of curiosity.
'Will do, Ciaran.'

Ciaran then asks the same of his other friends in the village, as they weave their way down the short high street. 'Hello, John', 'Och hiya, Aoife' and 'About ye, Niall'.

When they're both in their mezzanine beds high in the rafters and Fern thinks he's asleep, sometimes he hears her sobbing. It was her birthday last week. Maybe kids get more emotional around that time. When he asks if she's OK she says 'I'm grand' and he chooses to believe her.

~ ~ ~

When the net starts to close in, he gets some notice, at least. Nine months after his brother's death, the inquest on Rory comes back with: unlawful killing.

Ciaran is officially declared a person of interest in what the Antrim police had originally thought was an open-and-shut case of 'drunk man falls over stairs'.

He knows all this because every week at Annie Kelly's, he speaks to his ex-wife on the phone. She's the person he trusts least in the world – and also the only one who can help him and Fern out of this predicament.

The Housekeeper

HOW IT WAS
September 1990
Glenfoot, Northern Ireland

Crunching up the gravel drive to Ferndale, she feels the need to scrub some surfaces, beat some rugs, bleach and de-stress. Today, on the final day of the inquest, they found Rory's death was by misadventure. Ruth is very troubled by this verdict.

The trees lean over her, raindrops released as chaffinches squabble in the branches. 'The Dark Dredges' Ciaran used to call the driveway's long column of overarching branches, since they vaguely look like a budget version of the famous 'Dark Hedges' down the road.

The Dark Hedges draw tourists from here to Timbuktu. Ruth has never understood why visitors drive three hours from Dublin to see it, pose for a picture on a Kodak throwaway and then drive off again. They then go to the Giant's Causeway and do the same flamin' thing.

She stops in front of the O'Malley house – the house where Ciaran and Rory grew to become men. Ciaran was always her favourite, but he's been waylaid from who he was supposed to become. 'The man takes the drink until the drink takes the man' as the saying goes.

Ruth is always struck by the sight of Ferndale. It is handsome. A central section has pretensions of a castle, but the more demure East and West Wings know what they are. Just a big house in Antrim is all.

No cars sit outside, no smoke plumes from the chimney, no warmth imbues it whatsoever. Ferndale has been empty for nine months now, since Rory died, and Ciaran and Fern left. The original O'Malleys – Ciaran and Rory's parents – are long dead. Cradling the heavy iron key for the oversized front door, Ruth lingers on the steps and remembers Ciaran and Fern's departure. It was 5 a.m. and still dark.

'I won't incriminate you by telling you where we're going,' Ciaran said, chucking binbags full of their stuff in the back of his sports car. 'Tell the police whatever you're comfortable with. I won't tell you what to say. But until we're back, until it's safe, treat Ferndale as if it were your own.'

He pulled Ruth into his chest, giving her a noseful of rotting fruit and spearmint mouthwash. 'You're family,' he said, his voice thick.

Fern came back from saying goodbye to the rabbits, eyelashes heavy with tears, and ran into Ruth's belly, nearly winding her in the process.

'I don't want to go. I like it here,' she muttered into Ruth's ribcage.

Half an hour before, Ruth had found Fern sitting on the landing of the West Wing, legs poking between the unbroken spindles. Behind her, a cursing and slamming Ciaran packed their things. But Fern was unmoved.

Still and serious, the ten-year-old had stared into the polished hallway below, as if trying to solve the riddle of her uncle's death. In *this* hallway, on *this* side of the house, nobody had died, there was no body, broken and splayed on the tiles beneath. Maybe Fern had been working on magicking away the East Wing, just as the twister takes the house in Oz.

But she's ten, Ruth reminded herself. So, actually, the likelihood of her sitting there pondering a solution to Rory's death was kind of preposterous. Did she even know he was dead? She was probably thinking about boy bands and kittens.

As they drove away, Fern with her nose squished up against the rear window of the car, Ruth waved and forced herself to smile.

The skies opened and rain lashed down.

Ruth polishes the mahogany picture frame in the centre of her mantelpiece. In it is a picture of her daughter, Nora. She went missing in 1978, aged just nineteen, and is presumed dead by half the village. But Ruth knows she's not dead.

Next to it is a bird-flocked urn, containing her late husband, Frederick's, ashes. To Ruth, this no more contains Frederick's soul than it does the Easter Bunny's. A closet atheist in a very Catholic Antrim village, Ruth would probably be chased out of Glenfoot if she revealed her lack of belief. More likely, people would just stop talking to me in the grocers, she thinks, twinkling at having pulled the rug out from under her own melodrama.

She keeps up the appearances of a Catholic; going to church and reciting back, 'Lord, have mercy' or, 'And also with you' upon cue. She even has a picture of a glowing Jesus and a 'House Blessing' prayer above a golden clam-shell in the hallway. You're supposed to put holy water in the shell. It contains tap water.

Regardless of her performance, she's still notorious for unholy hubris, as a Catholic who had the audacity to marry a Protestant thirty-five years ago. In response to their wedding, there was a rock through their window and a note on Frederick's car saying, 'We're watching you', when he visited his Protestant town.

The most imaginative prank was the removal van sent to The Millhouse, their cottage in the grounds of Ferndale. They gave the van man a cuppa, paid him for his mislaid time and trouble and stayed put. Scared? Yes, they were, but they were infinitely more stubborn.

The O'Malley family, who Ruth had worked for since she was a teen, welcomed Frederick and promised to protect the couple. The village respected the O'Malleys and many worked for them, or had done in the past, so when they saw that Frederick was now living on their estate, they fell into a grumbled acceptance of the couple. 'Ah well,' they said. But Nora inherited their scandalised stamp.

The thought of a primary-school-age Nora stills Ruth's hands in the bubbly sink.

The Passports

HOW IT WAS
December 1990
Ballymastocker Bay, Donegal

The lavender envelope slides around on the leather passenger seat as Imo's car bumps down a pockmarked lane. It's tactically spritzed with a douse of her Opium perfume (*Cosmopolitan* says this'll remind Ciaran what he's missing).

As the lane narrows, the hedge closes in on her as if in a bad trip. Once she and Ciaran had dropped acid in a forest. He'd seen neon birds the size of humans, while she'd thought the trees were murderous, their branches reaching out for her.

'Frigging road in the middle of twattin'-well-nowhere,' she yells, realising that she cannot go deeper down this lane for fear of not being able to reverse out.

She parks the car and grabs the lavender envelope, the pre-bought bottle of Powers whiskey and her Fendi handbag. Starting off down the lane, she swears as she catches her heel in a cow pat. 'Fuck.'

The lowing of a cow answers her a few feet away, clearly trying to sleep on the other side of the hedge. Probably a bull, actually. Does Donegal have bears? This is a nightmare. But a necessary one.

'I have to go to Ireland, Doug. I need to see Ruth, y'know that little old lady. She's not very well.' He nodded and handed over his conduit for emotional support: the credit card.

The real reason for Imo's visit is to deliver the lavender envelope to her ex-husband. Since the courts ruled Rory's death suspicious, Imo has grown concerned that Ciaran might be found guilty and convicted. An ex-husband who's a convict? Unthinkable. Plus, Fern would be returned to her.

During the inquest, Imo loved the role of wronged ex. Finally, a chance to wreak revenge on the man who rejected her. Yes, she would tell any law-upholder who asked her. Yes, she thought Ciaran had done it!

But as the 'unlawful killing' verdict became fixed in the crosshairs, and the possibility of a criminal investigation grew ever larger, her thoughts turned to the long-term consequences. In short: Imo realised what a horrible mistake she'd made. It didn't happen often but, when it did, she had the good sense to rectify matters.

Thankfully, around the same time, Ciaran called her begging for help. Since then, she's been feeding him information on a weekly basis.

A hovel looms out of the darkness, candles flickering in the windows. It's nearly 11 p.m., so eleven-year-old Fern will almost certainly be asleep, but Ciaran's drinking will still have at least three hours of work in it. She knows this from four years of being married to him.

~ ~ ~

It'd been easy to track Ciaran down. For a low-level genius, the man is a naïve fool. He trusts people far too easily. When he called asking her to send Fern's passport and birth certificate, Imo saw her opportunity.

'Where are you?' she asked, covering her mouth with her cupped palm so that Doug wouldn't hear from the kitchen.

'I can't tell you,' he said. 'Just send it to Portsalon Post Office in Donegal. You got a pen to write that down? I'll be passing by on my way back to Belfast next week. *Please.*'

She found her map of Ireland, circled Portsalon and the surrounding towns. *Gotcha.* Then contemplated her options. She hated to do Ciaran a favour. But she also wanted him to take Fern with him. So yes, she could help.

'You know you won't be able to travel internationally under *your* passport?' she reminded him. 'You're wanted for questioning. Her passport will be on airport alerts too. So what are you going to do?'

Turns out the imbecile was planning on flying out from Dublin, thinking the North and South don't share information.

'That's far too risky, Ciaran,' Imo said, stubbing a cigarette out. 'There'll be an APB out for you. The British equivalent of a BOLO.'

'A what-lo?' he asked.

'Y'know, a Be On the Look Out. Like for a wanted person. Christ, have you never seen a detective show?'

She tucked her hair behind an ear. Ciaran was silent on the other end of the line. A thank you would be nice.

'Look, I'll send you a couple of fresh passports. I know a guy. Send me some passport photos and leave it with me, I have some pictures I can use for Fern. But it'll take a while, OK?'

Overjoyed, Ciaran sent her his photos quickly. Tearing them open, she felt a jolt of power travel up her inner thighs. She was holding his fate in her hands.

It gave her another tiny thrill, only posting Fern's new passport and doctored birth certificate, knowing that Ciaran would be distressed when he tore the Jiffy bag open and found no passport for him.

Felicity Felstead, she called Fern on the forgery, using the middle name Imo had chosen, plus her maiden name. Gosh – that is so much nicer than Fern Felicity O'Malley. They should just change her name to that anyhow.

Pushing the incomplete padded envelope into the postbox's mouth was as cathartic as pushing a pin into a voodoo doll. She would never stop wanting to be near Ciaran, and she would never stop wanting to hurt him.

~ ~ ~

Bouncing up the flagstone steps, Imo catches her first glance of Ciaran. Sitting in a rocking chair beside the fire, he's drinking from a clay cup and reading. Her entire body reacts. There's a cafetiere of coffee next to him. He always could ingest enough caffeine to rouse Tutankhamun. Normally it's spiked with something but, curiously enough, he now looks sober. She uses the glow of the candle spilling from the cottage to check her face in a pocket mirror. *Yep. Still got it.*

She's already a couple of martinis down, thanks to a pit-stop at a positively primitive pub called Annie Kelly's. The wind-beaten face of the landlady failed to respond to any of her charm, staying as deadpan as a shovel.

Imo finds it difficult to warm women up – they're so cold, so suspicious of her beauty – but men are easy. So, once she'd ordered her martini, she turned to the middle-aged, starburst-cheeked man beside her and started working on him. It took an hour – and two double ports on Imo's tab – for him to finally divulge where she might find Ciaran. Men are easy.

VERSIONS OF A GIRL

She pulls her outfit into place, organises the bottle of whiskey so it's label out, takes a deep breath, arranges her mouth into a smile and lifts the door knocker.

The Ultimatum

HOW IT WAS
A second later

Rap rap.

Who the chuff is that? thinks Ciaran.

His glance automatically shoots to Fern, a sausage of blankets and hair up above, but he knows very little wakes her. It's become family lore that, given Fern slept right through a riot outside a hotel in Belfast, 'she can sleep through a bomb'.

Fetch lies at Fern's feet. At the sharp knock her amber eyes snap open. She low-growls. 'Hush, Fetch,' he says. She at-eases.

Ciaran pushes back a thick forelock of curly black hair, suddenly tense, just realising this could be the police on a late-night tip-off.

Not a fat lot he can do about that now, given he's in a stone box with only one door and windows only a seven-year-old could wriggle through. Perhaps he could dig his way up and out of the thatch roof like a mole through undergrowth?

Ducking down to peer out into the blackness, he's reassured that there are no telltale blue lights, no high-vis jackets. Maybe it's the caravan park barmaid at long last, the minx. He opens the door with enthusiasm.

Boys a dear. Imo? No, thanks. Anyone but her.

*

An hour later, Ciaran's put away three-quarters of the bottle of Powers.

'No, no, just tea for me,' Imo protests. 'I'm driving.' Although she seems like she's had a couple already.

She *is* looking well, he concedes. Imo's always been a fox – and she knows it. Her chocolate dress cuts in and out at the waist, as if she's a curvy double bass.

She draws the lavender envelope from her boxy bag.

'I wanted to bring this personally, to make sure you and Fern get away safely,' Imo says, leaning towards him. Her hair smells like strawberries. If Helen of Troy is the face that launched a thousand ships, Imo is the hair that made a thousand men lose their wits.

He rips the envelope open. When he sees what it is – a convincing British passport under the name of Oscar Wolff – he removes his square black frames, ducks his head and presses his thumb and forefinger into his eyes. *Don't cry*.

'Thank you,' he says, voice choked.

There's a blur of fire hair and next thing, Imo is in his lap. Then they're up against the wall beside the front door, in the only part of the cottage that Fern's sleeping nook doesn't overlook, moving against each other urgently.

Imo's head is tucked under his shoulder, she traces loop-the-loops on his clavicle. They're lying in front of the dying fire on a sheepskin rug. He feels like an ancient king who's just conquered something. Perhaps it's the other way round.

'I like my new name,' he says, flipping open the passport. 'Oscar Wolff. It's dashing.'

'Like Oscar Wilde, I thought,' she says. 'Y'know: "I can resist everything except temptation." Just like you.'

She lights a cigarette in a slow – practised – move.
Ciaran chuckles. 'Aye, like me.'

'I don't get it, Ciaran,' she says. 'Help me understand. I know you couldn't have pushed Rory. So why are you running? Just explain to the police – or the guards, whatever you call them here – what happened. They'll believe you, I'm sure.' She pauses. 'We could even, y'know . . . try again. It could be the three of us, like before.' Her voice cracks.

He ho-hums, diverts his gaze and scratches his beard. Reaches for his cigarettes, lights one. The whiskey's beginning to wear off; he needs another. Imo's face shimmers and splits. He closes one eye to see a full her.

'That's a nice notion, honeybunch,' he says, soft. 'But we've been there, done that, got the divorced T-shirt. And I can't tell them what really happened that night. I just can't.'

Imogen sits up and coils the golden tail of her hair into a tight bun, securing it with bobby pins from her bag. Pulling an arched foot into her lap, she looks every inch the ballet dancer.

'You can tell me. And frankly, you must. I know the new name you'll be travelling under. I *gave* you that name.'

He flinches at the subtext – *and I can take it away again*. Here we go. She's still got it, the knack for deniable yet powerful manipulation. Imo will use anything to extract information. Your deepest secret, keenest longing, oldest wound, she knows exactly what to twist.

When they were still together, Imo would call him at the pub to ask him to come home. Three years into their relationship, he started shaking his head as the bar staff lifted the phone in his direction. Imo found not being able to reach him maddening. So she invented ever-more clever ways to do so.

She left messages, which the bartenders would scrawl on coasters. 'Call me, I have a surprise!' or 'Urgently call home.' The surprise was always non-existent, and the urgency a fiction. Imo had just wanted to pull a string and have him pick up the phone.

'Well. It wasn't me that pushed him. You know that much,' he offers.

'Who was it then?'

Ciaran hangs his head, heavy with information. Imo takes his jaw between her forefingers and pulls his gaze out of his lap and into her face. He knows she won't give up.

'You can trust me, Oscar Wolff. Why else would I bring you a forged passport?' Imo sits back in the lotus position. 'I want to help.'

Ciaran blows every inch of air out of his body, like a horse finally at rest. Help, my arse, but he has to tell her, otherwise she'll ruin their escape to America.

'Can't you see. It was *her*,' he says, jerking his head towards the sleeping shape of Fern. 'She pushed Rory. But she doesn't remember doing it.'

Boxing Night, 1989
Glenfoot, Northern Ireland

Ciaran wakes to the sound of a gunshot. No, a door slam. So hard the house seems to twang.

He hears a distant shout of 'Da! Da!'

Fern, fuckinhell, where is she? He thought she was in here.

HOW IT WAS

If Rory's been at her . . . he springs up and out of the room, adrenaline sobering him up.

His daughter sprints down the hallway and climbs him. He's relieved to see she's still wearing her nightgown and bed socks. Holding her on his hip, he can also feel the seam of her underpants.

'What happened? I told you not to leave our room! Are you OK?'

In the spaces between sobs, Fern tells him. She hurt Uncle Rory. He pulled her nightgown up, so she pushed him with all her might and now he's probably really angry.

'Och, I'm sure he's fine, pet! Let's go read our books in bed and then we'll check on your uncle in a little while, yeah?'

Fern nods. Ciaran carries her back to their room, stroking her hair.

While she chooses a book from the shelf, he comes into the bathroom, screams silently into the mirror and punches a tiled wall beside it.

That's it. Rory can have this bloody house. They're going to hit the road first thing in the morning and never come back.

The Split II

How Flick Loves

HOW IT IS
July 2007
London, England

Hundreds of eyeballs swivel towards twenty-eight-year-old Flick as the heavy oak doors open on to the ballroom.

She wonders what they think about her dress, about her hair, about her face. She wonders if she has something in her teeth – is it too late to check? She wonders what they said when they received the invitation: whether it was 'oh lovely!' or 'poor bloke'.

She wishes she could read the minds of everyone present, but is also petrified of the contents. All she has to go on is their expressions. Their eyes are hundreds of curved surfaces providing information about how well – or badly – she's doing.

Sita had one of those seventies mirror balls in her room, and they spent many hours lying on her tie-dye duvet underneath it; touching a luminous firefly landing on a hip, stroking a sprite of light on a nipple tip. Reading dirty poetry and listening to The Doors, brushing each other's hair and biting each other's lips. Flick can still taste Sita's skin.

Doug pulls their linked arms tighter as the Wedding March starts, striding forward as if she's a musket and he's about to go into battle. Why is she thinking about Sita right now? Is she here? Is it because she can feel her? Oh, no, that's right. Imo downgraded her to reception only.

'She's a bit of a one, that girl,' Imo said. 'You only want her around once people are tipsy. Then she'll be amusing. But at the wedding itself? She'll probably be swigging from a hip flask, pocketing the silver and swearing like a binman. Save her for evening colour.'

Flick wondered if the racist jibe was intentional but, as always, it was just deniable enough. *Just.* If she pulled on that thread, it would bring this down upon her head: 'Colour can refer to things other than race, dear. Don't be so sensitive.'

But then, maybe her mum had a point. This was the diazepam part of the day. This was the part she needed to glide, rather than bounce through.

Yes, Sita was more suited to the cocaine part of the day, the part when Flick intended to stop floating and start swaggering, gathering her skirts into her hands and using them for go-go dancing down alleys of clapping hands.

The hands of her friends, all in their late twenties, many of them without a whisper of a partner, let alone a proposal. 'I bet they're all so jealous,' Imo said with glee.

James stands at the end of the white-rose-festooned aisle. Dependable James, like the human equivalent of a kitchen appliance. White, sturdy, widely positively reviewed, guaranteed for at least ten years.

On the other side of the aisle, her mother is resplendent in an indigo gown with shooting stars sewn into it. A night sky in a field of blah floral, she's basically taken the rules of a summer wedding, set them on fire and shotputted them out the window.

Flick's just relieved she's not wearing white. Imo joked that she might.

~ ~ ~

Sita challenged her on the match with James.

'You're only twenty-eight,' she said. 'Why do you want to bind yourself to him for ever?'

'Because he loves me,' Flick responded. 'And my family love him.'

Sita tore up a beer mat into titchy shreds.

'I didn't ask you what he thinks of *you*, or what the ImogenandDougs think of *him*. What do you love about him?'

Flick thought hard on this. His opinion, their opinion, *then* her opinion was her order of priority. What she thinks seems irrelevant.

Something about Sita's question made her brain fizz and ding, like when she'd called Flick 'manipulative' for dropping gossip around the ballet company about her chief rival for a role.

'What do you mean, manipulative?' she'd asked Sita.

'Massaging the narrative for your own means!' Sita had said.

Flick didn't understand why that would even warrant comment. Wasn't that what everyone did? Wasn't that just being good at life?

Finally responding to Sita's question: 'He'll never leave me or cheat,' Flick paused, licked her finger and played the rim of her wine glass until it made the sound of a banished fairy. 'He makes an excellent living and we make a great couple.'

Sita sighed. 'This reminds me of the Klimt.'

'The what?' asked Flick, looking at herself in a pocket mirror, trying to smooth down a wizardy eyebrow hair.

Sita grabbed the mirror. 'D'you remember when you were about seventeen and you wanted that Klimt print, the one of the two babes embracing, with the bare nipple and all the seaweed? It was magical, that print.'

Flick nodded.

'But your mum said it was "coarse", so she made you get *The Kiss* because there was no nudity and it was all flowery rather than witchy, and it featured a man and a woman, so nobody would *talk*.'

'I don't get the comparison,' Flick said, shrugging.

'Oh my God. Can't you see? James is *The Kiss* all over again. He's your mother's choice, not yours.'

Silence.

'Why do you keep negging on my mother?' Flick asked.

'Because she's a narcissist and always has been! If nuclear Armageddon comes to pass, all that'll be left is the cockroaches and your mother's ego.'

'She's done so much for me, though, Sita. A beautiful home, clothes on my back, meals on the table, holidays, even.'

'What?' Sita flicked her friend's forehead. 'Earth calling, hellloooo. Do you have Stockholm Syndrome?'

'She has been an amazing mother.'

'Have you forgotten that she abandoned you for seven years?'

'And she's been incredible ever since.'

'Flick, I'm not denying that you've grown up on a cushion of privilege like a pampered designer cat, but all those things you just mentioned – giving you a home, clothing you, feeding you, taking you with her on holiday – are just normal parental activities, OK? They're pretty basic. My parents did all of that for me too. And they don't make me feel like there's some eternal debt that I can never repay.'

~ ~ ~

When Flick had come home with James in her jaws, Imo literally squealed.

'I looked his family's business up on Companies House,' she whispered to Flick over dinner, while Doug and James talked stocks. 'Last year's net profit was two million. He'll be worth a fortune. Marry this one, dear.'

It's been a different sort of relationship so far. Flick's exes have been few. There was Sita, then a couple of guys who Sita had nicknamed 'Player A' and 'Player B'. When Flick defended their honour, Sita pulled out her phone, looked, then produced a dating profile.

'Player A literally calls himself a player on MySingleFriend. He even spells it "playa". There's also a photo of him riding a sad drugged elephant.'

She scrolled to find the next. Flick regretted sending her screenshots of their profiles.

'Player B has a photo of him at a Playboy fan meet-up with bunnies, plus a photo of him at the gym topless.'

Over the years, the people Flick dates changes, the house-share she lives in shifts and the company she dances with alters, but the storyline of her love life always stays the same.

1. **The dreamy stage:** Sita/the players adore Flick and she them. Wild nights out and wicked sex turn weeks into months.

2. **The chill:** They mention an ex, who Flick becomes fixated by, wondering if they pine for them, love them, think of them in bed.

3. **The compliment fish:** It's OK, she just needs recalibrating. Some praise will do the trick. She

starts to prod for compliments. 'Why do you love me?' 'What's your favourite thing about my body?' She writes their answers down and rereads them, but not enough come, they don't fill her up, it's not working.

4. **The Facebook police:** Daily, sometimes more, she'll patrol their profiles. Clicking on the people they've befriended. If they're ugly, she won't investigate further, but if they're hot she's been known to scroll to the end of what's open, then migrate over to MySpace, Google searches, Linkedin to stalk this potential threat.

5. **The drunk inquisition:** When drunk or high – or both – she quizzes Sita and the Players as to whether she's the most beautiful person they've dated, are they going to get married, what will their wedding be like and when will it happen.

6. **The dissent:** All three of Flick's exes said something during the inquisition that threw her sovereignty into question.

    Sita refused to say Flick was the best sex she's ever had, maintaining that each partner was 'different'.

    Player A admitted he wasn't certain they were going to get married.

    Player B was denied sleep until she ferreted out the dissent she could smell like a bloodhound; that he missed his ex.

Flick would then finish it, she had to, because how dare they? She had to be their best, because anything less meant she's second best, which meant they want/wanted someone more, which meant Flick can't cope.

Within a few days of the split, Flick would beg for them back. They'd reconcile. All was well for a few more months. Then the cycle would begin again, the gap between reparation and break-up shortening each time, until Sita and the two Players became so exasperated they couldn't continue.

But with James, there was no drama. He was infatuated, clearly punching above his weight, and she was his willing muse. She has finally cracked it: find someone attractive, rich and stupid who loves you more.

~ ~ ~

Flick sways as if she's on a boat, trying to stay still to reapply her nude lip gloss. She dabs at a rosé stain on her second wedding dress; short, long-sleeved, lace and a little bit seventies, to show everyone that she can do both classic and cool. Day *and* evening doll: tick, tick.

It's possible she's misjudged the tricky equation of how much diazepam, cocaine and booze to mess with during an all-dayer. But what the hell, it's 8 p.m. and everyone's drunk at a wedding by now, aren't they. She just hopes she doesn't get a nosebleed. They've been happening more and more frequently lately, as if her body's attempting to tell on her.

Clicking back along the corridor towards the dance floor, which is now throbbing with middle-aged people gyrating to 'Here Comes the Hotstepper', she sees Sita ahead of her. Aside from a brief hello, they've not caught up tonight.

'Sit-aaaaa,' Flick calls. 'SITA!'

Sita spins and lets her group go ahead, waiting on Flick.

'Diyouknow,' Flick says, her words slurring together, 'that a marriage isn't legit and can be ammulled.'

'Annulled,' Sita says.

'Like I said, *ammulled*,' Flick emphasises, 'until the bride and groom shag? Diyouknow that? So technically I am still single.'

'Dancing Queen' by ABBA has cleared the hallway of toilet-goers and small-talkers, like a giant drunk-person magnet. Flick pushes Sita up against the statement wallpaper: snapdragons with gold hummingbirds.

Sita moves to free herself but melts when Flick runs a hand from her thigh up to her hip.

'Flick, you smell like cocaine. I could get high just by kissing you,' Sita says, trying to push her off.

'I really want to do this, Sit. I'm tired of pretending that I don't want you,' Flick says.

Sita pauses. 'Really? You actually want to put a stop to this whole circus? Because if you genuinely do—'

James's cousin Brent bursts into the hallway with his tie on his head, singing 'Dancing Queen'.

Flick finds the nearest door and shuts herself and Sita into it. It's a broom cupboard.

'Oh, no, you didn't,' Sita says, stepping her strappy sandal out of a mop bucket and sending it clattering into the corner. 'Did you just push me back into the closet? This is too much.'

'Calm down, Sita,' Flick says, pouting. 'It's my big day.'

'In the history of calming down, when has that phrase ever helped someone calm down?'

Sita yanks Flick out of the cupboard and back into the bright hallway.

HOW IT IS

'I am not a plaything, Flick. People are not toys. You don't get to pick them up and put them down whenever you please.'

Cousin Brent has stopped in his tracks, eyes wide. 'Ooooooooh!' he says, pointing at Flick and then Sita. 'Saucer of milk for table two.' He miaows.

'Don't you look exotic?' he says to Sita.

'How so?' Sita asks.

Her hair is loose and her linen dress plain.

'You glow.' He reaches out to touch her cheek.

She blocks his hand.

'Don't touch me.'

Brent backs away, hands up. 'Precious, aren't we?'

Sita turns to Flick. 'You need to sort yourself out or you'll lose everyone, apart from your mother. It'll be you and her alone in a room, congratulating each other for being beautiful.'

Flick perks up at the compliment.

Sita throws her head back. 'Give me strength! That's all you got from *that*? Sort your shit out, Flick. I mean it. Or I'll be gone for good.'

Sita turns and exits the building.

How Fern Loves

HOW IT IS
July 2007
Los Angeles, California

'Tidy desk, tidy mind,' her colleague parrots, when Fern has to burrow down through papers and coffee cups to find her keyboard.

'You don't have to be mad to work here, but it helps', says a poster of Einstein bobbing his tongue out. Digby snores beneath it in a box lined with an old scarf. Fern's now got a Masters of Science in psychology and is halfway through a PhD, having stripped her way through school.

Aged twenty-eight, she's supplementing her PhD with a teaching assistant role in UCLA's Psychology Department. Her entry into the atmosphere of office politics has been bumpy.

Like when a supercilious colleague asked if she knew who Steven Pinker was.

'Of course I do. Do you?'

'You can take the girl out of the trailer park . . .' he said, when she turned away.

Fern responded with maturity, by rolling a gum wrapper into a ball and flicking it, hitting him right between the eyes while he was saying some more pretentious wank, earning her a laugh from everyone present.

'You need to meditate,' he said, rubbing his brow.

'You need to bite me.'

HOW IT IS

She was hauled up on a disciplinary later that day.

'Oh, c'mon, it was a joke,' Fern said when the professor produced the miniature foil missile.

'You may be Hooters alumni,' he said, looking at her résumé. 'But that kind of behaviour won't fly here. Pun intended.'

He smiled, then placed his hand on her thigh. She stared at it until he removed it.

Since then, Fern's role has mainly been behind the scenes. She suspects this is also because of the clothes she wears. But given rollerblading into work, Digby bouncing alongside her, is an athletic endeavour, and she hates to be too hot, she's not about to switch her cut-offs and slouchy band T-shirts for scratchy dresses anytime soon.

'What other people think of us is none of our business,' Ciaran always taught her. And so Fern does precisely as she pleases, ignoring the up-and-down scans from colleagues and the roundabout feedback from the professors enquiring as to whether she's cold.

'Tidy desk, tidy mind' colleague Phyllis is actually rather lovely. They have regular brainstorming meetings where they suggest lateral solutions to each other's latest PhD snafu.

'Can we do a breakfast meeting instead of a lunch meeting tomorrow?' Phyllis asks Fern.

'A breakfast what?'

'A 7 a.m. meeting,' Phyllis explains.

'No can do, sweetheart,' Fern says.

'You have other plans?'

'Yes, I have plans. I plan to be asleep. It's Saturday.'

*

She and Buck watch a werewolf movie, turning Fern's living room into a den of cushions and blankets, before flopping down.

'I feel like you're going to sacrifice me,' Buck comments, nodding to the two dozen electric candles surrounding them.

'You're no virgin,' she replies, lobbing popcorn at his head.

Buck's toe leans against Fern's. She feels the presence of his toe like a hand travelling up her inner thigh. Maybe all that talk about the feet being connected to the rest of the body is real. A stir of danger in her hips. *No*, you'd eat him alive.

She worries he wants to have babies with her. While also worrying he doesn't want to have babies with her.

'Love is just an illusion,' Ciaran has taught her. 'It's lust telescoped into something it's not. I thought I was in love once, but it was bullshit.' He stroked his generous moustache and pushed his glasses up.

'When they do neuroimaging of those in the first flush of love, they find their brains most resemble those who are clinically insane or high on cocaine. So, there you go,' he concluded with a flourish, as if that was the final word that ever needed to be said on the matter.

They watch the main character of the movie start The Change to werewolf; having to hide their increasing hairiness, sudden speed, hunger for fresh blood. During one scene, where the newborn werewolf has to pretend not to have their head turned by a butcher's cut of raw meat, Fern places her Merlot off to one side, reminded of The Change in her drinking.

HOW IT IS

Then the protagonist chains themself to a metal post, in order to wait out the full moon and The Change without hurting any other sentient beings. They wake up naked in a forest, covered in fur, blood and feathers – a solo running shoe beside them.

This scene reminds Fern of when she locks herself down at home for a 'quiet drink' and then finds herself sprinting towards town in a cab to hunt her victims. *Come, my pretties*: she cruises the club looking for drinking buddies or hook-ups. Smiling wide in a black mini-dress and occupying herself with a drink or five, until they make their way into her night, or she theirs by asking for a light.

She uses late-night classes at the gym, washing her hair and leaving it wet, and even 'forgetting' her credit cards at work, as barriers between her and the clubs. Right now, she's using Buck as a person-sized anchor, to keep her in for the night and relatively sober. Buck has other ideas.

'Look, I can't stay long, and before you get too far into that,' he looks at the bottle of Merlot, 'I need to tell you something.'

Fern struggles to keep a straight face. Serious moments like this undo her.

'I think I'm going to move back upstate,' Buck says, twizzling his hoodie drawstrings. 'Not *home* home, but to San Francisco. Like you're always saying, that's where a young chef should be right now. Here, it's finally moving on from brunch beneath palm trees, and getting more complex than California rolls and green juice, but I have ideas that are just too big for LA right now.'

What is happening? Fern's face begins to crumple.

'Also, you know how I feel. It's beginning to get too painful watching you take guy after guy home, and girl after girl, while I remain friend-zoned. We'll always be friends, but I need to move on, move away for my own sanity. Out of LA.'

The next day, Fern pours the last of the vodka-spiked blue popsicle into her mouth. More of a slushie than a popsicle, given the vodka won't freeze. She's holding Digby against her chest like a rugby ball, but he finally wriggles from her grasp and goes to flop on the cool bathroom tiles with a grunt.

She picks through the wreckage of last night. Hugging Buck and pretending she was stoked for him. Feeling too depressed to go out. Not wanting to walk to the 7-Eleven and definitely not being able to drive, so ordering a pizza from Napoli Sunset on Westwood, in order to be able to purchase another bottle of wine.

Scrolling through her phone for dudes to summon: Traffic Stop Pete, Cafeteria Brent, Twerk Johnny and Producer Kai. Kai was the only one who picked up, so it was his lucky night. Just now, she's finally gotten him to leave.

A fan sweeps the room back and forth – *jjjhmmjjjhmm* – seeking her out like a searchlight. She stretches her legs up the tattered Klimt poster. Every time the fan searches this area it lifts the bottom right-hand corner of the picture. Fern holds it down with her black-and-pink big toe, a glamorous mix of toe fungus and cotton candy polish.

Her ex, Sofia, gave her this picture. 'I know you love Klimt . . . and she reminds me of you,' Sofia said, before breaking up with her.

Looking down her nose at Fern from the poster is some sort of snake-charming empress. Her mouth a determined line, her jewellery stacked high, she is the definition of a broad you don't mess with.

At first you think she's alone, and then you see hidden faces and figures in back; people she's left behind. Because you can't really trust anyone, not really. Alone is safer. Buck has asked her to intentionally endanger herself by letting him in fully. She can't do it. He's as close as anyone has ever gotten.

In Fern's opinion, this poster is the very definition of a backhanded compliment. It says, 'you're charming, yes, but probably a megalomaniac'. Regardless, she still loves it.

The results of the maternity test that she and Scout arranged seven years ago still sit in her bedside drawer, potentially pregnant with meaning and yet also meaningless. Kinda like the lubricant on top of them. At least now she knows that Imo isn't her biological mother. Explains a lot.

But it's also led her and Scout into a blind alley, given Nora has been missing for twenty-odd years and she still doesn't know how her birth came about. Ciaran shut them down with, 'Fuck off with ye, you're a pair of headcases!' when they'd tried to show him the maternity results, refusing to look. And even though secret kung-fu ninja Ruth is her grandmother, she won't reply to any of her letters. So, what's the point of this exciting revelation that has led exactly nowhere?

They also found themselves in a dead end when it came to finding Rory's real killer, with the Irish trip turning up zero credible new leads. Everyone on Ruth's list that was, or had been, connected to the house had an alibi for the night in question. And double-checking them with witnesses was damn-near impossible.

'Was Jimmy Reilly in a lock-in here on Boxing Day night eleven years ago?' the custodian of The Lurig Bar said, while drying glasses. 'Jesus wept, lass, I have enough problems remembering eleven minutes ago.'

There's a knock at the door. Fuck-a-doodle-do. She's never enjoyed an unannounced visitor, but lately her apartment has become feral: more of a lair lined with bones and pheromones than a socially acceptable place for other humans.

Any therapist poking around her apartment right now would probably have her tied to a gurney and taken away. She once lost Digby for a full hour underneath a gigantic fatberg of knotted clothes. He yipped indignantly until she managed to dig him out.

Bottles, traces of illegal substances, crusted dog food, even used condoms are common features. As are scrawls of 'detective thriller!' book ideas she has at 3 a.m., which look like a serial killer's musings come morning.

Buck caught a glimpse of her bedroom recently and said, 'You know there's some British chick who's put her bedroom in a famous art gallery as the epitome of fucked-upness, and her bedroom is less fucked up than *this*.'

He'd then told her that the Klimt snake-charmer woman is a Greek goddess. 'Her name is Hygieia,' he said, pointing at the poster. 'It's Greek for hygiene. She's the goddess of cleanliness.'

The irony of this is so cartoonishly obvious that it warrants no comment; it may as well be running around their ankles, hitting them with a miniature mallet.

On a blackboard in the kitchen, she's jotted down a quote, probably misremembered, from Sylvia Plath.

'Like a sword swallower's sword, it makes me feel godlike and powerful.'

This is why she has to protect her secret. Why she has to hide The Change. Because if anyone takes the drinking away from her, she'll be a sword swallower without a sword. A nobody. A nothing. A non-person.

The buzzer goes again. She creeps downstairs in bare feet and, wincing with the delicacy, slides the teardrop-shaped cover off the peephole, hoping that the radio still playing in the kitchen isn't audible.

Her single eye sees a goldfish-bowl distorted Scout, bringing his eye up to the peephole as though he senses her.

'I know you're in there, Fern,' he calls.

Shitballs. No wonder he made detective, he has a sixth sense.

She darts upstairs, yells, 'COMING,' and whirls through the apartment like a dervish, throwing on a gauzy dress, belting it, slipping on scruffy gladiators, grabbing the biggest sunglasses she can find, downing a shot of mint mouthwash, whistling for Digby and then stepping out of the door, keys in hand.

'Oh hey, Pops! I'm just on my way out for coffee. Come with?'

He raises an eyebrow at her.

Fern's Sandwich

HOW IT IS
Ten minutes later

Scout watches Fern order a club sandwich, a Coke 'with a straw, please' and an iced frappuccino and knows exactly what she's up to.

He sees it all. The micro-tremble in her hands as she passes the menu back. The tactics in what she's ordered – food she can eat without handling a knife and fork, drinks she can suck through a straw without picking them up.

This is the hangover cure of champions; the carbs and sugar designed to steady her low blood sugar and soothe her shakes, then the mind-slapping caffeine to fix her tiredness.

Back in the day, he too congratulated himself for inventing these coping strategies, thinking he was invisible. Just as Fern does.

'Look, I'll keep it short, I can see you're having a . . . morning.'

Fern squints at him, shakes her head as if to say 'who, me?', but leaves the booby-trapped statement there.

'There's been a development,' he says. 'My buddy from the Irish police called.'

The waitress delivers Fern's sandwich and she falls on it like a seagull on chips. Her bloodshot eyes roll back with pleasure.

'And?'

'I asked him to set up an alert on Nora Brady's passport.

HOW IT IS

He told me on the downlow that she's not a missing person any more. Ruth rescinded her missing status in 1984.'

Scout mimes his mind being blown.

'But what's even more exciting is this: Nora just arrived at Belfast International Airport.'

Flick's Undoing

HOW IT IS
October 2007
London, England

Rolling off the trampoline she's just 'died' on as the white swan, Flick is panting. That's not unusual, given the exertion of the final scene, but she is tearing feathers and diamanté off her bustle.

'GET. THIS. OFF ME,' she calls out.

'Woah there, slow your roll and let me help . . .' a stage-hand says.

Flick roars with frustration, managing to rip the bodice just as her co-star lands on the backstage trampoline too. The orchestra swells.

Her co-star takes one look at her, shaking and crying, and tells the stagehand, 'Go get her mother. Or her husband. Or both. They'll be in the family box.'

Minutes later, Imo and James arrive to find a topless Flick drinking champagne from the bottle, her tiara lopsided, her tights ripped, laughing to herself.

'Stay back,' Imo tells James, and goes to her daughter.

'What's wrong, darling? You were exquisite,' Imo says. 'I bet the write-up in *The Times* will be sublime. Aged just twenty-eight and commanding your own press sensation!'

'I couldn't breathe. Through that whole final scene I was hyperventilating.'

'Really? Nobody noticed. I would have noticed, you know that,' says Imo with a chuckle.

It's true. Mum's always the first to notice.

'It doesn't matter if nobody noticed,' Flick says. '*I* noticed. I hate this. I'm quitting.'

'No you're not. No. You're not. We'll talk about this at home.'

Imo throws her pashmina over Flick's bare chest and ties it at the back of her neck, pulling her to her feet.

James drives them back to the Kensington townhouse while Imo hushes her in the back seat. Flick stares at Hyde Park, the autumn leaves unfastening themselves from the trees.

'It'll be fine. Just a bad night is all. You're a star, sweetheart,' Mum says. 'I'll help you get better.'

'I got an email from Da,' Flick says, hiccuping, still swigging from the bottle. 'He said it's terminal. The cancer, I mean. I need to cancel the rest of the shows and go see him.'

Imo shakes her head. 'How can you tell an addict is lying?'

Flick looks at her, unsure.

'Their lips are moving.'

Her mother strokes her hair.

'I got the same email. I very much doubt it's true. I'll phone Ciaran's . . . Oscar's . . . whoever's doctor tomorrow and get to the bottom of it. We'll sort it, my darling.'

Flick sighs, relieved. 'Thank you.'

Five weeks later
Paradise, California

'Thanks for making the trip,' Wally says, his handshake firm and sincere. 'You . . . well, you've become a lady, haven't you?'

VERSIONS OF A GIRL

Flick gives him a tight smile, to match her tight charcoal dress and tight bun.

'And married too! So young! It's great to meet you, James.'

Why do people keep saying twenty-eight is young to get married, for pity's sake? It's the perfect time.

He ushers them into the function room of Paradise Falls. She can't believe that as a kid she spent so much time with this elderly motel-keeper. And that she actually drank from glasses – ate from plates – in this establishment. It's a wonder health and safety didn't shut it down decades ago. She wonders if there's a giant rat out back in a chef's hat, fixing more limp offerings for this buffet tray.

James grabs a cheese sandwich. 'Put that down,' Flick says, taking her pocket mirror out to check her lipstick.

'He seems nice,' James says, ignoring her command.

'He is, I guess,' Flick says. 'But it's just so weird that we hung out so much when I was, what, thirteen, fourteen? Do you think he's a . . . y'know?'

James frowns. 'Do you want a drink?' He gestures to the bar.

Flick sighs as if he's been pestering her to have a drink forever. 'OK, OK, just get me a vodka, lime, soda. And make sure they get it from the optics at the back, rather than a dodgy bottle under the bar.' She could use a sharpener. The last line she did after the cremation is wearing off.

Her life has become a dance between the white and black swan. The white – diazepam until sunset – and the black – cocaine after nightfall. With a few visible drinks thrown in here and there, so that people don't wonder why she's such sensational company at a party.

'I've had a few,' she says, shaking her wine glass and laughing when they ask what she's on and can they have some. Flick has never once shared her diazepam or cocaine. Because with sharing comes the risk of exposure.

The two drugs together provide the perfect balance of light and dark. When she wakes up shaky, the gnaw for more cocaine on her, she subdues the beast with a few milligrams of diazepam. Just enough to stop its snarl . . . then some cocaine later to put lipstick on it, plait its mane, get it dancing for the public.

Some musicians (who look like tramps) are setting up on a platform in the corner. Great. So this isn't going to be an in-and-out, as she'd hoped. They'll have to watch a whole show.

Flick's still sore that she wasn't invited to the red-carpet tribute gig in LA that Oscar Wolff's agent organised, with rock stars and emotional speeches by weeping actresses. When she read about the event in the *Telegraph*, Flick sent Ciaran's agent a strongly worded email about how disappointed she was not to be included. It was a thousand words long.

The response came: 'Sorry, but I have no idea who you are.' The cheek!

Ciaran (a.k.a. Oscar) must have burnt through a few agents since the one Flick met at Chateau Marmont seven years ago.

'Oscar Wolff dies aged just forty-eight', headlines mourned. There were all sorts of rumours about how he died – auto-erotic asphyxiation, overdose while having a fivesome, jumping off the roof of the Chateau Marmont – so when the inquest finally revealed that he'd died of alcohol poisoning

– of trying to put more alcohol into his body than it could handle – the press were deflated.

The inquest's 'alcohol poisoning' outcome got shoved up the gutter in two-hundred-word nibs. When it later transpired that Ciaran had been diagnosed with terminal cancer a few months before his death, but the alcohol got him first, the press were even less happy. That barely made the news.

'The middle classes don't want to read about Oscar Wolff dying of their favourite legal drug,' a broadsheet columnist observed. 'They want to read about him dying from a heroin overdose, so that they can feel superior while drinking their gin-in-a-tin on the 6 p.m. train back to Guildford.'

The red-top newspapers continued to peddle rumours that other drugs were the true cause, via the opinions of his ex-girlfriends. 'Never mind what the medical examiner thinks, let's ask someone he shagged for a couple of months,' the same broadsheet columnist wrote.

Flick continues to be surprised that nobody from Oscar's previous life as Ciaran has sold him out. Ciaran's friends and family could get five figures at least for something as explosive as, 'Dead rock star faked identity', or 'Troubled rock star's secret past life'.

Imo often joked that missing out on the limelight was killing her.

'But we have to stay quiet. It would be napalm for your career, darling, being the daughter of that lush.'

And so, they stayed under, stayed quiet. And stayed in the cheap seats of Paradise Falls at the Ciaran O'Malley wake, rather than in the VIP of the Troubadour for the Oscar Wolff tribute gig. More's the pity.

HOW IT IS

The bar staff of Paradise Falls turn the lights down and Pink Floyd track up, labouring under the delusion that anyone is enjoying this awful noise. Wally takes to the stage, the spotlight bouncing off his head, his black suit with yellow tie and pockets making him look like a six-foot-three bumblebee.

A flashback visits Flick, of Wally trying to teach her all the American words.

'Now, those are pants,' he said, pointing to her jeans.

'These are *trousers*, Wall,' she said. 'Pants are what you wear on your bum.'

'You mean your butt,' he corrected her.

Flick knows full well that there was nothing sexual in it, but her expectations of the world are now so rigidly defined – grown men do not hang out with teenage girls without being perverts, end of – that she can't see it as innocent.

'Thanks for being here, folks. I know Ciaran loved you all,' Wally says, pointing at a forty-something blonde wearing a skirt that nobody should wear past thirty. A twang of recognition in Flick. Oh, what: it's Dina.

She really ought to dress her age. Still, though, Flick will never forget how kind she was to her. She gives Dina a charity wave. Dina waves back, a little shy.

'Before we get started, I just want to read something out to you,' Wally says, the paper quivering in front of him.

Terrific. Nothing worse than watching someone who can't do public speaking doing public speaking.

'We all know that Ciaran had his demons,' says Wally, starting to choke up already, 'but we all also know that Ciaran was a beautiful soul, beneath all the lyin', cheatin' and griftin' that came hand-in-hand with his addiction.'

He turns the piece of paper so that the crowd can see it.

Flick rolls her eyes. *Forgodsake*, we can't read it. Get on with it, man.

'This here is a poem called 'Bluebird' by Charles Bukowski,' Wally says, pushing half-moon spectacles onto his face. 'People are saying that Ciaran's demons killed him. But I don't think that's true. I think his bluebird dying is what killed him. The hopeful, true, vulnerable, good-no-matter-what *heart* of him.'

There are nods of recognition in the crowd.

Kill me now, Flick thinks.

'We all have a bluebird inside of us and it's imperative we don't let it die.' Wally looks directly at Flick.

She flushes and tosses her hair. Who does he think he is? Trying to impart spiritual lessons upon her as if he's the Dalai frickin' Lama.

'So when I read this, it's because I want you to remember the goodness at the core of him,' Wally says. 'Yes, he could be a jackass of the highest order, and he owed most of us money.' There's a rumble of laughter. 'But we loved him – and his bluebird – right up until the end.'

Wally starts to read the poem about the bluebird. He breaks down over the line, 'he's singing a little in there, I haven't quite let him die', and has to regain his composure. Dina goes up on stage to hold his hand as he continues.

James pulls Flick into him, handing her a tissue.

'What's this for?' Flick asks, puzzled at the tissue.

'You're crying,' he whispers.

She feels her face, surprised to find it's wet. Then there's a scratch on her shin, a nose pushing its way into her hand.

HOW IT IS

What the— She looks down to find a tubby, elderly Jack Russell bouncing with excitement, eyes glossy with cataracts. Digby.

And that's when the truly ugly crying begins.

Fern's Undoing

HOW IT IS
November 2007
Los Angeles, California

Fern wakes up in a foetal position on the stained rug.

'I bet the previous tenant used this for transporting dead bodies,' Buck once said of the living room's mangy rug.

'We really should hand this into the police,' she replied, gesturing to what looked like bloodstains.

When guests offer to take their shoes off in their apartment, the couple quip, 'Keep them on for protection against the rug.'

Where's Buck? Why's she not in bed? Why is she naked? She's colder than a witch's tit.

As she sits up to go find clothes, there's a snort behind her. It's not Buck – she knows that instantly. She daren't look. She looks.

A man she doesn't recognise, hench and steroid-pumped, his arms crisscrossed over his face to block out the morning sun slicing through the blinds. He smells like sperm and coconut tanning lotion.

Bile rises in her stomach and burns its way out of her throat. She runs for the bathroom. Hangs over the toilet, wishing her stomach would empty, but no such luck. Buck is tucked up in the bedroom next door, with the door wide open.

How did this happen? Who the fuck is that? How did he get back here?

HOW IT IS

She's asking these questions while also knowing the answer is always: her. She happened. Invited it in. She's the only common denominator in these hundreds of tiny life fires. This, though . . . this is the biggest act of self-arson yet.

She pulls on week-old pyjamas from the bathroom floor – they smell like Cheetos – and splashes her face. The guilt can wait until later. It sits on the horizon. It's coming. But first thing's first. Put out the immediate fire.

Pulling the bedroom door shut as she passes it, Fern creeps back into the living room. The guy has curled up into a ball and has his back to her. *Tap, tap.* He doesn't stir. *Nudge, nudge.* He groans.

'You need to get outta here. My huge boyfriend with anger issues is right in the next room,' she says in his ear.

He looks at her. *Serious?* She nods, solemn and convincing. Digby lies in the corner, head resting on daintily crossed paws, ready if needed. As Fern's guest rises to stand, a low growl catches in his throat.

Her guest dresses fast. The only positive to this clusterfuck is that he woke up wearing boxer shorts, so she *hopes* that means they didn't. He tries to peck her on the cheek, but she turns her face so all he gets is a mouthful of hair. He thumps down the stairs, Fern wincing with each step.

Once the front door is shut, she rests her forehead against it. This has to be it, right? The lowest hole she's prepared to dig for herself. And she's gotten away with it. So, now's the time, before Buck finds out.

A few months ago, her greatest fear was being with Buck. Now it's *not* being with him.

~ ~ ~

She managed to behave like she didn't give two fucks about him moving away from LA for the entire month-long runway of him preparing to leave. Until they were filling a removal truck with his belongings and he came back from a box run to find her sitting in his leather La-Z-Boy, sobbing. He lifted her out of the chair, placed her on the sidewalk and started unpacking.

Having already given up his apartment, it made sense for him to move straight into hers. You don't have a courtship stage when you've been best friends for fifteen years. It goes from zero to committed pretty fast.

~ ~ ~

She hears Buck opening the bedroom door, padding to the loo, flipping the seat up. Tiptoeing past the ajar bathroom door as he *pissshhhes* into the bowl, his back to her, she re-enters the living room to sweep for any remaining clues.

A flash of Da runs through her head, of him sitting on a lacy bra before Dina saw it.

It peeks out from beneath the couch, a cheery yellow corner. An empty condom wrapper. Fern only just has time to push it back under with her toe, before Buck enters the room.

'Morning, little bird,' he says. He ruffles her hair.

Flowers open through her – then wither under how undeserving she is. Digby stares at her, unblinking, then glances at the hidden condom wrapper. *I know*, she mouths at him.

'Do you want a coffee?' Buck shouts from the kitchen.

She takes a deep breath.

'Yes, please,' she calls back, voice splintering.

She buries her face in Digby's fur. This is why she can't have nice things. She always breaks them.

She tells everyone she's done with drinking.

'Great decision,' Scout exhales, leaning back and half smiling, half frowning.

'Up to you, honey,' Buck simply says.

But the reactions of her friends range from a spit-speckling 'BOR-ING' to the bewildered 'Can you still . . . y'know, go to parties?'

'It's like I've betrayed them by quitting,' she tells Scout. 'Like I've just told them I've decided to start clubbing baby dolphins in my spare time.'

Scout rubs his beard. 'Yeah, that's a thing. You're opting out of an unwritten contract.'

'Just have one,' she's told over and over again, as if it were that simple, like she could stop that train once it's left the station, push that waterfall back uphill, un-pop that jack back in its box.

Despite her public resolutions to stop drinking, she continues to drink, but harder. She'll put together a couple of days alcohol-free, then slalom out of control once more. Naming her addiction seems to have emboldened it. It's come out of hiding, grown teeth and claws and is now openly feral.

'You've gone to the dark side,' she's told.

'You're no fun any more,' she's told.

Support for her drinking dies. But she has no support for her non-drinking either, other than Scout and Buck. The number of people she can drink in front of dwindles. The grand total of people she can be herself around without alcohol is two. Scout says nothing, other than 'I'm here' as he watches her ricochet.

When she drinks now, only the hardcore party monsters remain as viable company. Those who tap cocaine onto their hands in public, who order pitchers of beer that are gone within the hour, that swipe the bottle if another table leaves a glass at the bottom.

Until one day, with a few days of non-drinking under her, Fern walks along Venice Boardwalk after a yoga class, mat slung across her back like a protective sword. During savasana the teacher crept up behind her and massaged her temples, as tenderly as a mother might touch her newborn baby.

Fern found tears racing down her cheekbones to rest in the nape of her neck, tidal sobs coming up from her centre.

'Sorry. Jesus Christ, I don't understand, I never cry,' Fern whispered, while the yogi wafted lavender oil under her nose and the rest of the class pretended not to notice.

She still feels shaky from it. She stops for a green juice, and while she waits she browses a stall that exclusively sells toe rings. Turning to survey the boardwalk, she looks for something to restore her faith in the universe, but right now she can only see the ugly.

An elderly British couple sit on a table next to her.

'I rented a film for us to watch tonight, but I don't think you'll like it.'

'Whyever not?'

'It's about mobsters.'

'I have nothing against lobsters.'

And there it is, her faith-restorer. She tucks this away to give it to Buck later, but she can't feel it herself; it doesn't even make her smile.

Walking on, that's when she sees them. Her friends. Using a crater of the skate park as a dive bar. One sways as another yells a coyote version of 'Riders on the Storm'. A streak of piss beside their drinks cooler, no doubt from one of them. A pair canoodle, a breast is removed, an erection in pants is massaged. Skaters crisscross around them, wrinkling their noses, laughing at them.

'Fern!' one yells, holding his joint aloft, stumbling as he tries to get up. She taps down her baseball cap and runs away, her mat bouncing, the juice spilling.

That night she drinks.

~ ~ ~

Wally once took Fern to Sacramento fish market.

She loves to eat fish, but found the market stunningly depressing, with its stadium of staring eyes and open mouths.

'It's not much fun meeting the food you eat, is it?' she said.

As she looked into a bucket of tangled crabs, Wally said, 'They never get free, y'know.'

He explained that if one crab so much as stood an outside chance, another crab would pull them back in, in their attempt to escape too.

'They keep each other in.'

They stood and watched the crabs a while.

~ ~ ~

And so begins the era of only being able to drink with her dog. Always watching but unable to comment, he sees directly into her soul anyhow. No point hiding. Fern doesn't have to pretend to be happy. She can be exactly who she is; a person who needs to drink to be OK.

In the morning, she gets dressed in her uniform of athleisure. It means she can wear a cap to hide her face, have the sweats without judgement, and be socially championed for looking grim.

'Tough class, huh?'

'Yeah, whew!'

This morning, she loaded her reusable sports bottle with ten shots of vodka and a half-litre of Sprite. To anyone a few feet away she looks like a hiker, out pounding the boardwalk with her waddling Jack Russell, who keeps darting into outdoor seating areas to snuffle for mislaid fries.

'Heel,' she whisper-shouts at Digby, as he attempts to dive into an open kitchen to seek out floor food. Floor food is his favourite. She buys him gourmet kibble, which he rejects, but he'll hoover up any old furball-covered food from the street.

As her buzz deepens and she goes further out of town, Fern can almost fool herself that her sports bottle is alcohol-free as she puffs up the Hollywood Hills, can almost believe the hype that her veins aren't spangled by vodka, that she's just a normal twenty-eight-year-old on a normal hike.

She pushes her way through the trails swigging away, now unfazed about possible rattlesnakes. Kill me, see if I care.

If she sees anyone she knows, she pulls her cap down and breaks into a jog, even if they say her name, while Digby grunts himself reluctantly into a canter.

When she gets home, Buck squints at her over their early dinner, opens his mouth to speak. Her phone pings. She dives for it.

> **Billy from Reno**
> Why did you completely ignore me today
> on the trail?

Fern completely ignores him.

She tells Buck about the mobsters/lobsters couple. He chuckles and opens some mail.

'Oh, our lease is up for renewal,' he says. 'Do we want to stay?'

Their apartment is a bargain for LA. Next door, there's a lady who wails out of her window about being lonely, upstairs they move furniture around for fun, a family of racoons have taken the bike store hostage, and the shower is either arctic or scalding. The rent is just $2500 a month.

Bathing for an unnecessarily long time while Buck gets ready for the late shift at the restaurant, she waits for his cheerful call of 'Seeyalater' and the *kerdunk* of the door.

Dripping wet, she throws on her robe, goes to the kitchen, and retrieves the box of wine from the back of the cupboard, then decants it into her cup and lies on the couch with it dangling from her arm.

She's almost out of savings and doesn't know how to tell Buck. In July she got fired from her teaching assistant role for drinking on the job. The shakes had struck at work, so she scouted around for something to steady her. The only liquor on site was a pricey bottle of prosecco sitting in the staff fridge, probably earmarked for academic coups, or maybe spontaneous nerd parties. Gold and special.

Fern smuggled the prosecco into a tote bag casually, like she'd just taken her lunch.

'Bye!' she waved to her colleagues, holding the bag still so it didn't swing.

She went into the accessible restroom to pop it, drink just a little bit, get her hand steady enough to write, then the plan was to smuggle it back into the fridge. It would be flat, but still mostly there.

Unfortunately, the cork got away from her, ricocheted around the room and landed on the panic button beside the toilet. *Parp parp parp*, went the alarm, while a red light flashed like a strobe.

A few seconds later, a security guard burst in, the flimsy latch clattering to the floor, and found her swigging from the bottle, trying to figure out how to disable the alarm.

Explain *that*. There's no bullshitting your way out of that one, turns out.

Instead of telling Buck all of this, Fern lied that UCLA didn't have a job for her this semester, and she has been pretending to search for a new position ever since.

She even went to see Misty at the Landing Strip, to see if she could pick up a few shifts just so she didn't hit zero.

'Nope,' Misty said the moment she saw her. 'I love you, girl, you know that – the clients do too – but you're a mess right now. What are you on?'

Last time Fern looked in her account she had $1592. It's not nothing, but it's not something either. She could take credit, of course, get a loan, get a card, she knows she could; but every cell in her body resists that. Never done it, never wants to. She needs to make money the way other people need to breathe.

Digby appraises her, then steals a sock and tosses it into the air, trying to get her to chase him. Athleticism doesn't come naturally to him, given he's like a baby seal on toothpicks, so at first this makes her laugh. Until it becomes tragic that her dog's trying to cheer her up.

She ignores him and watches *Lost*. He tosses the sock ten,

eleven, twenty times . . . until he gets tired and lies down, nudging it with his nose, still hopeful.

'Up, up,' she says to him, patting the couch. He hauls himself up beside her and instead of curling up like a regular dog, lies flat on his side like a person, his head on the cushion too. The little spoon to her big spoon.

'You don't know you're a dog, do you, Digs?' she says, tucking her body around him and kissing his velvety ear. He stretches back and licks her nose.

His barrel body rests against her, solid and unquestioning. A feather of love tickles her stomach. It's the first time she's felt anything other than constant craving for weeks now. She exhales. He quivers.

~ ~ ~

A parking lot, 10.17 a.m., merciless sun, the rumble of a passing truck sending a puff of dust her way. Why's the door open? Fern's in the back seat, trusty sports bottle charged with vodka beside her. Raking her hand through her snarled hair, she runs through what she remembers of last night.

Buck went out with workmates texted her she felt sad but relieved she could drink more watched three back-to-back CSI episodes ran out of wine drove to the 7-eleven bought vodka saw a convoy of cop cars down the highway freaked out about driving home decided to stay here turn the radio up and dance beside the car some men cat-called she told them to go fuck themselves and fell asleep Digby was pawing at the door to have a pee she told him to shut up he wouldn't shut up so she . . . where's Digby?

'Digby . . . Digby!' she calls. Her voice is like smashed glass. Removing herself from the car takes a *whumph* of effort from her. He'll be snuffling around here someplace for floor food.

And then she sees him. By the side of the road, ignored by the speeding cars. Lying on his side, just as he does when they spoon. Nose pointing at Wendy's on the other side of the highway. Still and hopeful.

She lies down on the road and curls her body around him.

How It Began

The Boarding School

HOW IT BEGAN
March 1978
Wesley College, Dublin

'It's like she burgled a bunch of fortune-teller caravans,' Imogen Felstead says to her classmates, 'and put on every item of clothing.'

An oblivious Mrs Beauchamp swishes back into the classroom in a peasant blouse, tasselled skirt, patchwork cardigan and charm bracelets. Despite her kinder self, Nora Brady snorts. Mrs Beauchamp toys with her crescent-moon necklace and looks worried, having sensed the atmospheric change.

They're like the otters, Nora realises. And Imo is the head one. She gives the signal to attack.

Nora had seen a nature documentary on the BBC about the otters. They seem nice enough – cute, friendly, holding hands as they drift down the river. Until they form a pack and bully another otter out.

'We don't know what the ostracised otter has done,' the narrator had said, 'but they mobilise as one to oust him. As predators, they can be vicious.'

Outside, the rain pelts the grass of Wesley College and a nun scurries across the courtyard with an inside-out umbrella. Irish rain laughs in the face of umbrellas. The sky growls and darkens further. Nora uses the reflection in the window to watch Imo.

Imo's sharp tongue often turns on her classmates too, especially when a package arrives from parents.

'Looks like he found it in an Edwardian hospital next to a corpse,' she says, throwing down a vintage bear from one girl's father.

Another receives a tea set from a grandparent. 'Well, your induction into domestic servitude is complete.'

Nora has gathered that Imo's home life isn't charmed. She caught the tail end of a conversation while walking to the sports field.

'So, why'd you join at sixteen?' one of Imo's disciples asked. 'I mean, y'know, I just wondered, because it's just strange is all,' the girl babbled, sensing she'd just got herself into trouble and trying to dig her way out by using more words. 'Because most of us have been here at Wesley College since we left primary school.'

Imo deep-sighed and said, 'My parents moved back from South Africa and I think they wanted the house to themselves.'

The girls looked startled. What? Imo, sensing her mistake, added, 'And I shagged my private tutor's son, so, y'know, I was quite the delinquent non grata.'

The girls twinkled with laughter, Imo winked, then increased her pace. Her sidekicks panicked and broke into a trot rather than fall out of her orbit.

Nora and Imo are then randomly placed together on a life-drawing school project ('Girls, this is not permission to draw each other nude,' Mrs Beauchamp stresses, the tiny bells on her blouse jangling. 'You must remain dressed.')

Now Nora can stare at Imo uninterrupted by socially permitted time limits.

~ ~ ~

HOW IT BEGAN

'Are you a scholarship?' the girls ask, leaving a polite enough delay, but always after they see Nora's weekend clothes.

'Kinda,' she says.

Four years ago, her mother's employers offered to pay for her to go to Wesley College. Her mum resisted the offer at first, but then gave in.

'Half-breed', the kids at the local high school were calling Nora, knowing about her Catholic mother and Protestant father. Glenfoot is a Catholic town.

'If you dig for treasure in Glenfoot you'll probably find chests full of Virgin Marys,' her dad used to joke.

She didn't understand this when she was a kid, but now she's eighteen, she does. It's not just a Catholic town in sentiment, it's Catholic in sediment.

'Wesley is one of the best boarding schools in Ireland for young ladies,' Ruth said to Nora. 'Your father would have wanted it,' was the trump card.

Her mother rarely played the 'your dead father would have' card but, when she did, Nora knew it was game over.

~ ~ ~

Nora climbs onto a stool in a deserted art room that smells of chalk and white spirit. She knows how to do this, without actually being seen. She simply goes to that place she has inside herself. The cave.

Growing up at Ferndale, she became expert at going into the cave. Which, she suspected, was also part of the reason she was sent here. Nora finds that adults insist that you tell the truth, until the truth threatens to inconvenience them.

'Crikey, how are you staying this still?' Imo says, her voice full of wonder, after an hour's sitting. 'It's like you're already a painting. There, finished.'

When Nora sees what Imo has done, the bold lines, the light and dark dancing in her eyes, the rendering of the core of her – despite her having hidden – she knows for sure that there's more to this girl. She feels seen.

Imo hops up onto the three-legged wooden stool for her turn. Lately, she's taken to ripping up, knotting and defacing her 'trust-fund brat' image. This too, speaks to Nora.

Today, Imo's wearing a red gingham blouse from which she's chopped off the puffy sleeves and midriff, plus black corduroy flares she once would have worn with heels, but now wears with mustard Golas. Her eyeliner is kittenish and smudged. She looks like the girlfriend of a Rolling Stone. Sister Mary'll have a stroke if she sees her.

Aboard the stool, Imo laughs nervously. Strikes dramatic poses with her hand against her forehead, then sits astride the stool like it's a horse. But when Nora says nothing – doesn't laugh – and Imo's only option is to stay still, her face stiffens.

A pink shadow creeps up her neck, her eyes brim, and something in Imo breaks. Just three minutes in, Imo rises, kicks the stool over and runs for the toilet in the corridor.

Nora waits, silent and unmoved, until Imo returns, make-up fixed.

'Sorry. I was over-served last night,' Imo says. 'This hangover is savage.'

Nora says nothing but slowly approaches Imo. Imo's eyes narrow with warning but, undeterred, Nora takes her into an awkward hug.

HOW IT BEGAN

'Ugh, what are you doing?' Imo says.

But Nora waits. Waits. Waits some more. Until Imo's body lets go.

The Tunnel

HOW IT BEGAN
Four months later – July 1978
Antrim Coast, Northern Ireland

'And you're *sure* your mum won't mind?' Imo asks, as they snake around the Irish coastal road in her car; a present from her folks for her eighteenth to ensure even more independence.

Nora rolls her eyes and says, 'For the millionth time, she won't. She likes me bringing friends home; it means she doesn't have to think too hard about our relationship.'

'My parents are the opposite,' says Imo. 'They don't want anyone to see.'

The girls share a look. A click.

Imo's got to admit, Northern Ireland hasn't been what she expected.

They're less than an hour outside of Belfast, the land of The Troubles, home of the IRA and the UDA, the city of grey-faced news reporters outside Stormont. For starters, nobody has given her grief about her English accent. Second, nobody told her how beautiful it is here.

The Antrim Coast Road hugs the cliffside, almost slipping into the sea. Nora tells her that further down the coast there's a castle whose kitchen *did* fall into the sea.

So far on this trip they've seen a fat seal spinning in the surf, they've driven through tunnels blasted through rock, and they've swum beneath a waterfall in a fern-wallpapered glade, which is announced by a sign as 'Cranny Falls'. Nora calls it 'Fanny Falls'.

They stop for lunch at a stately home that Imo would've sworn was English.

'It looks like one of ours,' she says to Nora, tipping her head back and taking her sunglasses down.

'What did you expect, peasants and thatched roofs?'

After lunch, she and Nora take a 'turn' in the grounds, exaggerating their Austen-esque gait despite both wearing denim flares and stripy halternecks. Their style is so similar that they've decided to run with it, rather than fight it.

'A turn in the grounds is so good for one's countenance, don't you find, Gertrude?'

'Oh, yes, Ermentrude, a stroll on a fine day is but the most perfect refreshment.'

Polished women smile at them; they're sitting beside an ornamental pool with a statue, fountain and lily pads, taking tiers of afternoon tea.

'I dare you to get into the water and start doing lengths,' Imo says, her voice low.

Nora removes her brogues, stacks them neatly on the side of the pool, and hops in.

~ ~ ~

Imo hasn't been home since Easter. She hasn't been invited home either.

During that two-week break, she saw a quote from Bette Davis in a *Tatler* article: 'If everyone likes you, you're not doing it right.'

She stared at the sentence for a good ten minutes, trying to make sense of it. Then tore it out and pinned it to a cork board above her vanity dresser.

Not everyone has to like you. Huh. What a revelation. A revolution, even, for her brain.

When her mother, Penelope, saw it, she shook her head and ripped it down, the cherry-red pin falling to the floor.

'Have I taught you nothing?' she said over her shoulder, taking the quote with her but leaving a cloud of Givenchy behind.

~ ~ ~

'This place is . . . well, it's splendid!' Imo says as Ferndale rolls into view.

'Whoa there, hold your horses,' Nora says. 'That's not my house. That wee totey one there is.'

She gestures to the much dinkier house beside a stream that looks like it'll have mattresses stuffed with straw.

Imo smiles and says, 'Ah, right,' but resolves to work it with the rich brothers who live in the manor house, so that she can sleep there, not this cottage.

'And their parents died in a plane crash, right?' Imo asks, removing her glob of pink bubble gum, rolling it into a ball and throwing it on the ground.

Nora picks the gum up and pushes it back into Imo's hand, closing her fingers upon it with ceremony, like she's given her a precious stone.

'No, they died in a ferry accident,' Nora says, 'three years ago, so it's still a bit raw. Don't mention it unless they do.'

HOW IT BEGAN

A-ha. One of the brothers will have inherited this estate, or the bulk of it, and Imo needs to find out which one.

~ ~ ~

If Imo's mother doesn't have her face on, or hasn't had time to do her hair, her line is: 'Oh, I'm a fright, I do apologise.' As if her hair or face are central to everyone's enjoyment of the day.

Imo now does the same. 'I'm sorry I haven't washed my hair – what a horror I am.'

'It doesn't matter,' they say.

But it does, to Imo.

~ ~ ~

Imo has Nora pinned down and is drawing a perfect golden sweep along her eyeline. Kate Bush wails from the boombox like a banshee. They've pinched blue curaçao from the mirrored drinks cabinet in the lounge and mixed it with orangeade. Nora found some Hawaiian-style cocktail umbrellas for their blue, green and yellow concoctions.

'There,' Imo says, stepping back to admire her handiwork. 'You don't look unlike a pale, weak Wonder Woman.' She pats Nora on the head.

Nora appraises herself in a dressing-table mirror; batwing black minidress, gold eyeliner, spiky lashes and pale shimmer on her lips.

Clicking the lid back on the eye pencil, Imo watches her friend turning in the mirror and feels a squiggle of discomfort in her stomach. It's OK, she soothes herself. No matter what she puts Nora in, or applies, or pencils, or tongs, she'll never be a rival. A worthy wingwoman, yes, but never a threat.

There's a roar in the darkness outside the wobbly moss-flecked window. Two cars speed up the path and swerve to boy-racer stops on the gravel, sending a surf-wave of stones.

'They're back,' Nora says, hushed. A cackle of voices spill out into the night. 'And they have company.'

Imo whoops and twirls, her russet blouse blending with her ribcage-length hair. 'Let the games begin,' she says.

'Er, is this the part where you kill me?' Imo asks as they go further and further into the woods on a dirt path. 'The house is thataway, y'know?' she adds, pointing at the orange eyes of Ferndale, getting smaller and smaller as they walk.

'Sssh,' Nora says. 'I have something to show you.'

Nora's torch swings through the grey gnarl of ancient oaks, ash and pines. It feels rude to wake the tangled limbs of the trees, as if they've burst into a bedroom and disturbed an orgy. Starved of the rosy light of day, the forest looks grotesque, like Freud's nudes.

The torch alights upon a decaying red ribbon tied to a branch. 'Bingo,' Nora says, crouching down and moving away some loose branches, then shifting a propped-up, six-foot-wide pane of scrap metal. The metal boings and clanks to announce its status as an unnatural part of the woods, but a second ago, Imo could've sworn this was just another part of the forest floor. A squadron of earwigs flee from beneath it. Steps lead sharply down to a double-breasted cellar door.

'Blimey,' Imo says. 'An air-raid shelter?' she guesses.

'Nope,' Nora says, proud to be the bearer of unexpected news. 'It's a tunnel from penal times. We're talking the 1700s or 1800s, when Catholicism was outlawed. The O'Malleys' ancestors built it so they could sneak from the house to the woods without being seen. To attend Mass, when it was banned.'

Imo looks around at the shapes sketching themselves into the night, now that her eyes have adjusted. 'But there's no church here?'

Nora sweeps her hand into the distance. 'Yeah. Dunno. Someplace out there, Mum says there's a Mass rock, basically an outdoor altar. The priest would have met them there, along with other villagers, for the Mass. Probably at night, by candlelight.'

'That's wild,' says Imo.

She follows Nora down the steps, watching her retrieve a crude key from a cubby hole and open the wooden doors. Below are more descending stairs.

'You're not serious,' Imo says. 'We'll get all dirty. Well, even more dirty.' She kicks a clod of mud off her platform boot.

Nora tugs her arm. 'C'mon, m'lady, it's cleaner than you imagine down here,' she says, 'and it opens up pretty quickly. What's at the end is worth it, I swear.'

'If we meet a rat, I'm sacrificing you to it,' Imo says, after five minutes of the mildewed drip-drip-drip of the corridor.

'You're a gas,' Nora says. 'We're here.' The bouncing halo of her torch ascends some stone steps.

At the top, she uses another key hanging from a hook to open an identical pair of doors. They step out of the tunnel and into the smell of bread, raisins and baskets.

'We're in the pantry,' Nora says, face impish.

Vague cigarette smoke curls under the door from a couple of rooms away and, closer, a pin is placed on a spinning Ramones record, mid-track. An explosion of laughter.

'So the boys, their friends, they don't know we're here?' Imo asks, gleeful now too.

Nora laughs and shakes her head. 'They don't even know this tunnel exists. Mum showed me, but she said not to tell them as "they'll only use it for badness", whatever that means. Let's sneak past them and out of the front door, then ring the doorbell.'

Imo and Nora sidle out of the pantry and crawl along the floor of the lit-up kitchen. They freeze as a door is slammed nearby, then dart along a corridor into an entrance hall. Legs-crossed ladies and legs-spread hunters stare down at them from paintings. They let themselves out of the front door.

They spend a few minutes collecting themselves enough to ring the bell. As soon as one stops laughing and catches her breath, the other starts again. There are three more cars in the driveway than before.

'Guess the party's getting started,' Nora says.

'The perks of being orphans over eighteen, I guess,' Imo says. 'Does your mum ever get involved?'

'Nah,' Nora replies. 'She used to when Ciaran was a minor, but not now. They own the place.'

Ding, dong sounds the sombre bell, while Imo pulls the ghost of a cobweb out of Nora's night-sky hair, so black it shines blue.

'How do I look?' Imo asks, hand on hip. 'Bag o' shit, or bag o' chips?'

Nora shoves her playfully. 'Aside from the chip on your shoulder, you're grand.'

Imo hugs her. 'You're right, that tunnel was worth it. I've never had so much fun.'

And then, what opens the door changes Imo's trajectory. She hadn't known she was directionless until now. Until Ciaran.

Still astonished by the effect this walking pheromone has had on her, Imo trails behind Ciaran and Nora, speechless. He has a dancer's body, like her – lean and lithe – a tall drink of water with mobile hips. His mouth is pink and sinful. She wants it on her.

Dark-eyed, drunk, coarse people – who she can only assume are locals, given their apparent lack of class – are draped over claret velvet sofas in the next room, drinking beer (from the bottle – uncouth) next to a fireplace you could stand up in. Imo smiles at them. She may need them for something, someday.

Quite sweet really, the lengths men will go to in order to secure her attention. Ciaran has barely looked at her, other than the initial glance and greeting, choosing to pretend to be fascinated by Nora. She's had this one before, the faux freeze-out, only for the man to swivel to her, of course. She'll wait, it's fine.

Finally, something elegant. Ciaran leads them through a dining room that has dispensed with the po-faced manor malarkey and gone playful. Now *this* is a room for some debauchery. Pink walls painted with pampas grass, from which a flock of starlings has just burst. Low-flying drop lights are tasselled and gold, above a cherrywood dining table with ten plush chairs.

Imo follows Ciaran and Nora through room after room,

ignored. But where's the fun in the man you don't have to chase? It's like going to the butcher to buy a slab of venison rather than tracking a deer through frost-tipped woods.

Marrying big money has been Imo's plan all along, as well as her mother's. Last year, her mother, Penelope, had left Imo's phone number on the deck of a yacht; the captain was a recent bachelor. Imo's mother hadn't met him, only his yacht.

She can do better than Ciaran. She's met richer, more handsome men. But within minutes of meeting him, she wants him above all others.

They're now in the kitchen, cool flagstones beneath their bare feet, lips tinted purple by red wine, heels kicked off in order to dance to 'Dreadlock Holiday' by 10cc.

Imo's busting out big, extravagant ballet moves.

'I start my classical ballet degree in September at the Royal Ballet School,' she tells Ciaran over the music.

Ciaran grins and spins Nora into him, then back out, like a party streamer.

'You're very graceful,' he shouts back to Imo.

'And what about you, you dark horse,' he says to Nora. 'I had no idea you had these moves.'

Somebody turns the volume of the record down. They boo in chorus. Putting a different record on is a man taller than Ciaran, just as slender, clearly related to him and with a peppering of freckles on his flinty face.

Nora pulls back as if slapped.

'Rory, this is Imo,' Ciaran says.

Imo approaches, hand outstretched, head bowed in deference. She knows an alpha when she meets one.

*

HOW IT BEGAN

Imo and Rory are absorbed in conversation, working out who they both know in London.

'If these two drop any more names, we'll be tripping over the double barrels,' Ciaran says.

Imo throws a smile over her shoulder. Maybe he's jealous.

He and Nora head into the pantry, muttering about sandwiches.

A few minutes later, Imo registers that they're very quiet. She goes into the pantry to look for them. The double-breasted doors to the tunnel have been shut and locked. They've gone.

Rage rises in Imo. How could Nora do this to her?

The Rose Garden

HOW IT BEGAN
Six weeks later
Glenfoot, Northern Ireland

Nora and Ciaran kiss s-l-o-w-l-y in the driveway of Ferndale, saying goodbye.

'We're disgusting,' she says, as she starts to move away before he pulls her back in for another.

'You're not wrong,' he says. 'Meet me in the rose garden after dinner.'

She pulls a face.

'I know you don't like it there, but I have something to ask you. Please, at eight?'

She smiles and nods.

Sun-toasted and sea-salted, Nora crunches down the drive home to The Millhouse, wearing two things that Imo left behind in July by mistake – a cream kaftan and a chocolate string bikini. She still has honeycomb ice cream on her lips and recent sex sticky between her hips.

Drunk from a jug of icy cider consumed in a grassy beer garden on the way home, she feels incapable of anything but the biggest thought: *This summer, I have become a new person*. It's as if being around Imo and Ciaran has built her a chrysalis, so that she can transform and catch up with them.

Nora diverts into the woods, not ready to go into her beige house for beige soup just yet. She lies down on the

HOW IT BEGAN

forest floor, her bag as a pillow, and relives every moment of the day she's just had.

~ ~ ~

At the beach, she and Ciaran spread their picnic of cheese, crackers and grapes out across a scratchy woollen rug entirely unsuited for the sun. They sweat onto the wool, eat cheese and kiss with full mouths. Slim candy-coloured houses stack along the curvy harbour in front of them, glossy as sticks of seaside rock.

'Oi, Jim!' Ciaran calls to a group of teenagers drinking and smoking nearby. 'Lend us your kayak, mate?'

Jim gives a thumbs up and Ciaran drags an orange kayak off the rocks and towards them.

The teenage girls have just noticed that someone they used to bully at school is now beaching with an O'Malley brother. They whisper behind cupped hands, even though she's twenty feet away.

'I can't hear you!' she wants to shout. 'Do you think me being half-Protestant gives me superhuman hearing?'

Instead she lets Ciaran pull her kaftan off her – and her into the kayak. She stares back at the girls the whole time. I'm not scared of you now.

Her string-tie bikini is a scandal compared to their thick swimsuits, so they're now open-mouthed at her audacity. Nora smiles and waves at them as Ciaran pushes their kayak into the cannonball-grey sea, then hops in himself, kicking off the snarls of seaweed that reach for his feet.

The kayak smells like rope and fish. Ciaran pants as he paddles them around the rocky headland. They circle granite fists that have punched their way through the surf. Now in open water and out of sight of the beach, the sea beneath them is deep lavender.

'Are you sure about this, Ciar?' Nora calls, over the *swish, swash, swish* of the paddle through the misbehaving sea.

'Look!' he points with an oar. A three-storey white house sits on the shore, surrounded by near-vertical russet and lime cliffs.

'But . . . I don't understand, how do the owners get there?' Nora asks.

'The only way is by sea or through the tunnel deep in that rock there,' Ciaran says, pointing again. 'Look, there's no car in the drive,' he adds. 'We're going in! I think it's a holiday home these days.'

He aims the prow at a steep shingle beach that leads up to the house.

Wincing as she picks her way barefoot up the shingle, Nora silences the part of her that wants to play by the rules and get off this private land as fast as possible.

'Amazing, isn't it?' Ciaran's asking, dragging the kayak up the beach. She shields her eyes from the sun, taking in the house; the kind of forever home children daub with crayons.

'I'll buy this for us one day,' he says, lighting a cigarette and waving it at the house.

'It was owned by a poet laureate, I think? He wrote this great poem about a "salt-caked smoke stack butting through the Channel". I think about ships he saw from these windows. How cool is that? This place also used to be a home to nuns – the Sisters of Mercy.'

HOW IT BEGAN

'Dunno about nuns, but that'd be a hell of a name for an all-female biker gang,' Nora says.

Ciaran laughs. They walk around the perimeter of the house, which sits quiet, watchful, wondering what they're up to. There's a window ajar at the back.

'C'mon,' he says, reaching inside and lifting the latch, opening it wide to create a crawl hole. 'You first.'

Nora feeds her head, shoulders and hips through, swivelling on the window ledge to drop down into a chilly ceramic bathtub.

Tiptoeing at first, they get bolder as the house reassures them of its emptiness. Ciaran sprints upstairs and Nora follows, their bodies slicing through dust hanging in the air.

Flopping onto the marigold-stitched eiderdown of the master bedroom, he pulls her down on top of him.

~ ~ ~

Finally in her beige house, Nora is eating her beige soup.

'I am glad that you and Ciaran are dating, dear,' her mother, Ruth, says. 'I really am. I like Ciaran. I just want to be clear that there's nothing unseemly going on. Men don't buy the cow if they can get the milk for free, y'know?'

Nora places her spoon down, picks up her bowl of shin soup, tips it and pours the remainder into her mouth. If her mother's going to compare her to a cow, she'll eat like a cow.

'Well, I . . . what on earth do you think you're doing, you little savage?'

Nora picks up a half-loaf of wheaten bread and tears a bite out of it.

'Are you drunk? Heaven's sake, you're absolutely banjaxed, aren't you?'

VERSIONS OF A GIRL

Nora laughs, spraying crumbs and soup everywhere, then hightails it out of the kitchen before she gets a wallop.

It's after 8 p.m. Nora sits on the swinging bench at the end of a tunnel topped with a tangle of honeysuckle. A bee bumbles around her, tipping its face into a foxglove, its furry legs waggling behind it. *You're totally exposed, buddy.*

He's late. The sunset hides behind a hedge but sends up flares of pink and orange neon. A plane's trail leaves an underline of cloud.

There he is. She does a swing of celebration. But as the shadowy figure comes closer down the tunnel, she realises . . . this person is too tall to be Ciaran.

The Spider

HOW IT BEGAN
Ten minutes later

Ruth tugs her wellies on. It'll be dark soon. She's going to have to go find this wayward daughter of hers, make sure she doesn't fall face-first into a stream. She's never seen her so clattered. Ciaran's influence, no doubt.

Ruth takes the grass verge bordering the woods, peering into the fading forest.

If she finds Ciaran, she'll find Nora, and so she goes up to the house. Room after room – empty. Until she finally finds him in the study, a book spreadeagled on his stomach, snoring like a chainsaw, an empty whiskey glass and red ring box beside him.

She snaps it open and recognises his mother's engagement ring.

Chrissake, they're children! Well, not in the eyes of the law, but in the eyes of anyone with a jot of sense.

What is he thinking, the silly git? Was he going to propose? Despite herself, she smiles. If he stopped drinking, she'd bless the union.

Closing the ring box, she nudges him with her foot. Waking from a dream, he looks baffled.

'What have you done with my daughter, you gobshite?'

They go looking together. There's nobody in the tiny maze. Nobody by the pond. They circle the rose garden and see nothing. They're about to leave when Ruth senses movement under the pergola.

Walking down the hedged tunnel, they see two figures tangled on the floor at the end. The figures are in shadow, so the effect is of an eight-limbed creature.

'Oi!' Ciaran shouts.

Rory looks back at them, Nora now visible beneath him. His clothes are still on, but she's only partially clothed.

Rory runs off, Ciaran giving chase, and she can hear a fight breaking out between them on the lawn. It's not the first time they've physically fought, but it is the first time they've fought about Nora.

'Get up, you absolute disgrace.' Her daughter's brown bikini is pulled all out of shape, but still on. 'Make yourself respectable, please.'

Nora is dazed, crying, confused.

'One brother wasn't enough for you, then; you had to have them both,' Ruth says.

She pulls Nora to her feet, grabbing the kaftan from the floor and covering her up.

'I didn't want to, though. It wasn't . . . Mum, I didn't,' Nora says.

'Give over, I've heard that one before.'

Ruth wakes at 6 a.m., as usual.

Makes toast with marmalade, a cup of strong coffee, teeters upstairs with them. Nora will be feeling rough. She wants to apologise for being so hard on her. Teenage hormones are rampant, after all. Her teenage years weren't flawless either.

HOW IT BEGAN

Such a shame about Ciaran, though. He'll never get over seeing that.

Thank Christ Rory's trousers were still on when they found them. The alternative doesn't bear thinking about; a child out of wedlock from her employer's son? No, thanks.

She knocks on the bedroom door. It's ajar so she pushes it open. Nora's gone.

The Birth

HOW IT BEGAN
Nine months later – June 1979
Pimlico, London

Imo arrives in time to cut the cord. She pulls up to the squat in Pimlico at 11 a.m., keeping on her navy suede driving gloves.

The council have already evicted the squatters once and boarded up the door, then bricked up the ground-floor windows, naïve enough to think that would stop them from finding their way back in.

'Squat now while stocks last' is daubed in hot pink across the front door of the former mansion; a sign it's reopened for guests.

Imo raps out the code knock. Two long, three short. A makeshift peephole has been poked into the stained-glass window bordering the once-grand door. Imo sees an eye, a flash of a silver nose bar.

'Simon, it's me, for Nora.'

Simon, wearing a purple velvet suit and banana yellow boots, ushers her inside.

'She's in the master bathroom,' he says. 'This has been intense. A miracle? More like a massacre.'

Imo pats him on the back, glad of her gloves – yes, it's all about you, Simon, thanks for that – then walks up the stairs past Trudy, nodded out, her mohican curled between her legs like a sleeping hedgehog.

HOW IT BEGAN

She finds Nora in the clawfoot tub, which she's relieved to see is white among the mud-coloured rust of the rest of the bathroom. Someone obviously had the forethought to bleach it.

A naked bulb stares down from above. Nora is crying, bloody water up to her midriff, the mewling newborn trying to find her breast.

'I'm here,' Imo says, stroking her friend's hair.

'Oh my God, at last,' Nora holds up the wet baby. 'Please. Take her. You know what to do. Take her before I change my mind.'

~ ~ ~

When Nora ran away from home last year, she called Imo from a payphone at Belfast harbour.

'Rory tried to rape me,' she said, the words strangled.

'Fucccck,' Imo said. 'What did your mum say?'

'That she didn't believe me.'

Imo drove through the night to pick Nora up from Stranraer ferry port, bringing her back to their London townhouse. But when her parents returned from Cape Town a fortnight later, she had to ask Nora to leave.

Besides, Imo wanted to go and visit Ciaran. See if he was OK.

~ ~ ~

She sits in her car outside A&E at the Royal Brompton Hospital. The windows are wide open and the newborn is in a Moses basket, swaddled in a polka-dot scarf that she's not overly fond of. Asleep, the baby girl looks both box-fresh and ancient, her squashy face at rest, the only movement her twitching mouth seeking a nipple.

Imo knows what she *should* do. Go inside the hospital and do as Nora has asked. Leave her in the basket someplace safe, without being seen. Inside an unlocked staff toilet, or on top of an empty bed, or behind reception when they're not looking.

So that this baby girl can be found and taken home by a mother who isn't nineteen years old; whose family pay bills and own garden shears, and don't get high more than they eat; who have most of their lives *behind* them.

But it doesn't feel right. To turn this baby into a foundling. What if she bounces around the foster care system, instead of being adopted into a good home? What if she lands in the opposite of a good home?

If anyone knows about parental abandonment, it's Imo. She's been parented by tutors, a housekeeper, nuns, even, but hardly ever her own parents.

This baby may not have a mother who can care for her – in fact Imo suspects that Nora is on the verge of some sort of mental breakdown – but it's still possible she has a father who wants her. Imo can't deny her that chance.

She starts the car. Long journey ahead. She'll need to buy some baby things – formula, nappies and clothes – and then she'll head for the ferry to Belfast.

At 1:32 a.m., Imo inches up the driveway, the pine trees leaning over the car's bonnet, as if they're listening and are going to tell. All she needs to do is make it into Ferndale before Ruth wakes up and comes out. She can't answer Ruth's questions right now, her sharp blue eyes cutting through Imo's stories like scissors.

HOW IT BEGAN

She turns off the engine one hundred feet from The Millhouse, grabs the Moses basket and continues up the grass verge on foot. The Millhouse is fast asleep, but a solitary light still burns in Ferndale. The study contains Ciaran or Rory, or both. It's impossible to tell from outside because of the heavy green drapes.

Imo drums her fingertips lightly across the windowpane. Nothing. She raps softly with her knuckles, knowing the baby will wake at any second and yell into the blackness, her rose-pink lungs like a bell.

Ciaran lifts the side of the curtain, a cigar smouldering between his fingers. A blink-and-you'll-miss-it frown, then his angular face breaks into a smile.

He meets her at the front door, swaying slightly as if caught in a wind tunnel. Stands there for a second, percolating the sight of Imo and a baby.

'Holy smokes, Imo. You have a baby. Wait – is that yours?' He hides his face behind both hands. 'Wait – is that . . .'

She shakes her head, sharply, wanting to say words that her knackered brain can't quite form.

But when he comes back out from behind his hands, he looks happy.

'From our weekend together? After Nora skedaddled? Wow, why didn't you tell me you were pregnant? I could've helped.' He takes the Moses basket.

'Oh my God, she . . , it is a she, right? She's precious.'

Imo's mouth gapes, useless. She can't right now. He's going to have a million-and-one questions, and the epic twelve-hour journey has her done for.

She'll tell him everything tomorrow.

*

VERSIONS OF A GIRL

In the morning – after a broken night rocking, shushing, changing and feeding the baby bottles – Imo's woken up by Ciaran. The baby's finally asleep now it's daybreak: of course. He holds a tray. On it are a coffee and a red ring box.

The Police Station

HOW IT ENDS
Nearly thirty-five years later – March 2014
Ballymena, Northern Ireland

Her bum is freezing. She wakes the car back up, the headlights turning on in the gloom like eyes snapping open, the fan heater blowing. The radio turns on too, Taylor Swift crackling out. She presses a knob to silence her: love you, Taylor, but not right now.

A piece of cardboard twirls from the rear-view mirror, advertising the car rental company this vehicle is from. Ironic, that, given it's illegal to hang things from rear-view mirrors now. A taxi driver she once chatted to had been fined £50 for having a pair of furry dice hanging. She pulls it off, making the elastic snap.

She's read that the psychological bias that keeps us stuck is mostly down to 'loss aversion'. The fear of what we'll lose if we move, if we change.

It's what keeps gamblers feeding coins into one-armed bandits, scared of losing all the coins they've already fed in. It keeps people in relationships they should leave, the thought of all those years down the drain. And it's what is keeping her in this car, rather than doing what she absolutely ought to.

For fun – and because she has a chronic habit of trivialising the serious – she makes a list on the back of a parking ticket.

VERSIONS OF A GIRL

Losses of handing self in	Gains of handing self in
Will have to wear handcuffs. Assuming they use them. They may take one look at me and assume I'm harmless. They'd be wrong	Bum will be warmer
Freedom – for at least five years, even if I'm well behaved, which based on past experience, I won't be	Chattering monkey of guilt will be removed from back
Walks in the woods	No more working
Won't be able to choose own food	Will not have to make own food
May have a cellmate and don't like most people	Won't have to see all the people out here that I don't like
The luxury of a long bath with a sheet mask on, then taking a selfie because it's funny that I look like Hannibal Lecter	The luxury of knowing I did the right thing
	Won't have to pay this parking ticket

How It Ends

Flick's Bluebird

HOW IT ENDS
January 2014
Richmond, London, England

It's mad, really, how such a small thing can send you over the edge, thinks Flick, lying on her side, looking at a blank wall, picking at the hospital corners she's been asked to perfect. Four layers of sheets tucked under the mattress, meaning it takes twenty minutes to make the bed when a duvet takes two.

'But I don't want my bed to feel like a human envelope,' she said, when they explained the rules to her. 'And I'm only going to mess it up again later.'

Yet again, she discovered that what she wanted was irrelevant. There were rules and she needed to follow them.

'Why am I paying you over a thousand pounds a week to make my own bed? This hotel is atrocious.'

She was reminded it's not a hotel.

How did she go from starring in *Swan Lake* aged just twenty-eight, to here – rehab for dummies – aged thirty-four? Baffling. The quiet in her bedroom presses down upon her. It's unbearable.

'Boo hoo, your luxury rehab room is too peaceful. What about the sauna, is it too warm for you, poppet? #firstworldproblems,' Sita would text.

Only, Sita wouldn't text her, because she hates her now.

The small thing that sent her over the edge (well, *things* technically) measured around three centimetres long. Made of imitation peacock feather and topped by two silver question marks – the earrings that had been in her mother's ears the day she'd whacked her head on that swimming pool aged six. The day she'd been left unsupervised and could have drowned, if the bride hadn't seen her fall in.

In the past year or so, Flick has been unable to get those earrings, that day, out of her head. So much has been erased, blocked out, lost, but some episodes are burnt onto her brain.

'Dissociative amnesia can cause some children to block out weeks, months or years of their childhood,' a book in the clinic's library told her. 'Frightening or overwhelming situations cause the child to dissociate – detach – from what is happening. However, stress can cause some episodes to become *more* memorable, not less; we call these enhanced memories.'

Flick walks down the corridor, smiling as she passes Eli, an *unreal* tattoo artist who has already drawn a tiny bluebird in Biro on her neck, a kid's version of the upcoming real tattoo once they're out.

Like the poem Wally read out at Da's memorial, Flick wants to get in touch with her inner bluebird. It's time.

She waves at Beryl in her office, hunched over a document as if it's the lost Holy Grail – the woman who fastidiously went through her bags upon arrival, removing her spiky tweezers, the vape filled with weed she was hoping to sneak under the radar and even the shoelaces from her trainers.

'What are you doing?' Flick asked, gesturing to the shoelaces.

'It's just for the first week or so until we deem you're not a risk to yourself. Withdrawal tends to be rocky. There can be some self-loathing.'

Flick shook her head. 'I don't feel any self-loathing whatsoever.'

By day four of zero drugs in her system, aside from a baby dose of diazepam to stop her going into full-blown withdrawal ('Two milligrams? Are you having a giraffe?' she said when they gave them to her), the self-loathing has landed.

Without the anaesthetic of a drug or a drink, Flick finally feels what she's been trying to dodge for a decade. She feels rotten to her core, like if you cut into her, you wouldn't find blood, only tar.

A tape plays in her head of her keenest regrets: that relationship she fucked up; that time she bit back with an unnecessary comeback; when she flirted too far with somebody else's partner; when she'd lost that friend.

It's really important to Flick that everyone likes her. Really, really. Only thing is, she frequently does things to make them dislike her. She's a people-pleaser who often people-displeases.

Even James, who she married as a safety choice – the one person who would never reject her – didn't like her once he really got to know her.

'Your mother's right about you,' he said, when he asked for a divorce two years ago. She didn't ask what Mum had said; she couldn't handle the response.

Spliced in with the adult regrets, she's haunting her own childhood like a trapped ghost. Watching over and over and over the little she recalls: the day at the swimming pool, the slap, bedtimes with no dinner, never getting Digby, transatlantic moves without being consulted or considered. Round and round and round they go.

VERSIONS OF A GIRL

The further she gets away from the past, the more her drug use drags her back. The drugs used to help her forget. Then they broke, and nowadays, they only help her remember.

The musical pitches of cocaine (disco!) and diazepam (and chill) became a discordant drone. *Unnnnngh*, like the dial tone of a landline. She snorted more, drank more, hooked up more to try and bring back the music, but nothing worked. The only diversion from the *unnnnngh* was the wretchedness of withdrawal when she tried to cut down, or the relief when she got a fix.

And then there was the night of waking up in the hospital, having been rolled from a car onto the pavement by her 'friends', who were more scared of being done for possession than they were of her dying of an overdose.

And so, here she is. In rehab.

She walks past the pharmacist's cubby hole and sees a fellow ~~guest~~, no, hang on, ~~inmate~~ nope, *patient* being given a clear bag with a rainbow selection of pills inside. Multicoloured pills . . . *wham*. The memory slides into her.

~ ~ ~

A couple of years ago, after the divorce proceedings began, her creative director at the dance company gave her a gorgeous gift set of vitamins from Selfridges, displayed like premium candy. It was the start of the end of her career.

'Clearly you need to boost your immune system,' the director said.

Understudies were filling in more than Flick turned up and HR red-flagged her unusual number of absences. She ran out of plausible reasons as to why she needed so many twenty-four-hour absences, following a bender.

News of her impending divorce was now common knowledge in Kensington and Chelsea. 'Is there nothing to be done?' sympathetic well-wishers asked, faces set to grieving, as they treated her marriage like a dying patient they should, *could* defibrillate back into life.

'It's mutual. We've just come to the end of the road,' she said, faux-bright, hoping they hadn't talked to James, hoping he had been discreet about the many, many nights she'd called him when off her face, begging for another chance.

It wasn't so much *him* she was worried about losing, it was more that, without James, people might figure out that she really was unlovable. He'd been her beard. In shops, in the salon, in the grocery store, she imagined that everyone around was talking about it, about her. When she sobered up, she felt flamed by the shame, so she just stopped sobering up.

Food poisoning became too frequent to be plausible, so she started to fall back on more complicated ailments: migraines and endometriosis, which required a lot of research to thoroughly pull off. She ran her lines in a mirror, to make sure she got them perfect. Looked up the names of medication a doctor might prescribe for such conditions. Memorised them.

Regardless, her dance company reached exasperation. 'I can't cover for you any more, Flick,' her boss said, rubbing her temples. 'That's your written warning,' she added, passing her a sealed envelope. 'You're one of the most talented dancers I've ever worked with, but you need to show up. It's a "sod you" to everyone else in the company when you don't.'

A week later, Flick called in sick with a migraine – and was told not to bother coming back. She'd been spotted the night before in Jewel nightclub on Piccadilly, doing flamin' shots and snogging an oil heiress.

A paparazzo had taken a shot of her and the heiress sitting on a pavement in Soho, wearing devil horns and eating a kebab. Given Flick was mildly well known and the oil heiress was a megastar, the photo had made its way onto the *Daily Mail*'s sidebar of shame.

The whole fiasco was wildly unfair. She barely even goes out any more! What were the chances of her being out the very night before she got a horrible migraine. Her Facebook status update had even *mentioned* the migraine – wasn't that enough proof? Does going out the night before mean you're not allowed to be ill the next day?

In response to being fired, she sent a vicious email to her ex-superiors at the ballet company, lobbing in mentions of legal action and unfair dismissal. They did not respond.

~ ~ ~

Flick sits on an orange reading chair, hand on a stack of adult colouring books on the coffee table beside her – then cringes as she remembers how she first reacted to them.

'Oh, happy days, I can colour in pretty ducks!' she said to Eli, two days in. 'Dunno about you, babes, but this colouring-in means I no longer feel the need to do cocaine.'

After Flick's divorce proceedings and dismissal, Mum became less and less responsive. When Flick was pirouetting in the broadsheets and culture gossip pages as ballet's rock 'n' roll It girl, Imo called her every day. Mainly to quiz her as to what newspaper she was in now, how many followers she had on Twitter these days, what celebrities she'd met lately, the compliments she'd had on her performances, her upcoming TV appearances . . .

Mum wanted to know everything. See everything. Be forwarded everything.

'We're so lucky that we're mother and daughter, but also best friends,' Imo would say.

And then for the past year, since the divorce had been finalised, Flick was lucky if Imo answered her calls once a week. Even then, her mother was often too busy to talk. There was something in the oven, or someone coming over, or an imminent appointment.

So Flick had bided her time, waited until she had her mother in person, a butterfly under a pin.

Opening the adult colouring book – seeing a cartoon buddha – she wants to stop the memory there. The rest is still too painful. But the memory tugs at her.

If she doesn't go with it now, it'll only tap her awake at 3 a.m. She sits, closes her eyes and follows it down the rabbit hole.

~ ~ ~

A few months ago – November 2013

Imo and Flick are seated in the Charlotte Street Hotel, with a view of boutiques, black cabs and people walking one mile an hour faster than they do outside of London. The day's rainbows are now lying in the puddles and a Bernese Mountain Dog is taking its owner for a walk.

Imo sits, adjusts her silk kaftan and sniffs.

'What do you think of my winter hair colour, dear?' she asks, cocking her slightly darker head. 'You haven't mentioned it.'

'Oh, gosh, I'm sorry. It's lovely,' Flick says.

Flick orders a buck's fizz because it's acceptable to drink those before midday, while Imo orders a lemon cooler.

'Mmm, yummy, do you want to try some?' Imo says.

'I don't like lemon, Mum,' Flick says, for the hundredth time. She has one dislike – one! – and her mother never remembers.

Imo appraises her daughter. 'Why're you not wearing that gorgeous top I bought you? The floral one?'

Flick has never worn a floral item in her life. Simple neutrals are her thing. The top still hangs in her wardrobe.

'Sorry, I will,' she says, her voice small.

She wonders if her mum left the price tag on the top on purpose. 'You take the sales sticker off and leave the full price on,' Imo once taught her.

An eel of nausea slides through Flick. This hangover – this comedown – is nasty.

'I need to talk about that day at the swimming pool again. Please. I have this memory I can't shake, of your clothes folded, the peacock earrings on top,' Flick says.

Imo sips her drink, quizzical in winter copper.

'And then you said you'd been watching me, but you hadn't. You left me alone in a swimming pool aged six. I'm lucky I didn't drown.'

Imo considers her nails, and then goes in, a little jingle of laughter at the outset.

'As for folding my clothes before jumping in, I did no such thing. And I've never even owned such earrings, dear. Peacock feather? They sound ghastly. You were always so creative with your stories,' she says. 'Do you remember you used to write lesbian love stories in your diary as if they'd really happened?' She hoots with mirth. 'Nancy Friday eat your heart out.'

Mum looks around the room, as if this conversation has now expired and she's scanning for other people to talk to.

'You've imagined these earrings, dear, just like you did those sapphic sex scenes.' Then she turns to look at her evenly. 'Or maybe those stories were real?'

Flick throws herself in. 'No, no, they weren't real.'

Imo smiles. 'My little drama queen.'

She pinches Flick's thigh.

~ ~ ~

Flick walks through the rehab facility, nodding and smiling at the staff and fellow patients. Tears are pooling in her eyes and she needs to get outside before they spill.

The grounds here are lovely. A Japanese maple flames, overlooking a partially frozen pond and Adirondack chairs on a deck. She sits, blows on her hands and revisits it all again.

Even after that conversation, the earrings refused to let her be. She dreamed of them, googled what they might look like, even absent-mindedly doodled them on a pamphlet.

Drawing her legs up to her chest and placing her head between her knees, Flick goes back.

~ ~ ~

November 2013

A fortnight later, while over for Sunday dinner, Flick goes upstairs to look in her mother's jewellery box.

And there they are. Exactly as she remembers them, secured in a tiny silk bag. The earrings Imo claims don't exist.

Flick crushes and snorts some of Imo's diazepam from the bedside drawer, then comes downstairs with the earrings, sitting on her palm like two question marks, the same way she saw them that day.

She shows them to Mum.

'How dare you go into my room and rummage through my things?' Imo says.

For the rest of the day, Imo's outrage spreads through the house like a bruise. She refuses to look at Flick, let alone talk to her. These maternal silences can last days – weeks, even.

~ ~ ~

Flick kneels down beside the pond and uses a pebble to tap the ice, see if it cracks. Nothing. She holds her hand on the ice, waiting for the freeze to turn into a burn, and then brings the heel of her hand down on the solid pond. Still nothing.

After weeks of Flick calling and leaving message after message on the answerphone, or of Doug picking up and claiming her mother was out, Imo answered while Flick was recording another apologetic answerphone message.

She agreed to meet her daughter for a cocktail in Sloane Square.

~ ~ ~

December 2013

A giant icicle twirls from a tree in Sloane Square, a red double-decker bus manoeuvring its way round a tight corner. It's not going to make it – it makes it.

HOW IT ENDS

'Well, what do you have to say for yourself?' Imo says, biting an olive off a cocktail stick. 'Are you here to tell me what a bad mother I am again? Show me more earrings?'

'I never said you were a bad mother,' Flick says. She measures the words out carefully, like baking ingredients.

'You're a great mother, but . . .' she takes a deep breath and tells her mum how the lie about the earrings made her feel. Betrayed, minimised, gaslighted.

'I can't make you feel anything, Flick,' Imo says. 'Your feelings are on you, not me.'

The edges of her lips lift; Imo knows she's landed a point.

Recently, Flick re-posted a meme on Instagram from a pop psychologist, saying 'Your feelings are ultimately your responsibility', which Imo had clearly squared away for future head-fuckery. Flick's own Instagram witterings, weaponised against her.

The waiter comes over to take their order. Imo orders a cappuccino and switches her charm on like a flashlight. Flirting, bantering, cajoling. It's as if Flick and the atmosphere between them doesn't exist.

But then, here it comes: 'Are you single, young man?'

Flick reddens. Not aiming for doctors or pilots any more, her mother is now content to pimp her off to anyone giving them a frothy coffee.

As Imo walks back from the toilet, Flick looks at her. Really looks. Clever, determined, magnetic. Somehow, she loves her more from afar. From a distance, it's like seeing a creature from a safari Jeep. Up close, it's more complicated.

Wow. But no, thanks, that's close enough.

*

VERSIONS OF A GIRL

Flick left her mother in Sloane Square, bought some mojitos in a can and went back to her rented studio apartment to compare herself to other people on Facebook and cry.

Stalking her former dance company's social media, she sees a link to a group. It's called 'It shouldn't happen on a Wednesday' and consists of most of her ex-colleagues.

They've left the group open. Photos of nights out, links to discounted athleisure, plans for leaving-do whip-rounds, a meme comparing the career of a ballet pro to the lifespan of a peach:

WAIT
WAIT
WAIT
WAIT
NOW
TOO LATE

She's about to click off it when she spots her name in a thread-within-a-thread about pointe shoes. A tickle of excitement – then dread – as she clicks into the comments.

Where did Flick get her pointes, does anyone know, her heels were never baggy

    Only her morals

Ooh that's dark

    But delicious

Moohahahaha

    I have more where that came from

We nicknamed her Sick Note

HOW IT ENDS

    Never rated her as a dancer even

Too old now anyway

    Bit harsh guys, c'mon

I feel sorry for her husband

    Uppity bitch

Oh, he left

    Couldn't get away fast enough

🚜

😀

😂

That night, Flick overdosed on a cocktail of diazepam, vodka and cocaine, ending up on the pavement outside A&E. She spent two nights in hospital recuperating, then got wasted again before checking herself into rehab. And now here she is, in the best rehab facility her divorce settlement can buy.

Something black and feathered bursts out of the rushes and *plop!* dives into a break in the ice. Flick is still crying, but now she smiles. This is where she heals.

~ ~ ~

January 2014

'My best friend Sita . . . well, ex-best friend . . . I don't know if we're even friends now, we haven't spoken in years . . . anyway . . . Sita is a psychotherapist now. And she thinks my mum has narcissistic personality disorder,' Flick tells her rehab therapist. 'Until now, I've always defended Mum, denied it could be true, said Mum's amazing.'

A diminutive man who looks like an owl, her therapist, has been treating her daily since she landed here five weeks ago. Ninety per cent of his job appears to be asking her how she feels about things.

'And how do you feel about that?'

Ugh. You could programme a talking bear to do his job.

She sighs. 'It doesn't matter what I think, does it? You're the professional. Is she a narcissist?'

He removes his glasses and cleans them on his shirt. His eyes look indecent without them, like bare buttocks.

'I can't diagnose someone I haven't met, Flick. Even if I were treating your mother herself, it would take a lot of time to diagnose something like narcissistic personality disorder. Those who have it rarely seek therapy – beyond one session – anyhow. But having said that, if the episodes you've told me about are all accurate, then yes, I would say she fits the classic behavioural patterns.'

Mercifully, he puts his glasses back on.

'The flip-flopping between neglect and smothering, the invasion of your privacy,' he says, casting down at his notes. 'The obsession with how things look, the anger when you contradict her version of "reality", those all fit. But I can't say for sure.'

Flick pauses. Then goes in.

'Do you think I'm a narcissist too?'

'The fact that you're asking that question tells me you're not,' he says, his owl-eyes as wide as they go.

'Unless the asking of it is performative. However, you may have picked up some behaviours from her. Learned habits from her being your main caregiver, then carried them with you into adulthood.'

This is the most he's ever said in a session. Flick is loving the feedback. She lives for the feedback.

'Like narcissistic fleas?' she asks.

'I'm not sure that's a term we'd want to use. It's quite negative.'

She thinks. 'How about narcissistic flares? Like when it flares up within me?'

He nods at her suggestion.

Flick already knows how and where she's flared in this very room. In the first few sessions, the temptation to name-drop was too much. She wove in the names of great thinkers she'd met, authors she was friends with.

'Do you know him? He comes to watch me dance,' she said.

It was only five weeks ago, but it feels like a different decade. Back then, Flick needed this therapist to know that she was not off-the-rack riffraff.

Right now, she's not quite ready to face up to it.

'OK, I can see that there's some truth in that,' she says, careful in her tone. 'But let's not do that today. I'll need to think on that one; let it percolate.'

February 2014

Flick watches her mother flutter around the rehab's security guard, raising a tentative smile from his square jaw, then a laugh. Another one bites the dust. He's bewitched.

And now she goes in for what Flick suspected might happen, but dared to hope wouldn't.

VERSIONS OF A GIRL

Imo gestures over to Flick. The security guard looks – a lingering, evaluating look – while Mum delivers some sort of speech. He clasps his hands, looks down at them, shakes his head, then recites what's probably a line from his employee handbook.

Imo shrugs, beams and then discards him, having determined he is not of use.

'Did you just try and matchmake me with the security guard?' Flick asks, as she tries and fails to keep the anger out of her voice. 'I'm in *rehab*, Mother.'

Imo rolls her entire head in protest. 'No, but so what if I had been? I have every right as your mother to try and solve your conundrum of being divorced at thirty-four. But no, I didn't. It's not *all about you*, dear.'

Today is 'family day' at Havenheart Clinic, and it's not going so well. Before their family members came in today, some intensive group sessions were delivered around making amends. How to apologise. What to apologise for. Only, Flick feels like she's spent her entire life apologising to Imo.

Within seconds of entering the building, Imo managed to gain an audience with the clinic's director. The director delivered her to Flick as soon as possible, but before he could disengage himself, she'd overheard the tail of their conversation.

'. . . well, it's her father's genes, you see,' Imo was saying. 'He's a very well-known rock star. I can't tell you who he is, of course, but he was always a hopeless addict and even though I raised her, you know what they say about genes . . .'

Mother and daughter now sit across from each other in William Morris-print flocked armchairs. 'Blameless in foliage', Flick captions her mother, whose eyes scan the room.

HOW IT ENDS

'Are there any famous people here?' Imo asks.

Flick holds up a hand. 'A, I can't tell you, and, B, that's not why we're here.'

'So why am I here?' she asks. 'It's all my fault, is it?'

'I never said that; nobody has said that.'

'I'm a bad mother, am I?'

This is their regular script. Imo says she's a bad mother, Flick says she's not. End of conversation. Because now that she has been prompted to say Imo's a good mother, she can't hold her accountable for the times she's been a bad mother. It's kinda genius.

But this victim-fawn cycle needs to stop. Flick picked up a book here in rehab that explained there's a fourth reaction to conflict. Everyone knows about fight, flight and freeze. But not many people know about the fourth: fawn.

As a social experiment this time, Flick leaves her line unsaid. She doesn't fawn. She's not going to spend today consoling her mum that her parenting has been exemplary, because it hasn't been. Imo never hesitates to point out any flaws in Flick's daughtering, after all.

Her 'you're a good mother' line falls to the ground between them. Imo frowns. She hasn't got what she expected. Flick's going off script.

'How dare you?' Imo's voice drops, so no one else will hear. 'I've forgiven you for all the hurt and pain your addiction has caused. The silly and cruel things you've said when drunk. The embarrassment of your divorce. If you owe me and Doug anything, it's gratitude for supporting you out of this predicament. Not judgment.'

'Mum, I am sorry for any pain and embarrassment I've

caused. *I am.* But my being an addict doesn't mean you haven't done anything wrong.'

'And your dad was so great, was he?'

'Who said anything about him?'

Her mother looks at her long and hard, as if pondering something. Then leans in close.

'Well, let me tell you about what happened on your father's watch. You know that your uncle Rory fell to his death? Guess who pushed him.'

Flick sits there clinging to the sides of the armchair. She won't react. *She won't.*

'You did,' Imo says. 'Your father told me all about it. Said that's why he ran. And that's why he couldn't ever go back to Ireland, because he was covering for *you*.'

Dread begins to rise in Flick, closely followed by a shrill craving for a drug.

Imo stirs her tea, satisfied that the silence means she's won.

'Oh my, he's handsome. Look, Flick.'

March 2014

Three centimetres of earring brought her to her knees. And now, three short months later, she feels as if her insides have been poured out, zhooshed around and rearranged back inside.

If some reality show were to do a split-screen reel of her entering rehab and her leaving, it would look more like three years had passed. In December, she came into reception waving a credit card around, her nose bleeding from a cocaine binge, with teriyaki sauce on her gym leggings and a gin-in-a-tin in her hand, demanding that they make her all better.

'I don't want to quit altogether!' she said during her entrance interview. 'That's too extreme, too all-or-nothing. Everything in moderation! I just want to learn how to use my – prescribed, by the way – diazepam, and also some alcohol and maybe a sprinkling of party dust,' she'd winked here in a fun way, 'moderately, y'know? Like how other people do. If you can't do that for me, I'm not paying these extortionate fees.'

She folded her arms. They explained to her that what she did after the stay was, of course, up to her – given they could not control her future – but their aim at the facility was to prepare people for abstinence, not moderation.

'Yeah, OK,' she said, signing the piece of paper, thinking she'd outwit them and use it as a moderation programme instead. *Fools.*

Now, she's saying goodbye to the friends she's made – friends who know her darkest corners and brightest hopes; not just a sequined and wisecracking version of her propping up a bar.

She's leaving a 'thank you' card behind reception for her talented therapist, who somehow nudged her to the places she needed to go, without her ever noticing she was being guided.

'You've done a lot of hard work here,' he said, as they said goodbye. 'I've enjoyed our time together.'

She has a pocketful of first day, week and month chips chinking against her leg. Most of all, she's ready to tell the truth. Not only that, she's craving it, straining towards it. She can't wait to get there.

VERSIONS OF A GIRL

Right now, instead of handing herself into Chiswick Police Station, which is an eight-minute walk, according to Google Maps, she's on her way to the airport. En route, she'll pick up some things from her mother's Kensington house, knowing Imo will be out at her weekly manicure. They haven't spoken since 'family day' and Flick doesn't intend to change that.

Now she knows what really happened. On some level, she feels as if she's always known. She killed Uncle Rory by pushing him to his death. And she did so in Northern Ireland, so that's where she'll go to confess her crime, face the consequences.

Like the 'little drama queen' she is. One day, she'll have that stitched onto a cushion.

Flick's Emancipation

HOW IT ENDS
Last month – February 2014
Richmond, London, England

Imo wants to find the director before she goes. It would be rude to leave without saying goodbye.

The security guard winks at her as she leaves the visitors' lounge. Seems he was more interested in her than Flick, oohee. She is only fifty-three – still got it.

'Family day' has been a farce. If she were paying for this rehab, she'd be asking for her money back, given Flick is getting worse rather than better.

Her daughter just sat there, frosty and unfeeling, and accused her of being a bad mother. She had to tell her about her part in Rory's death – how else could she get through to her? Imo was expecting an amends speech today, so the whole experience had been deeply hurtful. Heartbreaking, even.

Flick's memories must have been warped by some ten-a-penny therapist who wants her daughter to feel like a victim. She's read about false memories induced in therapy. Imo can't – and won't – put herself through that again.

She can't find the director. His secretary says he's out, even though there's someone moving around in his office. A cleaner, perhaps.

~ ~ ~

VERSIONS OF A GIRL

At a literature festival a few years back, Imo caught a reading from a professor who had written a book called *Your Memories and What They Mean*. Evening descended, the autumn air was nipping and Doug was at a deathly dull lecture about World War II.

She wasn't interested in self-help – or as they'd tried to re-market it, 'smart thinking', as if calling a thing 'smart' can make it so – but the heat of other bodies drew her into the marquee. Pulling her alpaca coat close, a glass of fizz in her hand, Imo found a chair at the back.

'Think of a book in a library,' the professor read. 'That's how we see our memories. Writ in black and white. Truth. How it was. But the reality is, each time we take that book – our memory – down from the shelf we change it. Turn down favourite pages, neon-highlight passages and redact others, write notes in the margins for additions. Our memories are not facts. They're stories we tell ourselves.'

The thought of it made Imo shake. She knows exactly what has happened to her. What kind of crackpot would say otherwise.

Feeling a sweat form on her brow, a stain of redness steal up her face, she had to duck into the aisle and leave the marquee, her breath torn ragged.

~ ~ ~

Making her way from the rehab clinic back to her car, winter copper head high, the peacock feather earrings jostle in her dress pocket. Bringing them was a bad idea.

She thought maybe her and Flick could smash them together, perhaps with a rock from that pretty garden, a symbolic ceremony so they no longer have to talk about the past.

Imo doesn't want to relive it all – hasn't she been through enough? Those years were hell.

On her way to the clinic, she even toyed with the idea of presenting the earrings and telling Flick she *was* right: she hadn't been watching her in the swimming pool, she was sorry for that, she'd failed her that day. But she was just trying to secure a new husband so that they could have a nice life, which she'd managed, hadn't she, so all's well that ends well.

When it came to it, she couldn't do either. Flick attacked her, so her only option was self-defence. Her fist closes around the earrings in the silk bag. She crushes them, the question-mark hooks collapsing, and throws them in a bin.

She can't. She won't. Just as she needn't defend this 'you folded your dress' nonsense (Doug folded it, for heaven's sake), she doesn't have to defend her parenting choices either. Since when does a parent have to explain themselves to a child? She did the best she could.

It has been easy to keep her secret safe all these years about the birth. Nora is long gone, probably dead, and Ciaran is now dead too. The only living person who could possibly pull the last thirty-four years from under them would be Ruth.

And Ruth has always been tucked conveniently away in Ferndale, the house Flick is in line to inherit. Not that she knows about that. When Ciaran died, Imo made sure to intercept all letters from the solicitor about his estate.

It's pretty standard for her to steam open Flick's post, read it, then glue it closed once more. Imo's only been keeping an eye on things, protecting her daughter from her own financial fuckwittery. Any mother would do the same.

Ferndale's a money pit if ever she saw one. Flick's better off without that albatross. Imo and Doug would probably end up paying to maintain the estate if that tiny trust is empty, which it probably is.

But the existence of this unclaimed inheritance troubles Imo. Soon, that blasted solicitor – or meddling Ruth – will find an email address or phone number to get through to Flick.

And then, Flick will meet Ruth, and Ruth will see how unmistakably she is like Nora, and the whole thing will come tumbling down.

Having binned the earrings, Imo's posture straightens, her chest expands, a hand goes to smooth her hair.

She cut her hair short five years ago, because her mother had told her that 'long hair never becomes one later in life'. Feeling drained of her power without it, like Samson, she regrew it, but only after these internet searches:

Can fiftysomething women have long hair

Is long hair considered witchy on older women

Do men like long hair on middle-aged women

What do they say about older women with long hair

She determined that, these days, it's OK to have long hair later in life. A further series of searches revealed she was also allowed to wear minidresses still, as long as she does so with opaque tights.

Her mind whirrs as she considers what to tell Doug about cutting ties with Flick. She barely got away with the first estrangement all those years ago, having to make up some poppycock about Ciaran gaining full custody because she hadn't sought his permission to move over to England.

Doug just about swallowed it, accepted it, as did the Kensington bitcheratti, but what can she say this time round?

HOW IT ENDS

A-ha. She'll tell them about Rory's death. Say she's scared of what her daughter might do. Perhaps they had an argument at the top of a flight of stairs, Flick snapped and shouted at her, and Imo now fears that history could repeat itself.

Yes, that's what she'll say. That's true, after all. Flick did push her uncle. Which means she could absolutely kill another family member.

Fern's Bluebird

HOW IT ENDS
February 2014
Paradise, California

As Scout slows for the turn into The Rest Inn, Fern scrolls through her favourited pictures of Digby: with a squeaky bone as a puppy, swimming in the sea as a teenager, curled up on her lap as an old man.

It's been seven years since his accident brought her to her knees, or more literally, caused her to lie in the road. For a second on that tarmac she'd thought he was gone. But then *ga-jung, ga-jung*: a faint heartbeat.

His pelvis was broken. But after surgery, two weeks in the veterinary hospital and many more weeks of bed rest at home, Digby was able to walk again. The bill was astronomical; Fern had never paid a bill more gladly in her life.

Alongside his recovery, she started her own. Instead of sitting on the edge, dipping her toe in, getting in and getting back out, she launched herself fully into being sober. No excuses this time. No going back.

She took every hour she would have spent drinking and spent it going to addiction conventions, meeting up with potential sober buddies from Facebook, listening to other people's stories. Every cent she would have spent on getting lit went on therapy, dozens of books, a course on anger management, the bougie gym she'd always insisted she couldn't afford.

HOW IT ENDS

All the energy she'd previously launched at getting wasted – the atomic equivalent of a nuclear missile – was instead redirected towards *not* getting wasted. And this time, it worked.

Fern was two years sober when Digby died of old age. He went during the night, swirled up in the small of her back.

'I've never known a Jack Russell live this long,' the vet said, when she brought him in. 'Sixteen, that's something.' He gave a low whistle. 'He must've been happy.'

~ ~ ~

Getting out of the car, she wonders if this could be the last time they come to the motel, other than to visit Wally. Because if they have their way, today her dad is going to go home to Ireland, and Dina's (hopefully) going to agree to go with him.

It's taken them years of graft, and Fern feels older than her thirty-four years because of it. But they've finally got together what they think they need to get Ciaran back home.

In Fern's hand is a fat brown file.

'Go get 'em, tiger,' Scout says, patting the file. They both look at it with hopeful eyes.

'I'm gonna go look for Wally and get a coffee,' he adds. 'I'll come find you two in a half-hour once you've broken the subject open.'

Scout walks towards the dark motel's reception in search of Wally, while Fern splits off in the other direction.

She holds the file to her chest, like it's a person she cherishes. In it are some freeze frames of CCTV footage – secured by way of some bribery – of Nora Brady at Belfast International Airport.

'He loved her,' Fern said to Scout, when they finally got the footage. 'So it'll be a useful carrot to dangle.'

The rest of the file consists of Ciaran's case notes and their years of subsequent research. There'll be some questions to answer about Rory's death when Ciaran re-enters Northern Ireland, for sure, but this file can help him deal with them.

'It's all circumstantial,' Scout said of the case against Ciaran. 'They have no witnesses, no physical evidence tying Ciaran to Rory's fall, and a bunch of ex-staff who could have copied the key and gotten into the house without forcing entry. The police were so focused on pinning it on your dad – because he'd done a runner – that they forgot to consider the many other possibilities.'

'So we have reasonable doubt on our side?' Fern asked.

'Yup. Even if it did get to court, which it won't, we would have a *monster truck* of reasonable doubt to drive through their prosecution.'

Also in the file are the details of a top-notch Irish lawyer who Fern has talked into representing her father, by way of a sizeable deposit.

'I can coach him on all the tricks the police will use when they question him, how they'll try to trip him up,' Scout said. 'Unless he does something crazy like confesses, the burden of proof they need for the CPS is, in my view, unobtainable.'

Fern's been knocking now for over fifteen minutes. Her knuckles are grazed, her throat is hoarse from shouting his name and panic is beginning to grip.

He's in there, for sure. She can see his outline on the bed. These curtains don't do shit.

Scout re-enters the parking lot with a takeaway coffee cup.

HOW IT ENDS

'I couldn't find Wall— Hey, what's up, is he out?'

Fern can't talk. She knows what this is. She always knew this would be the way. Sliding down the wall, she curls into a ball.

Scout kicks the door down with one try. She hears him inside, trying to rouse Ciaran. Starting CPR. Realising it's useless.

Going inside, Da's body is face-up, lips parted, eyes open, his Viking skin grey.

Cops and medics arrive on the scene. Scout deals with the questions, while they wrap a shivering Fern in a metallic blanket, the type that marathon runners use as capes of glory.

'We're too late . . . too late . . . too late,' she keeps repeating.

'You did all you could,' Scout says, pulling Fern into him.

'But he still . . .' Fern starts.

'It was never something you could control.'

'But I could have . . .'

'You couldn't do it for him. People have to do it for themselves. You know that.'

Scout insists that they go and eat something, once the paramedic has given her the all clear.

They walk to Ted's Diner. She surprises herself by eating a full meal with gusto. An hour or so later, some colour has returned to her face.

'Why do you keep touching your stomach?' Scout asks, his tone soft. 'And you asked them to hold the blue cheese dip. Is this what I think?'

'I just found out. Buck doesn't know yet. I'll be a catastrophic mother,' she says.

'Why d'you think that?' he asks.

'You know me, Scout. I'm impulsive, reckless, selfish; people getting too close scare me. I love being alone, and I'm the product of two parents who couldn't do this either. So what hope do I have? I'll be like *them*.'

'You're not them, though, Fern. You're you. And if anything, the childhood you've had means you know exactly what a child needs.'

February 2014

Flanked by Buck and Wally, with Dina and Scout a few rows back, Fern flicks through an in-flight magazine. She stops at the album reviews. Wally reads one of the band names over her shoulder.

'Neon Tigers!' he says.

Leaving him hanging would be like leaving a kid with a high five in the air.

'What about them?' Fern asks.

'When you were in London that time, they asked your dad to come on tour with them as their support.'

'*They what?*'

'Yeah. I guess they were playing Sacramento or something, their tour bus slid into Paradise Falls' lot, and they sat and had fries and beers. Ciaran was performing – some of his own stuff for once – and they were really taken with him.'

Fern ponders this. 'He never told me. Why didn't he go? That could've been his big break?'

Wally shrugs. 'Said you wanted to stay still.'

HOW IT ENDS

She said that, it was true. And still they were, finally. For years, during which Wally gave Ciaran a job, a work visa, then Fern joined and graduated high school.

'But hang on, he couldn't, could he?' Fern says, finally putting it together in her head.

'Couldn't what?'

'Get famous. Be in the music press, the newspapers. Because he was wanted, Wall,' she says. 'He had to keep his head down.'

She finally gets it. That's why her dad never followed through, why he let opportunities pass him by, played but didn't punch up, did covers rather than his own songs. He had to stay low.

Buck's face falls forward, his snore accelerating into the nosedive, until the end of his neck wakes him up. She looks at him, her face softer with love than she dares when he's awake.

It's seven years since she stopped trying to set her life – their relationship – herself – on fire. Buck knows what happened with Digby, that Fern's neglect led to him being hit by a car, but he still doesn't know what she did in one of her previous rock bottoms. How she had sex with another guy while he slept in the room next door.

Scout told her that there is one simple rule around making amends as an ex-hellraiser.

'If telling them about *the thing* hurts them more than making amends for *the thing* would heal, then you keep your cakehole shut,' he said. 'Let them live on in ignorant bliss.' He popped a nacho into his mouth to punctuate the point.

VERSIONS OF A GIRL

Her insides feel scrubbed clean these days, with every drawer having been emptied, every cupboard decluttered from years of work, but this was – *this is* – the rat under the floorboards. She has to tell him, and soon.

She draws the creased sheet of paper out of her bag, wanting to practise some more in her head. Wally printed the poem out for her on the motel's PC. 'The Bluebird', the poem is called. Fern has doodled a bluebird on the back of the print-out. Tracing her finger around it now, she feels the urge for another tattoo.

Wally's right – these are the perfect words to send her father's body, currently in with the luggage, into the fire. And then they'll scatter him. Back home, where he should have stayed all along.

Fern's Emancipation

HOW IT ENDS
A few days later
Coleraine, Northern Ireland

Mourners crowd at the crematorium's doors, making tight-lipped and heads-bowed small talk, while Imo and Doug glide into the car park in their luxury rental.

Imo hadn't wanted Doug to come, but she could hardly manipulate the date of the cremation into a no-go diary zone of his. And it would look terribly uncivilised if she didn't show up to her ex-husband's funeral. She'd just need to stage-manage who Doug talked to.

They put their best sad faces on and get out of the car. People are starting to be seated. Joining the last few stragglers in, Imo is affronted by a giant slideshow at the beginning of the service. Pictures of Ciaran grinning, kayaking, graduating, cuddling, dancing, feeding Fern as a toddler . . .

Decades-sour tears wait behind her eyes. *Not now.* She never got over Ciaran; not really. Despite trying to bitch, wheedle and detest her way out of the sorrow.

The party line on their divorce goes as such. He ran off with an air stewardess, he wanted to drink himself silly rather than parent, he didn't think he was good enough for her. She'll emphasise one particular line depending on who she's talking to.

But the truth was: he just didn't want to be with her any more. He chose nobody, rather than her. The darkness of it sat inside her like an ink blot, spreading. So she started simply denying that reality and created a new one.

Faces at the front swivel to regard the latecomers.

'Is that Fern over from America?' Doug whispers.

Yes, it is. Imo hasn't seen her in over twenty years and Fern has become an unwashed tree-hugger. A purple sheen in her hair, the flash of a nose stud, what looks like an ugly great bird tattooed on her neck.

Fern sits next to Ruth, who's looking well, as always, despite her advanced age. Imo has always admired how attractive she is. Neither of them turn around.

Doug leads the way into the very back row. Dire Straits' 'Brothers in Arms' plays, a little too loudly in Imo's opinion, while Doug folds their clothing into an outerwear tower.

As the song rolls to a guitar solo close, one last mourner ducks in. The solo woman creeps into the pew in front of Doug and Imo, her posture apologetic, turning into profile to remove her jacket and sit.

She doesn't see Imo, but Imo definitely sees her. The latecomer is Nora.

Without stopping to collect her coat or Doug, or even really thinking at all, Imo slides out of the pew and is up and out of the doors, just before they close in on the silence.

As soon as Nora sees Fern, she'll realise what really happened to her baby. And Imo doesn't want to be here when she does.

The Night Rory Died

HOW IT WAS
Boxing Day 1989
Glenfoot, Northern Ireland

Ruth wakes up, the sensation of having stumbled and tripped. She shuts her eyes again. Oh. The noise is real. A yowl of pain. The clock that tick-tocks beside her bed says it's nearly 11.15 p.m.

Now here's a dilemma. She's not meant to be in the house at all.

'I've told her to sleep in my room over Christmas,' Ciaran explained, when Ruth asked if she needs to change the sheets in the nursery for Fern.

'Your room? Ah, good idea,' Ruth replied. The unspoken passed between them.

Regardless, Ruth made up a secret bed in the East Wing. At least this way she'll be close enough to intervene, should Ciaran be clattered and the girl need her.

'I'll be sleeping in here over Christmas,' she said to Fern, 'but don't tell anyone, OK? If you ever need me, I'm in here.'

She wouldn't make the mistake of letting the past echo. The definition of insanity is, after all, doing the same thing over and over and expecting different results.

What is this yowl? Maybe Fern has bitten down hard on Rory's hand. It does sound like him. The thought of it pushes Ruth upright. She can tell that the noises are coming from the landing beneath.

Deep in the West Wing, she can hear Fern calling, 'Da, Da!' The landing's banister is burst through, as if Wile E. Coyote had torn through it in pursuit of Road Runner heading over a cliff.

Ruth leans over the intact part of the banister and sees Rory lying on the landing below, his limbs at odd angles like a dropped and broken wooden toy. He's gurgling, his eyes screwed shut. She's about to shout to him that she's coming, when she sees it.

A dark figure darts from near where he lies. Someone else is here. Ruth makes her way downstairs, with as much stealth as she can, and draws the poker from the stand beside the kitchen fireplace.

The pantry door is swinging. She sidles in there and watches the winged doors to the tunnel being closed silently. Ruth holds her breath as whoever is inside turns the key.

She didn't anticipate having to ride a motorbike again at fifty-three. It's been thirty years since Frederick taught her. But what the hell, it's nice to be surprised.

There's a lick of fear in her gut, but the adrenaline is delicious. Slinging Frederick's old air rifle over her nightgown, she throttles the bike into a growl and roars off down the path.

She's not wearing any knickers. Oh, well. Who wears knickers to bed, just in case they need to leave the house in the small hours? She wonders what the ladies of Martha's hair salon would make of Ruth Brady on a motorbike in knicker-less pursuit of an intruder.

She's always doing this: being trivial in grave situations. Frederick used to say she would make jokes in the path of a tsunami, would wisecrack in the mouth of a volcano.

HOW IT WAS

Arriving at the tunnel's exit, she stations herself behind a tree, Frederick's gun pointed at the doors, Ruth wondering if there's actually any pellets in the thing. Not that she intends to fire; it's only a prop.

Ten seconds later, the doors push open. Ruth's heart lifts. 'Oh! Hello, darlin'. What are you doing here?'

The Late-Night Visit

HOW IT WAS
Boxing Day 1989
Glenfoot, Northern Ireland

Arriving at The Millhouse just before 10 p.m., banjaxed after twenty-four hours on the road, Nora gropes above the door frame for the spare key. The light above the stove burns bright. It's always on – Mum is paranoid about burglars. As if a solitary light will stop them, but OK, cool.

She waits almost an hour, thinking that maybe Mum's at the pub quiz – she does like a bit of trivia – but by 10.45 p.m. she knows that can't be the case. Her mother's a habitual animal and is always in bed by 10.30 p.m.

Nora takes the grass verge up to Ferndale – you can't quite see it from the lodge and she doesn't want the gravel up the driveway to alert anyone of her approach. Her car's down the road in a picnic area, just in case.

The overhanging trees part and she can see that candle-light still flickers in the study. There are two cars outside. One she recognises as Rory's, the other she doesn't know, but it's probably Ciaran's. Shite. She folds herself into the trees even though there's no way they can see her from here.

Taking the path, she heads in the direction of the tunnel. She'll need to get in and out without anyone knowing, check Mum's OK, given she must be in the house with Rory – that degenerate. And Ciaran too, but Ciaran will be half in the bag by now, if his drinking has continued.

HOW IT WAS

The key to the tunnel turns like a spoon in butter. It's been oiled recently. It smells like Satan's dirty socks in here, though. Dead rats, she guesses.

Within a few minutes, Nora's located her mother, fast asleep in a bedroom in the East Wing, for some reason. Closing the door silently, she's about to head back to the lodge when she hears a clank of bottles below, the door to the cellar closes, then somebody is on the stairs.

She wraps the floor-length curtain around herself and watches as Rory staggers up the stairs, clearly off his tits, and looks in the two nursery bedrooms. A bottle trails from his hand – red wine – and he stops to lean over the banister, stare at the fat moon, light up a cigarette.

Then she hears a little girl's voice. And there she is. Fern. Her daughter, who she hasn't seen in ten years.

~ ~ ~

Nora is now a celebrated chef in Bangkok. In interviews, she talks about her inspirations, giving other chefs some deserved air-time. She can't share the truth as it sounds too pretentious.

While she *is* inspired by those chefs, her recipes arrive to her fully formed. Like lost things she just needs to catch, re-name and home.

She's lived in Thailand since she gave Fern away. In the weeks after the birth she realised: she couldn't live in the same city as her daughter. Every London baby would trigger the wonder of 'Is that her?' So she worked double shifts at The Pig in Hammersmith, flirting with every punter to get tips, and saved for the flight.

Having never been outside of Britain and Ireland, a nineteen-year-old Nora – still sore from the birth in every conceivable way – landed in Thailand. She waited for a bus to Haad Rin beach after her red-eye flight and morning ferry.

A macaque monkey sat next to her on the bright blue bench, nonplussed, as if he too were waiting for the bus. While she tore into fried squid from a street cart, the monkey gently removed her sunglasses from the top of her head, then bounced up into a tree, squawking with amusement when she realised.

'You need pay him,' the street vendor said, handing her a slice of mango.

Nora offered the monkey the fruit and he returned her sunglasses.

Arriving at Haad Rin just before sunset, she saw tiki torches being lit along the shore. Gangly tans lounged in hammocks, hats tipped over their faces for disco naps, a bonfire and barbecue promised for that evening. Coconuts were being split with machetes by the smiley bar staff – *kerchunk* – with the strains of Bob Marley coming from a tinny radio.

It couldn't have been more different from Ireland, from England, and from everything she needed to forget.

~ ~ ~

Even if Ciaran had seen her over the years, Nora very much doubts he would have recognised her. Thrice weekly pilates and yoga means she's strong, lean, more machine than woman. She can press up into a handstand as casually as she stands up. She can also do a somersault, but never would in public.

Single and happy about it – no, thanks, she doesn't want your number – she still likes good sex. Her Irish skin held out for the first year, but then relented and created melanin.

HOW IT WAS

Nowadays, she's permanently hazel and her hair is bleached blonde, short and beach-chick messy.

This was what threw Mum the first time she came home to visit her. Her daughter, but in an entirely different palette, after five years missing and presumed dead.

'Nora, is that, no, dear Lord, I'm losing my wits,' Ruth said, when Nora knocked on the door.

'Can I help you?'

'It is me, Mum,' she said.

And for one of the first – and last – times her mother wrapped her wiry arms around her, squashing her until she couldn't breathe, making her shoulder wet with tears.

'Je-sus, you hug like a cobra,' Nora said, wriggling herself free.

Now Ruth wasn't crying, she was angry.

'Where the hell have you been, girl?'

~ ~ ~

She begged her mum to keep her return a secret. She wasn't ready to see Ciaran.

It haunted her, the decision she'd made about their baby without consulting him. When she was told that Ciaran and Imo had got married, had a kid, were still together, it allayed her guilt somewhat, but replaced it with resentment.

How could he, how could she? Wankers.

Then when Mum showed her a picture of four-year-old Fern, she just knew.

'She's not theirs, she's ours,' Nora said.

'What do you mean?'

'She's mine and Ciaran's.'

~ ~ ~

It was straightforward, coming back for visits incognito. Ciaran and Imo were living up in Belfast, and Rory worked overseas as a trader. Mum always knew when Ferndale was going to be occupied, so Nora just planned her yearly visits for when it wasn't.

'I'm useless at lying, so I just hide in plain sight,' Ruth said.

'You've lost me,' Nora said, buttering a toasted pancake on a floral plate and pouring the digestive-brown tea from the stove pot into her china cup.

'I tell them that you're not dead, only missing, and actually that I see you plain as day about once a year. They then finish their drinks and say they've got to be going. Or look at their watches and make up dentist appointments. I've no doubt they then go off and talk about me going crackers, saying I ought to go to Sunnyvale Home to do potato-print art, make some birdhouses out of cereal boxes.'

Talking about your feelings has never been encouraged in Glenfoot. Talking about other people is, however, prime social currency. Which is why, when her mum calls off the missing persons investigation, revoking the search for her, she also has the sense to invoke her right for privacy, before it's leaked and everyone's talking about the return of Nora.

Astonishingly, the local police comply. Ruth gets through to someone high up, explains the delicacy of the situation, asks him to do the paperwork on the quiet.

He's a good man, is DI Sean Wells.

~ ~ ~

As she climbs out of the tunnel, Nora thinks she's got away with pushing Rory; absolute pervert and waste of skin. Then she sees her mother, who she thought she'd outwitted by locking the tunnel door. How did she get out into the woods this fast?

Dad's motorbike leans against a tree, rakish as her father himself. She rode that thing? Mum has her flaws, but she's never not surprising. In another life, she could have been a spy, rather than a housekeeper.

'Oh! Hello, darlin'. What are you doing here?'

She kisses her mother's cheek, finding it soft but fragile, like just-risen dough.

'I wanted to surprise you for once, come check on you, with it being twenty years since Dad died. Bit of a silly idea, it turns out, given everyone's back at the house. I'll have to leave before light. It's too risky.'

Ruth nods, a sad smile that she's remembered the anniversary, pecking her daughter's cheek.

They walk back through the trees towards the houses.

'We need to go help Rory,' Ruth says. 'The ambulance'll be too long from Antrim, so I'll get Dr McAllister out of bed. Did he fall . . . or did you two get into it?'

'No, he didn't fall. I pushed him. He was pulling up Fern's nightgown. She's what, ten? I *told* you what he was like.'

Ruth stops, rubs her eyelids with sorrow. She has rehearsed this speech in her head many times, too cowardly to deliver it in person, but now here it is. And she knows she's going to bungle it.

'I'm sorry, so sorry. Please, can we talk about this later? I have things to say.' She places a hand on Nora's arm.

Nora moves away. 'Well, let's just hope Rory doesn't press charges. He definitely saw it was me.'

She pulls a wayward branch back out of the path, lets her mum go first. The stove light of The Millhouse burns up ahead.

'I'm sure what you saw will keep him quiet. We'll go to him now, talk him into keeping his mouth shut, before he wakes Ciaran up.'

As if summoned by his name, Ciaran's voice rips the night.

'Ruth, RUTH, help!' He's pounding the front door of The Millhouse, then pulls back and shouts at the upstairs windows. 'Rory's not breathing!'

Ruth and Nora look at each another. Any moment now, Ciaran will come round the back of the house and see them both there, standing on the path.

'Hide,' Ruth says. Nora goes.

~ ~ ~

Nora was thirteen when she first told her mum about Rory. 'He looks at me funny,' she said.

'That's how boys look at girls,' Ruth said.

Soon afterward, eighteen-year-old Rory suggested they go for a walk in the rose garden and pushed his face on hers, stuck his tongue in her mouth, put a hand up her top.

Nora told her mum.

'You shouldn't have been alone with him. Boys will be boys,' Ruth said.

When Nora was fourteen and Ruth was out for the evening, Rory took the spare key from the top of the door, let himself into their house, lay on Nora's bed beside her and moved his hand around fast until he moaned. He thought she was asleep, but she wasn't.

Nora told her mum.

HOW IT WAS

'It was just a dream,' Ruth said.

By the next school term, Nora was at boarding school – Wesley College – generously paid for by Rory's parents and gratefully accepted by Ruth.

Flick Goes Home

HOW IT ENDS
March 2014
Gatwick Airport, England

Flick drops the coins into the payphone at Gatwick Airport. Her phone got cut off while she was in rehab. She's amazed payphones still exist, frankly, but she guesses: old people.

Her hand wants to slam the phone down when Ballymena Police Station answers, the number she'd looked up back in rehab scrawled on her hand.

'Detective Inspector Sean Wells,' a voice says, sounding bored.

'Oh, hi, my name's Fern Felicity O'Malley. And I'll be along tomorrow to hand myself in for the manslaughter – or maybe murder, I'm not sure – of my uncle, Rory O'Malley. I'm just travelling in from London today.'

Stunned silence fills the other end of the phone.

'Hello?' says Flick.

The detective clears his throat.

'Right you be, Miss O'Malley, er, we'll look forward to that then. So we'll see you soon, thanks a million for calling,' he says. 'Oh, and come see me personally when you arrive. DI Sean Wells.'

The phone fills with a dial tone. Flick looks at the payphone. She expected more, frankly. Talk about a little drama queen's anti-climax.

HOW IT ENDS

Swinging in a canvas bag at her side are the only belongings she deemed worthy of rescue from the Kensington townhouse, her supposed home for over a decade. Mum had already changed the locks, but the cleaner was in and welcomed Flick inside.

First up and symbolic: she got her Birkenstocks. Even in high summer, she has never dared to wear open-toed sandals, let alone such functional ones. Professional dancing has left her with the feet of a Gruffalo. They're as muscular and splayed as a creature that might live barefoot in the woods, with the gorgeous addition of bunions and corns.

'Lovely feet,' other dancers say about her arches *en pointe*. Nobody else thinks they're lovely. But Flick is prepared to no longer care. From now on, her comfort comes before her attractiveness.

Next to the sandals is the ultimate disobedience: the photo of Mum and David Bowie. She knows how much her mum treasures that thing. She knew taking it would be the end. Flick stood there for a full five minutes, tears rolling down and dropping off her jaw. And then she picked the picture up. Bagged it.

On her way out of the door, she plopped her pocket mirror into the vase containing the artificial flowers and water. It floated for a second – then sank.

Flick also packed the half of Ciaran's ashes that Wally gave her, the tin that is now stowed in her hold luggage. How bizarre that such a bombastic person can be reduced to a tin formerly used for tea.

'Scatter these where he grew up, maybe,' Wally suggested.

She's never found the time. It wasn't exactly urgent, was it? He isn't going to be un-dead any time soon.

Now, she's making the time. Before it's too late and the truth has her in handcuffs. But she has no intention of scattering Ciaran at Ferndale. She'll scatter him where she'd seen him happiest.

Ballymastocker Beach in Donegal – the cottage beneath the road to the sky.

Four hours later

Flick looks over a marsh plain that could almost be lunar, if it weren't for the straw-blond grasses and cotton wool balls of distant sheep. The fence posts keel along the edge of a field, trying to stay in line but failing, like drunk soldiers.

She sees a double rainbow in the distance, above a felled pine forest. The baby rainbow beneath is brighter. The bigger rainbow fades into the purple post-storm sky.

Every hectare or so in the vast graveyard of pines, the tree fellers have left an intact tree, sticking up like a telephone pole. Why would they do that? A distant memory stirs of her dad telling her the farmers do that on purpose, because the birds still need a place to perch, rest and look for food.

It strikes her that she's looking for her own tree, too. A place to rest. It's a shame she can't spend more time in Donegal, but maybe she'll find stability in police custody. Some roots, at last, that aren't uprootable by her mother's mercurial whim.

She stands there, watching the dusk draw a blanket over the landscape, feeling a low thrill in her stomach at being unguarded under the moon path, in the middle of noplace.

The same animal thrill she felt while racing around Soho

looking for more danger, more cocaine, more people to admire her, want to kiss her. She's surprised to be able to feel the same sensation while having placed herself in no danger whatsoever.

Turning to get back into the car, she sees, at least a hundred feet away down the road, another figure in the moon path, leaning against a car. A silhouette, black against dark grey. She waves. The figure doesn't acknowledge her.

Flick shivers. Maybe they didn't see her. She starts the car.

Flick's Journey

HOW IT ENDS
March 2014
Donegal, Ireland

'Shite,' Nora says, as her daughter's tiny silhouette starts waving at her. She thought she was being subtle, but it's plain as flour that she's been made.

The blue rental car beetles on up the hill. Nora'll hang back. Now that they're this far, she knows exactly where they're going. Not to the police station, or at least not yet. They're going to the little cottage on Ballymastocker Beach. Ciaran took her to the cottage a couple of times, during their summer of intense courting.

'My father left me this,' he said, gesturing towards the house. 'Didn't want Rory to know, for some reason. I think it's like my safe house, in case my brother ever turns full psychopath.' Ciaran pulled a face like Edvard Munch's *The Scream* and chased Nora up the steps.

~ ~ ~

Three hours ago, Nora and her mother Ruth were stuffing a chicken when the phone rang.

'Och, hiya, Sean!' Ruth said, delighted.

Then – quiet.

Ruth looked at Nora, face sorrowful. Turned her back on her.

'Alright, yes, I understand. Thanks for letting us know, Sean.' She replaced the phone.

'Letting us know what?' Nora said, her hand halfway up a chicken. 'Has the cat got your tongue?'

'That was Detective Inspector Sean Wells,' Ruth said. 'You remember Sean, the one who helped us keep your return on the downlow.'

Nora nodded, bracing for the impact of the *something* coming.

'He said Fern just called Ballymena police,' Ruth said, her voice as gentle as it goes. 'Well, she calls herself Flick these days, but whatever. She's about to get a flight over here, hand herself in . . . for the killing of her uncle Rory. She's taken a fit of the head staggers and thinks it was her.'

Five minutes later, having chucked some underwear, clean clothes and a toothbrush into a holdall, Nora sped out of the drive, her mum hustling after the car as best a septuagenarian can, trying to stop her.

Best guess would be that she's landing at Belfast International Airport, on a flight from London. Nora's mission? To get to Flick first, before she gets to the police.

Only problem is, Nora thinks, following the blue car from as great a distance as she dares, now she doesn't know how to tell her.

She doesn't know where to start. That she's still alive (er, self-evident), that she gave her away as a baby . . . or that she was the one who pushed Rory?

Flick Is Planted

HOW IT ENDS
March 2014
Donegal, Ireland

The next morning, Flick wakes in the cottage early, her conscience clean, the first time in years that she's woken up out here in the real world without a stain to expunge.

She stretches into the silence, then climbs down from the 'penthouse', as her dad used to call it.

She and James lived in an actual penthouse in Canary Wharf during their marriage. A box of glass, stainless steel and bossy kitchen appliances that beeped until you attended to them, Flick had hated it. Being up in the sky with the birds made her feel adrift, as if in a zeppelin.

The feeling she gets in this cottage is the exact opposite. It feels like being planted, her bare feet on the terracotta tiles that surround the fireplace, as she builds a fire that smells like honesty.

When she arrived, the key was under the plant pot. Here in this part of Ireland, no one locks their door. At most, they lock up and place the key under a plant pot, like so, where nobody will ever find it. Apart from, y'know, everybody.

She doesn't know how or who, but in the past twenty-odd years someone has been keeping the cottage respectable. Annie Kelly maybe, from the pub? She and Ciaran were always close. Or that old guy with the donkey . . . what was his name? Nah, he'll be long dead by now.

Annie is her best guess. There is even ground coffee that is only about a year old, in a tin beside the stove kettle. Maybe Annie comes up here to read, escape, rest, who knows?

Flick fills the stove kettle and lights the gas hob with a match, letting it burn right down to her fingers before blowing it out. 'Still a thrill-seeker, I see,' she hears her therapist comment. She brews the stormy coffee, as bitter as it is black.

The North Atlantic waves fling themselves upon the beach, then do so again, again, again. It reminds Flick of herself for the past . . . decade?

'We're not sure diazepam or cocaine are your primary addictions after all,' the rehab's programme director told her, a month into her stay. 'We think it might be love.'

Flick snorted with surprised laughter, like a sat-on whoopee cushion, but once he explained, it made a lot of sense.

Her love addiction is because she's an 'anxious attacher'. Meaning she thinks anyone who 'loves her' is faking it, she needs 24/7/365 reassurance, and she fears them leaving like most people fear death. *Fun.*

Her rehab prescription is a) put herself first, for once, b) set some boundaries, c) spend a whole year single. During a kooky afternoon of being taught transcendental meditation, she was given the mantra: 'I will disappoint other people before I disappoint myself.'

She curls up on a window seat and watches the seagulls swooping, crying out what sounds like, 'Call! Call!' Is it a sign to call Sita? She mentally slaps her own hand. Bad love addict.

Last night she had to literally sit on her own hands to stop herself from doing so. In the end, Love Addict Flick and Rehab Flick struck a deal. She wouldn't call Sita, but she would email her. After all, she owed her an amends, didn't she?

Three thousand words and approximately twenty-nine bullet points later, her amends was done. The swoosh of the sent email felt like redemption.

Love Addict Flick checked her inbox for a reply from Sita at 1.15 a.m., 1.44 a.m. and 2.01 a.m., until Rehab Flick finally intervened and locked her phone into a tin money chest, lobbing the key into a patch of dewy nettles outside.

Now that she's had her coffee, Rehab Flick allows the retrieval of the key. Wearing rubber gloves, she fishes the key out of the patch.

Love Addict Flick holds her breath as she unlocks the tin, the phone sliding around inside it.

There's a reply. *Schweeee.*

'Thank you for all of this, Flick, and huge congrats on your three months sober,' Sita has written.

As usual, she cuts through Flick's bullshit.

I won't wait for you, so don't entertain any notions of that. I'm not your Manic Pixie Dream Girl whose role is to ease you through recovery. But I will see you once you have a year sober.

Balls. Sita's obviously aware of the 'no relationships for a year' rule after rehab. What the hell's a Manic Pixie Dream Girl? Flick opens a tab to look it up. 'Fantasy playmate who saves a male protagonist by showering him with glitter and how-to-love-life lessons.' Often played by Kirsten Dunst, it seems. The email continues:

Also, proud of you for going no contact with your mum. I know that must feel like amputating a limb. She does love you, in her own way, but she was never taught how to love. Somebody hurt her badly long ago. You are allowed to protect yourself from her.

You can borrow my mum anytime. Just be warned that she keeps randomly bringing up Ellen DeGeneres and Portia de Rossi ever since I came out. It's her only middle-class lesbian reference.

Until we meet again, then. Good luck, Flick. I believe in you, even though you've behaved like a right tosser.

The euphoria she feels about Sita's email is closely followed by the anger.

She loves Sita. Always has. Yet the fear of what her mother might think has kept them apart all these years.

Reaching into her canvas bag, Flick takes out the picture frame of Imo and David Bowie, throws it on the floor to crack the frame, then grinds into the pane of glass with the heel of her boot.

Laughing out loud at her audacity, she jumps up and down on the picture frame. It feels luxurious. Anger has never been a permitted emotion. Only *she* was allowed to be angry.

The photo in the frame isn't even a photo, she notices. It's a clipping from a magazine.

'*Tatler*, 20 May 1979', the folded-over edge of the article reads. Beneath the picture, there's a caption: 'David Bowie and *Swan Lake* star Imogen Felstead, after this month's performance.'

Flick brushes the icy scrunch of glass away, then sits holding it, wondering why this feels off. Then, it comes. 1979 was the year she was born, and in May, Mum should have been eight months pregnant.

But this photo shows that Imo's waspish waist could barely have carried a three-course meal, let alone a baby the size of a coconut.

She doesn't know what this all means. Right now, she doesn't have the headspace to figure it out. Maybe the magazine was printed up wrong. Flick clears up the glass and puts the magazine clipping to one side.

~ ~ ~

A storm is rolling in – violet clouds and violent sea spray – as if on a sped-up time lapse. 'Like white horses you could never tame,' Da used to say.

Shrugging on his khaki waxed jacket, the corduroy collar still smelling like pipe smoke, she throws the tea tin in a canvas bag, pushes open the door onto the wind attempting to close it, and steps out into a gale that tips her hair vertical.

The chaos of the beach feels exactly like her many, many regrets around Da's death. Like, she never went to say goodbye. She did her *Swan Lake* shows and the after-parties instead. By the time Wally was contacting her via Facebook and saying, 'No, but really, you need to come,' Da was already gone.

All those unanswered questions she never got a chance to ask him. Those unsaid sweetnesses – and bitters. Him never getting the chance to see her settled and happy, whatever form that might take. Her never getting the chance to see *him* that way.

She inhales the regret into every cellular inch. She's been drinking, drugging, shagging, denying and bullshitting her way out of feeling her feelings for years. Now, she lets them in. Even the regret.

HOW IT ENDS

She takes it in, through and out, as if she's the eye of a needle and the feeling is thread.

Opening the tin, Flick is surprised to find it's nearly full. And that's only half. The gale starts scattering Ciaran before she can. Some of it lands on her coat, bergamot orange still detectable from the Earl Grey tea.

Rushing to fling the rest into the waves, she then drops to the sand, squeals and balls herself up to avoid being covered with more blowback. When she looks up, the ashes are suspended like a dancing murmuration. And then, the spell is broken; they disperse.

The seagulls dive-bomb the surf one by one. Like boy racers doing drifts in a car park, they circle back to their crew after a turn.

She would have loved to have spent her single sabbatical here, dipping her drug-sore body into the icy waters, curling up on this seat reading, thawing herself by the fire and attempting to recreate her dad's stringy Irish stew of yore. It's unfortunate that she's not planning an adult gap year in Donegal.

Thunk. Something rectangular, white and heavy falls on to the furry doormat.

'Fern', it says on it.

Clearly someone who knew her before her name changed at the age of fourteen.

She opens it, expecting it to be from Annie, while munching on some shortbread she bought from the airport. This next year is going to be a 365-day tribute to all the calories she's ever missed as a working dancer. Flick intends to eat every dessert they serve in the prison canteen.

VERSIONS OF A GIRL

An oversized iron key falls out of the envelope, clanking onto the floor. A spare key? That's good of Annie.

Dear Fern/Flick,

You don't know me, and this may be hard for you to comprehend, but I am your mother.

My name is Nora Brady and I had you when I was nineteen. Imogen Felstead was my best friend. Instead of taking you to hospital so that you could find an adoptive family – which was my wish – she claimed you as her own.

Ciaran O'Malley is your real father. Imogen Felstead is not your real mother.

I know that you think you pushed Rory to his death, but you didn't. I was watching you that night and saw what he did to you. After you pushed him away, he recovered his balance.

It was me that ran into your uncle and pushed him through the banister. I'd do it again, too. He was a predator.

Ruth, who I guess you'll remember from back then, is my mother and your grandmother.

Ferndale is yours now that your father's gone (the executor of the will wrote to your Kensington address about this several times).

Here is a key. The solicitor will help you sort out the paperwork later. The address is: Ferndale, Mountain Road, Glenfoot, Ballymena.

Ruth is waiting there for you in The Millhouse. Go to her, please. She'll explain everything. Why I did what I did to Rory, who I am, who I was to your father . . . she has all the answers.

HOW IT ENDS

I am now going to the police to hand myself in. I cannot allow you to take responsibility for something that wasn't your fault.

I'm sorry I gave you away in 1979. I was a scared kid. I can't say I wouldn't do it again, because I would. And it would be the right thing to do, because I've never wanted to be a mother.

But you deserve all the happiness and all the freedom, so I hope you now find it. That's what I wanted for you right from the start. I just couldn't give it to you myself.

Nora

A car struggles to start in the lane, spluttering then cutting out. Flick throws herself out of the cottage's door, still holding the letter.

The Letter for Flick

HOW IT ENDS
Ten minutes before

Why did she sleep so long? Stupid jet lag, but that guesthouse bed was so fragrant and soft, it was almost worth the risk she now finds herself in.

Nora had set her alarm for 4 a.m., but when it sounded she was so tired that her dreamlike self had told her it was something else. It wasn't an alarm, heck no, it was a cymbal from the band she was pogoing to, and she should just plunge back into her bacchanalian dream.

Now it's almost 9 a.m. and Flick is awake and moving around the cottage. On the plus side, there's only thirty feet between the cottage door and the car, which is hidden behind the lane's hedge, so even if she comes out, Nora will get away.

Thunk goes the envelope as she slides it through the door. Fucksake. Why didn't she pad the key, wrap it in something? Another dunderheaded mistake.

Nora sprints for the car, slams the door, goes to make her getaway, and then it won't twattin' start. Of course.

~ ~ ~

Being confronted with the almost-you of twenty years ago is disconcerting. Nora jumps as Flick taps on the window of the passenger seat, then tries to open the door.

They stare at each other for a while, Flick mouthing 'let me in' while Nora has an existential meltdown.

HOW IT ENDS

The door's not locked, only stiff; this car is ancient. There's so much of Ciaran in Flick, more than she first realised; in the way she moves. Her daughter dislodges the door, but once the barrier between them is gone, the awkwardness begins.

It's so odd being back in this cottage. She and Ciaran had had sex there, there, there and there. Now she's sitting here with the beautiful result of that hedonistic time, but it's a result she never wanted – and never will want.

~ ~ ~

Nora has known since she was three that she didn't want to be a mother. One Christmas, she was given a doll that cried 'real tears' (er, not real tears) when you poured water into a hole in her back, then pushed a button. 'Tiny Tears' she was called, and on reflection, she looked like Princess Diana.

Instead of playing with the doll, Nora staged ever more elaborate deaths for her. Boiling in a pot, thrown from the upstairs window, poisoned by a bottle from the kitchen marked 'Do not drink'.

Until one day, her mum had found Tiny Tears tied to one of the water wheel's teeth, a crocodile toy attached to the doll's face, being dunked into the water again and again.

Nora told everyone that she never wanted a family. 'You'll change your mind,' was always the reply. But she hadn't.

~ ~ ~

Flick doesn't just move like Ciaran, she has, perhaps, inherited his talent for storytelling. He had never let the truth stand in the way of a good story.

They've been talking for two hours now and Nora wonders how much of what she's heard is true. Near-death experiences in swimming pools, a two-year road trip across America, stealing a minivan, credit card fraud, characters called Wally and Buck, a private investigator on their trail. Ahem. *OK then, sure.*

But Flick is clever and kind, also like Ciaran. She has a tic of touching her nose and stroking her upper lip, like she's wiping something away. She tells Nora that she's three months and one day sober.

'Wow, well done,' Nora says. 'I wish your father had found himself where you are.'

'Me too. Will you come with me to Ferndale? Before you go to the police.'

Nora pauses. How much false hope is this giving.

'I can,' her tone is guarded. 'But as your friend, not your mother.'

As they drive away from the cottage and towards Clondallon, Flick following in her rental, Nora's phone finally picks up some signal. *Beep beep.*

You have one new voicemail.

She starts to listen to it on speaker.

'It's only me, darling, just calling to let you—'

Nora cuts it off. Her mum's always leaving voicemails, always saying the same thing, like caller ID wasn't invented back in the 1990s.

'I know it's you, Mum, my phone tells me. You don't have to leave voicemails every time you call,' she tells her over and over again.

She'll listen to it in full later, then call her mother back.

The Police Station

HOW IT ENDS
March 2014
Ballymena, Northern Ireland

Ruth only stopped running after the car when it rounded the bend. She found a tree to lean on, caught her breath.

Nora has taken *her* car, inexplicably. Maybe she couldn't find the keys to her rental. But Ruth finds them easily enough, on the kitchen counter.

She knows exactly where her daughter is going – the airport, to wait in Arrivals until she sees the image of herself in the shape of Flick. But that's an hour's drive.

All Ruth needs to do is to get to Ballymena Police Station, half an hour away. Wee buns. She'll beat her.

She brain-dumps a 'looking after Ferndale and The Millhouse' handover onto a pad beside the beige telephone, packs a bag and she's away.

~ ~ ~

Ruth had watched Nora pack. Or, more accurately, helped her unpack, pulling the clothes her daughter put into the holdall back out.

'I know what you're at. You're not going, child,' Ruth said.

'I'm not a child, I'm fifty-three!'

Ruth sat on the bed, holding Nora's electric toothbrush hostage.

'Exactly, darlin', you're still a youngster. I'm almost eighty, which is near-expired anyhow. Let me take the blame for this. I was there that night too. And they don't know you were even in the country, let alone on the grounds. They'll probably send me to some old people's prison where I can while away my days watching *Midsomer Murders* and doing crochet. It'll be grand. Free retirement home, hi.'

Her daughter shook her head, zipped up the bag and slung it over her shoulder.

Ruth's voice had gone up an octave. 'We both know that I'm to blame for what happened. Rory should have faced consequences for what he did to you. Before he went and did it to others too.'

Nora's back paused. But then she carried on, thumping down the stairs.

~ ~ ~

Rap, rap. Sweet Jesus: that made her jump.

A man asking if she's coming or going – his wife is doing laps of the car park in her mud-brown Lada. A cardboard advert for the car rental agency twirls from the rear-view mirror.

She's in this very serious predicament and all Ruth can bloody well think about is the plot of *Thelma and Louise*, and what a ride Brad Pitt was (still is, mind) and why there's not some sort of 'you don't need to go to jail' card for the dispensing of vigilante justice.

Taylor Swift sings about never ever ever getting back together. She presses a knob to silence her. Not now, Taylor love. She opens the car door. Ruth has always said that over-analysis leads to paralysis, and she's done with that nonsense.

She points her body at the police station. Now she won't have to pay that stupid parking ticket, happy days.

~ ~ ~

'Sometimes good people make bad choices,' Nora said to her last night, as they opened their second bottle of wine.

Ostensibly, they were talking about Ciaran and his womanising, but whenever she said it, her daughter looked straight at her.

It was the absolution Ruth had been looking for. Is this how people feel after confession, when they've been forgiven by the priest and said all their Hail Marys? Because if so, she wants it.

Maybe she'll find God in prison too. If she has time, what with all the weightlifting.

~ ~ ~

The snacks at the police station leave a lot to be desired. There's some (criminal) filter coffee and a vending machine with soggy (ought to be outlawed) flapjacks, but that's about the size of it.

Handing herself in for Rory's murder is all a bit disappointing, if she's honest. She hoped they would 'cuff her, read her those Miranda rights, and then give her an orange jumpsuit. It's possible that her expectations are based on American prison dramas.

'Sean, I'm telling you the God's honest here,' Ruth says, sitting across from DI Wells. 'I saw him put his hands on that wee girl and I saw her push him, so it's no wonder Flick thinks she did it. But once he regained his balance and she skedaddled, I ran with all my might at him.'

Ruth pauses for emphasis. 'I'm the one who sent him through those banisters, down to his death, Sean.'

'Was it in self-defence? Are you sure that's the whole story? Did he attack you first?'

'No, Sean,' she sighs. 'I even snuck into the house without them knowing. So you can add breaking and entering to the charge. There's a tunnel you didn't find that goes from the woods straight into the kitchen pantry. I hid the doors when you searched, put sacks of potatoes in front of them. You'll find it if you look again.'

Sean looks doubtful.

'Even the alibi I gave you – talking to my cousin in Florida – was pure fiction. Check it and find out. I don't know why it never got checked in the first place.'

Ageism, she speculates, with a side order of sexism. Thinking an older woman couldn't overpower a thirty-something man.

Frowning and scratching his beard at the mention of -isms, Sean holds up a finger to denote 'wait there a sec' and goes to a filing cabinet. A few minutes later he's back, the ruddiness near drained from his face, which has started to resemble the full Irish breakfasts he enjoys daily.

'Jesus. Well, you're not wrong,' he says. 'Constable Cleary is going to get his arse handed to him once I raise a report on *that*. We went to the phone company right enough, tried to check out your alibi, but they played silly buggers with us for ages and we never circled back for the final verify.'

Ruth raises her eyebrows. *I told you so.*

'Right, well, I'll need to get you a solicitor and we'll get ourselves into an interview room, take a full confession. Christ, Ruth, you've fair pulled the rug from under me with this. You! I never would have guessed it in a month of Sundays.'

'Because of my age?' she asks.

'Well, now. No comment.'

'You've clearly never witnessed the Black Friday sale down at Debenhams.'

They smile. Sean clears his throat.

'We'll go over this again in the official statement, but you've said Rory was at Fern. Is that why you did it?'

Ruth nods. Their mouths straighten, they shift in their seats, neither of them comfortable with such topics.

She reaches across and puts her hand on Sean's. He looks at it, a very real breach of protocol; leaves it there all the same.

'I want to thank you for all the kindness you've shown me over the years, Sean. Keeping Nora's return on the downlow and all. But I need one last favour. Once Nora reads my note back home, she might try to come here and throw herself in front of this instead.'

Sean cocks his head. 'Is that so? An awful lot of people trying to take credit for this mischief, aren't there?'

'All you need to do is check my alibi with the phone company, *finally*, because it's false. I might even have my copy of the phone bill back home in the loft.'

Sean nods.

'So, when do I get my orange jumpsuit, and how do I arrange my one phone call?'

*

VERSIONS OF A GIRL

Ruth watches as what looks like a solicitor arrives, wearing a cheap suit.

Nora's mobile phone goes straight to voicemail. She expected nothing else – she'll be with Flick right now, or in pursuit of her.

'Hi, it's Nora, leave me a message at the beep. Or don't . . . actually, do whatever the hell you like. I'm not the boss of you. OK bye.'

Ruth takes a deep breath. 'It's only me, darlin', just calling to let you know that I'm here at Ballymena Police Station. I've told them what happened that night, that I pushed Rory over the banister. I'm in custody now.'

A pause.

'Let me do this. I was the one responsible. I failed you when you needed me most. I didn't believe you when you needed me to. This is the right thing.'

She puts the phone down. It clicks. Ruth smiles. This is exactly how it's supposed to end.

Fern's Ending

HOW IT ENDS
March 2014
Glenfoot, Northern Ireland

Wally has set up in the study, inhaling the leather-bound books as if they're the scent of a beautiful woman, Buck has disappeared into the forest that horseshoes the house, and Dina and Scout, who appear to be inseparable on this trip, are whooping and yippee-ing their way around every room.

Ruth is showing Fern around *properly*, which means slowly and in a very dull manner. Fern feels a stab of envy hearing how much fun the other two are having.

'Of course, you've stayed here before,' Ruth says. 'But that was over a decade ago. And, of course, you're now the official owner.' She talks Fern through the upkeep of the house, the trust that funds it, the occasional staff that come in and help, and the history.

'There's even a secret tunnel that leads from the kitchen's pantry to the middle of the woods,' she says.

They're now standing on the part of the landing Uncle Rory fell from. Fern runs her hand along the rough – then smooth – seam where the old wood meets the new. Ruth tries to chivvy her along but Fern stops.

'Y'know, I spoke to Uncle Rory that night,' Fern says. 'The night he died. We were standing here. I was up getting a glass of water. And it went sideways. But then the memory cuts—'

Ruth interrupts her. 'I was at the inquest so I know exactly what happened,' she says. 'It was nothing but a skinful of drink and a weird angle of a fall. You had nothing to do with it, dear. Ciaran didn't either.'

~ ~ ~

When they approached the turn for Ferndale – Scout telling Wally to slow down, that they were finally here, stop speeding forgodsake, man – there was a car pulling out of the drive.

They only caught eyes for a second, but it was enough. There she was, the magnetic girl from the side of the well, the one who'd inspired Da to draw a tiny heart, who'd given her away when she was only a few minutes old.

~ ~ ~

Now that she and Ruth are descending the stairs, their tour of Ferndale complete, Fern feels she can broach the subject.

'Was that your daughter – Nora – we saw leaving?'

Ruth stops on the stair.

'Oh, you saw.'

'Yes.'

'It was. She was over for Ciaran's service, but she had to be getting back to Thailand on the 7 p.m. flight. And I won't be expecting her back for another year, dear.'

'I'd love to meet her.'

'Maybe. She never did want to be a mother, though, Fern. Which is nothing to do with you and everything to do with her.'

Strangely enough, this time round, it doesn't hurt. Maybe because she never had this mother in the first place.

*

HOW IT ENDS

Buck appears from the forest with his megawatt grin and highlighter-bright T.

'It's like a Marvel character was just hatched in an Irish wood,' remarks Scout.

'Maybe his egg spaceship is still back there,' Wally says. 'We can use it when we wanna go home. *If* we wanna go home.'

'Baby! Come see this. It's unreal,' Buck calls, beckoning her.

Fern shrinks at his use of a sugary moniker in public, yet also swells. She wonders if there's a long German word for being affronted on behalf of feminism, yet also secretly pleased.

'I found a den!' he says.

Ruth is crunching down the drive back towards The Millhouse. 'That'll be the one Ciaran built for you when you were a girl,' she calls over her shoulder.

Fern doesn't remember any such den. Buck darts through the wood, expecting her to keep up.

'Whoa there, bullet!' she says. 'I'm with child. I need to be careful.'

He's gone, she can't see him.

'Yoohoo,' he says from above.

Fern looks up to see him framed by the circular window of what can only be described as a giant bird's nest. A treehouse, but one of the coolest ones she's ever seen. How can she not remember this?

She climbs up the twenty-foot rope ladder into the top of the tree, questioning the wisdom of such a high climb. Then finds herself in the centre of a ball, the walls tightly woven like a basket.

'What does this remind you of?' he asks, reclining back on cushions and a blanket. Fern looks around. The cushions are mandarin orange, the blanket a deep twilight, with stars stitched into it.

'The minivan.'

'You must've seen it when you were a kid and recreated it,' Buck says.

Buck pats the spot next to him. She crawls in. His warm fingers tuck under the waistband of her long skirt, around about where their apple-sized baby is.

'It'll be lovely for her to have a constant home here,' Buck says. 'Rather than the sliding homes we grew up with. I moved seven times before I was even sixteen. You?'

She smiles. Nods. Thinks. Maybe they *could* stay.

'I want to give her the childhood I didn't have,' he says.

'Same. But is here really the place? The locals are lovely, but so backward. I heard someone at the gas station ask what hot-desking is. She asked if the desk is actually heated.'

He laughs. She picks at the side of her nail. The skin never gets broken now, but the habit remains.

'Buck, I have something I need to tell you.'

'Will it hurt us?' he asks.

'It could. Actually, it will.'

'Was it something from when you were drinking?'

She nods.

'Then don't tell me,' he says. 'I have secrets from you too, y'know. Like what I look at on the computer when you're not around, how much I spend on vinyl and where the flowery bedspread disappeared to. Secrets aren't always bad things. Sometimes they protect something. Everyone's allowed them.'

Fern tries to interject. Nope, Buck's not finished.

'I saw something on Twitter about how every cell in our body regenerates every seven years. So, you are literally a different person now, a different version of yourself. If you believe everything you read on Twitter, which I most certainly do.'

They're quiet.

'This really is just like the minivan, isn't it?' she says.

Buck pulls her back so that she leans on his chest. He strokes the bluebird inked on the back of her neck.

Back in the house, Buck is taking a long bath. He's the only man she's ever known who loves a candlelit bubble bath.

'Don't be so binary,' she hears LA say.

Smoothing on body lotion and getting dressed for the 'special dinner' they're all about to have, she takes extra care. How she looks has never been of interest; her body's always just been a skin suit, her face a moneymaker. But now she takes her time. Given she's not doing it for others, it feels like valuing herself.

Her phone chirrups.

Buck's sent her a screenshot of a meme. Joan Didion smoking and looking awesome, along with a quote from her:

'I have already lost touch with a couple of people I used to be.'

She types back: 'I love that, thank you.' Then deletes it. And instead sends:

Thanks for the inspo, Oprah ;-)

She's made progress, but she's still an avoidant. Sincerity, emoting, intimacy, people getting close all still scare her, like clowns, spiders or enclosed spaces scare others.

But she saves the screenshot, looks at it for a long time.

Another message from Buck. What is he doing, wasting all this money sending her picture messages from the tub? She needs to have a word.

> If you ever feel sad, remember that 'penguin' is literally translated as 'business goose' in Chinese.

A long cherrywood table with ten plush seats stretches out before them. The walls are pink and a flock of birds fly from long grass. Fern still can't believe she owns this country pile aged thirty-four.

Ruth's cooked a brace of pheasants with all the trimmings. Goose-fat roasted potatoes, broccoli smothered in butter, peas in mint, boats of gravy.

'Nice to have people to cook for,' she says, 'I just stab microwave meals when I'm on my own.'

Everyone's in evening wear and as they finish the meal, there's a sense of ceremony, an air of something coming, like a distant thunderstorm that you've sensed in the weight of the air.

Buck is looking at her, expectant. *Oh, no.* If he does this, then he doesn't know her at all. A chair scrapes, but when she looks up, it's Wally standing, not Buck, and now Scout is standing too. Wally is holding something.

'Fern, we have something for you. I don't know if you're interested in this, or whether today is the worst possible timing – or the best – but it feels right to us.'

He places a piece of card on the table in front of her. It's an adoption certificate.

'Scout and I would like to adopt you. Now, there's nothing

legal about this certificate whatsoever, given it turns out you can't adopt a Northern Irish citizen aged over 18. But the intention is there.'

Upon closer analysis, it's an adoption certificate that has been badly photoshopped.

'We want to look after you until you have to look after us,' Scout says. 'I give him ten years,' he adds, flicking Wally with his napkin.

'You'll be in adult diapers within five,' Wally says.

The doctored certificate is edited from a real one. They've covered up whoever's names were there, and replace them with hers, Scout's and Wally's.

Her date of birth is even wrong. It's a shitshow.

'It's perfect,' she says.

Flick's Ending

HOW IT ENDS
Nine months later
Glenfoot, Northern Ireland

Flick tears the brown paper and the red 'fragile' tape off the six-foot, rectangular package that's just been delivered. Inside is a picture in a gilt frame, but she can't see what it is yet.

She peels away layer upon layer of bubble wrap; then squeals.

It's a Klimt print, of two mermaids embracing, a bare breast, a fish head, a lot of hair. '*Water Serpents I* by Gustav Klimt' says a card from an art gallery, which falls from the bubble wrap onto the floor.

A further card is taped to the frame, 'Flick' written on it in Sita's hand. She rips it open.

> *Happy one year*
> *I'm so proud of you*
> *I can't wait to see you*
> *Love, Sita*

Flick hugs the package. She'll call Sita later. They can plan her visit some more.

This gift feels extra decadent because she no longer buys luxuries like this. Let alone has them bought for her.

They made her cut up all her credit cards back in rehab. OK, maybe not *made* her, but suggested it, and she'd done it, because she likes to please people.

HOW IT ENDS

Having found out she owed sixteen thousand pounds across three different cards, they'd said she needed to seek out 'financial sobriety' too. So all she has now is a debit card – no credit – with access to the last scraps of her divorce settlement.

Tens of thousands went on the rehab. The repayments on her debt are horrible. But what's left has gone a long way towards rewilding herself in Ireland, and the house's trust helps.

Turns out that her grandmother Ruth – who's now in a minimum-security prison serving a five-year sentence for manslaughter and is apparently reading a book a day – was very sensible with the money in there. There's more than enough.

~ ~ ~

'That quote in the waiting room annoys me.'

'Which one?' her therapist asked.

'The one from Jung: "I am not what happened to me, I am who I choose to become."'

'Why do you think it annoys you?'

'Because it's not true. I can't delete thirty-four years of things that happened to me. I *am* what has happened to me. It would be naïve to think otherwise. Aren't people like hard drives in that even if you erase it all, a ghost trace is still there?'

'How would you change the quote to make it feel more accurate. To you.'

She thinks. Opens her mouth.

~ ~ ~

VERSIONS OF A GIRL

The mirror in the en suite reveals her ruddy, wind-tossed face, a constellation of acne, hair a wayward snarl. Should she . . . before heading into the village? Nah.

There's a quote on a Post-it next to her reflection. Flick stuck it there when she arrived at Ferndale nine months ago, having kept it from her stay in rehab.

The Post-it is now grimy, the words smudged from steam, but every time it's swayed to the floor and been trodden on, she's straightened it back out, stuck it back up.

Now, it's attached to the mirror with the post office's finest 'Xtra-Strong!' parcel tape. There's no falling down from that.

> *I am what has happened to me.*
> *But now, I choose who I become.*
> *Fern Felicity O'Malley*

She kisses the tips of her fingers, places them on the quote and smiles.

Acknowledgements

I thought fiction was going to be easier to write than non-fiction. Oh how the writing deities rolled on the floor laughing their asses off at that one. 'You just make stuff up,' I said. It was like I was asking for a humbling flick on the forehead. As my Dad would have said: 'Your head's full of sweetie mice, dear.'

Turns out that if you just make stuff up, the fiction isn't good. All fiction has to be somehow true on a granular level, even when the sum of parts is not; the way a person made you feel, a thing you saw and never forgot, an uttered line which stayed with you for decades. Nothing in this book is true, it's not auto-fiction, and yet it is *true*.

An author once said to me, whenever I asked her if she was 'ever tempted to commit literary revenge' that you have to be every character, at least *partially*, otherwise the characters don't work. Obviously the emphasis is on partially, especially with sub-human, deviant characters, otherwise Stephen King presumably wouldn't have been able to lay claim to the same character-writing secret in *On Writing*.

These two – and hundreds of others – lessons were some of my flicks on the forehead. This novel was scrapped and rewritten at least twice. My plotting board was dismantled and reassembled multiple times. But I can now finally – perhaps foolishly – say that come what may, I am very proud of this debut.

Jon Elek for seeing the potential in this manuscript even when it was buried deep. Rachel Mills, for being the best agent I could ever hope for and for her art of never sugar-coating; yet it always feeling sweet. Jason Richman, for seeing the potential for the big screen and all the dog chat. Ellie Freedman, for that rarefied work synchronicity in which even when we disagree, we somehow agree, because of an underground river of mutual respect. Your instincts are impeccable and your edits have unreservedly made my work better.

Marta Juncosa, for the truly imaginative marketing talent. Isabelle Wilson, for all the external validation and PR know-how. Amy Cox, for the artistic verve of coming up with the genius sliding panels. (I tried to take it in a different direction for edit two, literally. You were right, I was wrong, and I am so grateful for your brilliant initial brief). Petra Eriksson, for her stunning *New Yorker*-level illustration.

Headline Fiction in general, in particular Jen Doyle, for looking after me throughout the buy-out and making sure I always felt like I had a home. Mountain Leopard, for being my second home with a sexy new logo.

My first readers: Kate Faithfull, who has had my back with essential and clever suggestions right through the past decade. Sarah Linford, for thoughtful, smart and insightful cheerleading. Kathy Smallwood, for reading not just one, but all three drafts. Emily Johnson, for making the first 10K sing. Holly Whitaker, for telling me the things others won't. Tamara Vodden, for the country know-how, Benji Lamb for the (very) early read, Sam Purser-Barriff for the encouragement, and dozens of others who have since read and fed back on a few chain-mail proofs posted up and down the country.

And to my readers, who with every buy, post, story, review and mention, enable me to do this thing that I love truly, madly, deeply.